"Help me," the man called, his voice raised in panic

He glanced back to where Jak was hiding. "Please, you know what they'll do...."

Five white-clad figures emerged from the trees, descending on the armed man. They were women, young, tall and svelte, with long hair styled on top of their heads in elaborate braids. Their robes were light and gauzy, covering each woman from neck to ankle. The skirts and sleeves billowed around them like mist.

"Die! Damn you all!" the man screamed, rising from his crouch and blasting wildly.

The women kept gliding toward him, gracefully, swiftly, sidestepping the shots with breathtaking ease.

The man was shouting nonsense now. Jak could see him squeezing the trigger, but he had no ammo left. He dropped backward in an uncoordinated stumble.

The white-robed women converged on him. What happened next, Jak couldn't tell. All he saw was the billowing robes circling the spot where the man had gone down, fluttering there like waves.

**Other titles in the
Deathlands saga:**

JAMES AXLER

DEATH LANDS®

Siren Song

A GOLD EAGLE BOOK FROM
WORLDWIDE®

TORONTO • NEW YORK • LONDON
AMSTERDAM • PARIS • SYDNEY • HAMBURG
STOCKHOLM • ATHENS • TOKYO • MILAN
MADRID • WARSAW • BUDAPEST • AUCKLAND

Recycling programs
for this product may
not exist in your area.

First edition January 2014

ISBN-13: 978-0-373-62624-3

SIREN SONG

Printed in U.S.A.

Medicine heals doubts as well as diseases.
—Karl Marx, 1818-1883

For so work the honey-bees, creatures that by a rule
in nature teach the act of order to a peopled kingdom.
—William Shakespeare

THE DEATHLANDS SAGA

This world is their legacy, a world born in the violent nuclear spasm of 2001 that was the bitter outcome of a struggle for global dominance.

There is no real escape from this shockscape where life always hangs in the balance, vulnerable to newly demonic nature, barbarism, lawlessness.

But they are the warrior survivalists, and they endure—in the way of the lion, the hawk and the tiger, true to nature's heart despite its ruination.

Ryan Cawdor: The privileged son of an East Coast baron. Acquainted with betrayal from a tender age, he is a master of the hard realities.

Krysty Wroth: Harmony ville's own Titian-haired beauty, a woman with the strength of tempered steel. Her premonitions and Gaia powers have been fostered by her Mother Sonja.

J. B. Dix, the Armorer: Weapons master and Ryan's close ally, he, too, honed his skills traversing the Deathlands with the legendary Trader.

Doctor Theophilus Tanner: Torn from his family and a gentler life in 1896, Doc has been thrown into a future he couldn't have imagined.

Dr. Mildred Wyeth: Her father was killed by the Ku Klux Klan, but her fate is not much lighter. Restored from pre-dark cryogenic suspension, she brings twentieth-century healing skills to a nightmare.

Jak Lauren: A true child of the wastelands, reared on adversity, loss and danger, the albino teenager is a fierce fighter and loyal friend.

Dean Cawdor: Ryan's young son by Sharona accepts the only world he knows, and yet he is the seedling bearing the promise of tomorrow.

In a world where all was lost, they are humanity's last hope....

Chapter One

The road rushed toward Ricky Morales as he took the blast in his flank. A second later his face collided with the broken pavement. The burning flare in his hand sailed away, sparkling bright red as it rolled over and over across the tarmac like blood-drenched lightning. Beside it, the ball from the musket went rolling away down the road, splashed now with Ricky's blood.

"Come on, boy, keep up," J. B. Dix shouted, thrusting the barrel of his Smith & Wesson M-4000 shotgun over Ricky's head. A second later J.B. sent a roaring blast at the figures that chased them through the grove, momentarily silencing their sinister, animallike whooping.

Ricky winced at the noise of the blast, his eyes narrowed against the bright explosion. Behind him, at least a dozen human shapes were stalking through the grove. The trees didn't help matters. At some point someone had had the bright idea of hanging folks from their upper branches like a gallows, leaving the decaying corpses swinging in the wind in bloody warning. It was a warning that Ricky wished he and his companions had heeded when they had arrived in this place just a few hours earlier. But they had been hungry, and it had been pitch-black when they had emerged from the redoubt.

J.B. blasted another burst of buckshot from his weapon, carving a crescent moon through one side of a thick tree trunk and felling the figure poised behind it.

"You moving or am I leaving you?" J.B. snarled.

Ricky raised his Webley Mk VI revolver and sent four shots into the shadows of the trees, peppering the area with lead. He smiled with bleak satisfaction as he saw one of the scalies crash to the ground. Beside him, the flare continued to fizz, sending up sparks of red as it butted against the ground.

"I'm coming," Ricky insisted, pulling himself up to a standing position. He reached for the flare and stopped. His side hurt, and his belly was churning so much that he could taste that stolen meal coming back up his throat. *"¡Madre de Dios!"* Ricky cursed the pain that seared through him.

J.B. chanced a look at the youth between his scanning of the trees. "You look green," he said noncommittally. J.B. was a short man with wire-rimmed glasses and a fedora hat on his head. He looked to be about forty-five, but it was hard to tell—life in the Deathlands prematurely aged a person, especially the kind of life that J.B. led.

He was a weaponsmith, an expert in firearms and explosives and able to turn his hand to just about any weapon a person cared to name. He was the Armorer of the group, and he had traveled with Ryan Cawdor the longest.

Ryan was the nominal leader. There were six others in the group, including J.B., with Ricky the youngest and most recent addition. Ricky was sixteen with black hair and dark brown eyes. He was good-looking in a skinny kind of way, still more youth than man but growing every day. He had met Ryan and J.B. when they had visited Nuestra Señora, a small seaport on Monster Island. Nuestra Señora was Ricky's home, but with his sister missing and so much that had happened there, he had chosen to stick with Ryan and his companions as they traveled the Deathlands in search of a better life.

Just now, this was not that better place. "California"

was what J.B. had called it when they had emerged from the hidden redoubt. J.B. knew maps and geography, and he had a way of mapping their location using a device he carried called a mini-sextant.

It had been dark when they had arrived, emerging from the redoubt via its mat-trans system into what appeared to be a grove of oranges. The oranges were as big as a baby's head, weighing down the branches of the trees that lined the little ribbon of road. The trouble was they were radio-active oranges. J.B. had taken one glance at his lapel rad counter, left them on the trees and gone in search of other nutrition. They had found a scalie settlement located in a flat-faced pyramid beside a graveyard for rusted cars.

"Shopping mall," Mildred had explained when she saw it. Mildred Wyeth had grown up in the twentieth century and sometimes she made reference to things that Ricky couldn't make sense of. She was a handsome black woman who wore her hair in beaded plaits. She had been a medical doctor back in the twentieth century, specializing in cryogenic research. When she had suffered complications during routine abdominal surgery, the decision had been made to place her temporarily in cryogenic hibernation. "Temporarily" turned out to be about a hundred years, during which nuclear exchange between the U.S.A. and USSR had heralded the end of Western civilization. Mildred had woken up to a world that had driven through the gates of hell and just kept on accelerating.

J.B.'s hand pressed against Ricky's back, propelling him faster along the road with a mighty shove. "Head in the game, boy!"

Ricky's side was bleeding, wetness seeping into his shirt and making it stick. He ignored it; whatever wound he had, be it lethal or a graze, stopping now to check would get them both chilled.

Behind Ricky, the Armorer's other hand was working the M-4000, sending another cacophonous burst of fire at their pursuers.

"They've got our scent," J.B. yelled. "Forget the flare!"

Their pursuers were scalies: mutated humanoid creatures with hard, blistered skin. Scalies were just one of a whole variety of genetic twists that had happened to humanity since the widespread nuclear fallout had sent planetary radiation levels through the stratosphere. Humanity also suffered at the hands of genetically developed beings that were used as bioweapons.

Scalies were insular and some had proved capable of forming a society. This group clearly took it personally when anyone accidentally stepped into their territory. But then, the figures hanging from the trees gave that away, now that Ricky thought about it.

They had to get back to the redoubt, but the scalies were right behind them. They'd have to lure the muties away, then double back to the redoubt so that the companions weren't swarmed before they got inside.

J.B.'s shotgun roared again and a shower of watermelon-size oranges dropped from a tree like cannonballs, slapping two of their pursuers to the ground. The others continued to give chase, stopping every few steps to pitch fist-size rocks at the two companions. Surprisingly, a few of the scalies were armed with muskets. They were cobbled together, based on more efficient designs—probably something the scalies had found in the pyramid structure that had once been a shopping mall. Whatever they were, getting hit by a projectile from one was still going to hurt like hell.

J.B. was mentally counting his shots, and knew he needed to reload the M-4000. He fumbled with its breech on the run, his legs pumping as he sought the right pocket of his jacket for more ammo.

Ahead of J.B., Ricky skidded to an abrupt halt, his arms windmilling as he fought to keep his balance, the Webley revolver drawing circles in the air.

"What the hell, kid?" J.B. asked as he came up alongside Ricky. Then he saw why the youth had stopped. They were out of road. Literally. The blacktop ended in a sudden drop—a cliff that fell about two hundred feet to the ocean below. J.B. figured that hitting the surface from this height would be like hitting a solid wall.

DOC TANNER WAS struggling to keep pace with Mildred and Jak.

Jak had short legs but he moved like a jackrabbit on jolt, barreling down the slope toward the redoubt entrance. Jak Lauren was an albino, with hair and skin that were chalk-white and eyes a ruby-red that made him look almost ghostlike. A few inches over five feet tall, Jak had a slight, wiry build that was surprisingly tough, and the barrel of his Colt Python pointed ahead of him as he scanned the overgrown scrub that all but hid the entrance to the redoubt.

Mildred kept pace with Jak easily enough, head down so that the wind blew her plaits past her shoulders, regulating her breathing as she ran. "You all right back there, Doc?" she asked as they zipped between dead trees on the pronounced slope.

Doc nodded, breathlessly muttering that he was fine, but it ended up sounding more like a straining steam engine trying to speak than a man.

Mildred glanced at him, concern etched on her face. "We're almost there," she assured him. "Just a few dozen yards."

Doc nodded again, appreciating the heads-up. His vision was whirling a little, as if he was on one of those old fairground rides that used to visit his hometown back in his youth.

Dr. Theophilus Algernon Tanner, to give him his full appellation, was an unwilling time traveler who had been dumped in the Deathlands following a rather cruel experiment by the whitecoats of Operation Chronos. The chron jumps had affected his body, aging him prematurely. When he was trawled from the nineteenth century, Doc had been in his early thirties. Now he resembled a thin, silver-haired man in his sixties.

He wore a black frock coat, pants, a white shirt and black knee boots. Doc carried with him an ebony cane topped with a silver lion's head, and inside the sheath was a blade of fine Toledo steel. Besides his swordstick, he carried a replica LeMat percussion pistol, which included a second barrel that functioned as a shotgun, and which could blast a single shot when needed. The fact that both swordstick and blaster contained a surprise pretty well said all that needed to be said about Doc Tanner—he was a man full of surprises.

Up ahead, the redoubt entrance looked like a tunnel that had become overgrown with creepers and moss. A line of orange trees had grown in front of the wide entrance like a fence, masking it further. Three hours earlier the entrance had been all but invisible. When the companions had emerged from it, they had cleared some of the flora out of the way—enough at least that they could pass through.

Jak was first to reach the doors, pulling away creepers from a keypad that rested against the wall at shoulder height. His white fingers punched in the three-digit entry code. As the heavy door slid aside on aged tracks, Jak glanced behind him, checking for Mildred and Doc and confirming that no one was following them.

Jak saw a figure appear behind Doc, still a little ways up the slope where once a dirt track had lain. Jak didn't wait to see who the figure was; he just raised his Colt Python and fixed the shadow in its sights. Then he stroked the trigger and sent a single booming shot up the slope, cutting Doc's pursuer dead center in his chest. The scalie went down in a splatter of blood and bone.

Mildred joined Jak an instant later, breathless, her eyes wide. "What was that?"

"Scalie," Jak said, already slipping through the open doors to the redoubt. He spoke little, and rarely in full sentences.

Mildred waited in the doorway with her Czech-made ZKR-551 target pistol in her hand, scanning the landscape for further movement. Jak's eyesight was uncanny, but Mildred was confident she could spot a hostile figure in the overgrowth.

Doc joined Mildred seconds later and together they slipped through the open doorway and into the redoubt.

"FIREBLAST," RYAN CAWDOR muttered as he watched the scene play out below him.

Belly on the ground, he lay amid the grass, the Steyr Scout Tactical longblaster stretched out in front of him, his finger resting on the trigger guard. All around him, dead bodies hung from the trees, casting long shadows as the sun rose over the cliff. This whole excursion had been a mistake from the get-go, he lamented as he watched the sloping ground through the longblaster's scope.

Ryan was a tall man with broad shoulders and a mop of unruly black hair. His face had two days of stubble and a black patch over the left eye where he had lost it in a knife fight with his brother a lifetime ago. A scar ran up the side of his face, a pale line that cut through his emerging beard like an arrow pointing to the missing eye. Ryan had lived with it a long time.

Krysty Wroth crouched next to Ryan with her back against a tree, her expression fixed as she listened for an ambush. She was strikingly beautiful with vivid red hair and the kind of athletic frame and long legs that, once seen, men fantasized about long after the woman herself had departed.

The woman wore a red shirt and blue jeans, with blue cowboy boots whose heels added to her tall frame. She held a blaster in her hand—a compact Smith & Wesson .38 loaded with .158-grain lead slugs.

Ryan watched through the scope as J.B. and Ricky reached the end of the road. California was a lot different since the nukes hit. This place, for instance, was nothing more than a splinter of an island surrounded on all sides by blue ocean. For another, the place was maybe two miles long and a mile across, and it was covered in orange groves. Again, if they'd known that when they'd jumped into its mat-trans they might have had the sense to get the hell out of here before the scalies took umbrage at their appearance on what they obviously thought of as their own private island.

When the nukes had struck way back in 2001, a lot of California had gone missing. The San Andreas Fault had finally cracked, dropping a good portion of the western coast of the United States of America into the ocean and drowning millions with it. What was left now, besides the abbreviated West Coast itself, was a group of isles known as the Western Islands. This minuscule piece of land, it seemed, had once been the home to some out-of-town mall.

"Twelve Starbucks and a JCPenney" was the way Mildred had described it to him.

Ryan guessed that visitors to the mall had been oblivious of the redoubt on its doorstep. He took another breath, watching through the Steyr's crosshairs as the scalies swarmed toward J.B. and Ricky. He had known J.B. a long time, all the way back to their days with Trader when they had roamed the Deathlands, part of the crew of War Wag One. The two men were equals and as close as brothers, and they had an understanding that went beyond words.

The scalies were slowing now, wary of what J.B. and the kid were going to unleash on them. The flare had gotten their attention, which was just as they had planned it, ensuring Doc, Mildred and Jak could get to the redoubt safely without the scalies hot on their heels. Ryan watched the scalies emerge from the tree cover in ones and twos. He took another deep breath and slipped his finger behind the guard so that it rested against the trigger. Shoot on the exhale, he reminded himself automatically, when the body is at its steadiest.

J.B.'S BOOT HEEL scuffed against the cliff edge as he took another step backward, the sound of the ocean loud in his ears. Ricky was hunched over next to him with one arm around his belly. There was blood leaking through his fingers.

"Hang in there, kid," J.B. murmured as scalies swarmed from cover.

There were more than two dozen of them now, closer to thirty, J.B. estimated. They were hairless and buck naked. Some had added rudimentary tattoos across their bodies, blue swirls and lines across shoulders and chest; one displayed a shape across his face that reminded J.B. of a bat.

As he emerged from the trees, the bat man said something, but J.B. couldn't make sense of it. It sounded like a dog snarling, a low kind of growl. Around him, the other scalies began to laugh louder—now *that* was something J.B. did understand, the universal laughter of the mocking bully.

Several of the scalies were sticking close to the trees as they reloaded their muskets. They were cumbersome weapons, and J.B. could see that the shot they fired was large and ball-like, approximately the size of an old table-tennis ball. It was one of those that had hit Ricky, large enough to tear clothes and skin, but not refined enough to pierce through the flesh.

The Armorer calculated that Ricky had two bullets left before he would need to reload, which meant, unless he got his shotgun reloaded, the odds were lousy.

"We going to chill them," Ricky whispered, "or what?" The kid trusted J.B. to make these decisions. He had volunteered to carry the flare even when J.B. had tried to dissuade him. "Two blasters are better than one," he had told the Armorer, "and you'll have my back, right?"

Sure, J.B. had his back all right. And look where that had got them.

The leader with the bat tattoo was walking purposefully along the overgrown roadway toward J.B., its dark eyes flicking down to the open shotgun where J.B. had not had a chance to reload. "Outta time tuh load blasta," Bat Tattoo taunted as he approached the Armorer. His voice was rough, like sandpaper, the accent all but impenetrable. The leader's lips pulled back from his sharp teeth and he began to laugh. And then his head burst like a watermelon and a thunderclap echoed through the grove.

"Dark night, Ryan, but you took your sweet bastard time!" J.B. muttered as the mutie leader went caroming past him and over the cliff edge, his head a ruined mess of brain and bone.

Around him, the scalies were reacting with shock at their leader's death, scrambling this way and that as they searched for their new attacker. Another shot cut the air and one of the musket-carrying muties went sailing to the ground in a sprawl of limbs.

J.B. slipped new ammo into his shotgun's breech as he moved, then stroked the shotgun's trigger, sending a fearsome burst of fire at the two nearest scalies. They went down with yelps of pain, blood splattering across the blacktop.

Beside J.B., Ricky had sunk to one knee and was firing shots from his own blaster before switching to his second weapon, a reproduction De Lisle carbine. The De Lisle was about half as long as Ricky was tall, with a bolt action and mock-wood finishing. It boomed with each shot like a miniature rumble of thunder, and each time another scalie dropped to the ground. Despite the pain in his flank, Ricky felt alive.

THINGS WERE A mess inside the redoubt. Located underground, it was like a concrete rabbit warren, flickering lights illuminating gray walls on which were painted dusty stripes of red, green and yellow. Bird caws echoed down the corridors. There was sand and dirt splashed over the walls by the wind, and bird droppings and insect husks carpeted the floors. Some of the corridors ended in rubble while others ended in sheer drops that looked straight out onto the ocean. Mildred followed Jak, trusting his keen tracker instincts to retrace the path they had taken a few hours ago when they had arrived.

They had left Doc at the redoubt entrance, either to

welcome Ryan and J.B. or to blast the living crap out of anyone—or anything—else who tried to enter.

The redoubt itself was set half out to sea, one entire side cut away by the quake that had turned this strip of land into an island decades before. Despite that destruction, its automated facilities still functioned, including the ceiling-mounted fluorescent lights and, crucially, the mat-trans unit. Quite how the mat-trans could still operate when so much of the building had been wrenched away was beyond Mildred's comprehension. They'd built these old places tough.

The mat-trans was a twentieth-century invention designed to move troops and matériel between locations with the minimum of fuss. The matter-transporter units were located in dozens of abandoned military redoubts across the old United States of America and several other parts of the world. While the redoubts remained mostly untampered with by the locals, locked up and hidden away as they were, Mildred and her companions had utilized the mat-trans units for a number of years, zipping from location to location as they sought a better life away from the routine bloodshed of the Deathlands. Finding somewhere to settle had proved a lot harder than Mildred had expected.

Leading the way, Jak stepped into the redoubt control room. Twin aisles of desks ran lengthwise across the room, facing a screen that was blotched with the white stripes of bird feces. The desks, too, were smothered with droppings, and as Mildred entered the room she saw a gull flap its wings in surprise as it rose from one corner. The bird had a nest here, tucked out of sight. Mildred ignored the gull as it swooped around the room, cawing in distress.

The two companions made their way to the door to the anteroom, where they waited for their friends to join them.

IT WAS PANDEMONIUM. Scalies were running in all directions.

While most of the muties had scattered in blind panic, several came searching for the sniper who had executed their leader. Krysty watched from her hiding place in the bole of a tree, the Smith & Wesson .38 clutched close to her breast as two figures broke from the tree line where the bodies hung, running toward Ryan where he lay on the grass picking off their companions. One of the scalies held a knife, and it flashed as it reflected the sunlight. Glass, Krysty realized.

As the two scalies vaulted over a fallen log, Krysty emerged and popped off two shots from the .38. The first plowed into the chest of the scalie on the left, and he seemed to flip over himself as he was driven back and to the ground. But her second shot missed, whipping away just an inch over the right hand scalie's shoulder. Tough break—he was the one with the knife.

The scalie changed direction. He ran not for Ryan now but for Krysty, drawing the glass knife back in preparation to swing. Krysty whipped up the .38, but the scalie was on her before she could squeeze the trigger.

The two of them went down with a thud of bone-jarring impact. Krysty fell backward as the knife swished through the air just inches from her face. The scalie spread his legs to hold her down, crouching over her crab-style to stop her from escaping. The knife swung again, eight inches of blade flashing with the sun's rays.

Krysty brought up her blaster and squeezed the trigger. The .38 fired at point-blank range, but the bullet deflected on a callused section of her attacker's armor-like flesh. The scalie howled in pain and, in the same instant, reached out with his free hand and grabbed Krysty's blaster by the muzzle, shoving it aside.

Krysty groaned as her wrist was bent backward. The

scalie's grip was as strong as a vise and she could feel the bones of her wrist grinding together as he clenched tighter.

Looming above Krysty, the mutie brought his glass blade down toward her face, hissing through clenched teeth in some eerie victory trill, the blade racing toward her.

Gaia help me, Krysty thought as she watched the blade carving the air. Hear my prayer and come to my aid in my time of need.

Then everything seemed to slow down; the blade hovered in the air as if it was a static object.

Krysty had grown up in Harmony ville where her mother, Sonja, had taught her how to tap into a wellspring of energy that she called Gaia power. Quite how that ability worked, no one could explain, but it drew on the Earth Mother herself to feed her with a burst of incredible strength and stamina. That "Gaia power" had saved Krysty's life on numerous occasions, but it came at a cost—each time she used it, it ran out fast and she was left as weak as a kitten. Right now, Krysty figured that cost was worth it.

As she focused on her chant, Krysty could feel the power of the Earth Mother race through her like an electric current charging her veins. Krysty's emerald eyes seemed to shine as she snatched the scalie's wrist and pulled, altering the angle of the stabbing knife and yanking the scalie with such force that he went sailing from her with a howl of surprise. An instant later the scalie's flying body slammed against the trunk of a nearby orange tree, and Krysty heard his neck snap.

She lay there breathing hard as the Gaia energies coursed through her, making her feel every whisper of breeze, every blade of grass, as it seared through her body like a fire. Moments later the power ebbed, then was gone.

Still lying in the grass, Ryan picked off the last few

stragglers of the attacking party, watching through the scope as the remaining scalies ran for the safety of their pyramid-like home.

"You okay?" he asked, his single eye still fixed on the rifle's scope.

"Been better, lover," Krysty replied weakly. She was shaking, and her voice had that familiar tremble, the result of using the Gaia force.

When he looked at her, Krysty was checking her right wrist where the scalie had tried to break it.

"Time to go," Ryan said.

Krysty nodded. Her wrist was still working, although she may sport a bruise there for the next few days. Ryan bent to help her to her feet. He put his arm around her shoulder and they headed toward the redoubt.

THEY CONVERGED ON the redoubt entrance. Doc was using his faithful LeMat to, as he put it, "dissuade the locals from investigating too thoroughly."

"Good thing, too," J.B. said as he carried Ricky through the doors and into the corridor beyond. "Wouldn't do for muties to learn about the mat-trans system. Before we know it, the redoubts would be overrun with crazed scalies only too happy to consume or destroy anything they come across."

Other than sending another warning shot into the trees overlooking the redoubt entrance, Doc didn't bother to reply. He pulled back from the entrance, his LeMat still jutting out the doors in search of new targets.

A moment later Ryan appeared with Krysty at his side. As they entered the redoubt, Krysty looked exhausted; her hair hung limply now and her movements were slow and heavy, as if she was underwater.

J.B. caught Ryan's eye, an unspoken question there.

"She's fine," Ryan replied. "Just a little knocked out from her Gaia power."

When J.B. said nothing, Ryan smiled.

"Had a bit of trouble finding a good spot," Ryan said. "Did you miss us down there?"

J.B. shrugged. "I figured you'd come through for us," he said. "Just, you know, quicker would have been better."

Ryan nodded. "I'll keep that in mind the next time I save your life. Ricky, are you okay?"

"Millie'll look him over," J.B. replied for the teen, "once we're away from this rad-blasted pesthole."

Doc punched in the code to close the doors. Once he had done that, he turned to his companions and touched his free hand to the brim of an imaginary hat. "I trust we are all ready to leave?"

Less than a minute later the five companions joined Jak and Mildred in the anteroom, then they all entered the mat-trans unit and sat on the floor, except for Ryan. The one-eyed man was last in, and he firmly shut the mat-trans door, initiating a jump. He quickly made his way to Krysty's side and sat beside her. The mat-trans powered up.

All seven companions disappeared, leaving only the wispy trails of cooling gas and the whine of the air vents in their wake.

Chapter Two

As the companions didn't have the destination codes for the mat-trans unit, where they ended up was totally random. The jump could take them to a redoubt five hundred miles away or five thousand—or anywhere in the world, for that matter. The companions never knew where they'd arrived until they left the redoubt and got their bearings.

The effects of traveling by mat-trans made a person feel as though he or she had caught a swamp bug. The stomach rebelled, the body went weak and there was the urgent feeling that you were about to crap your pants. Thankfully, the journey itself was momentary, and once it passed—usually—so did the sickness.

The seven companions materialized in a shock of light, and even as they appeared the extractor fans of the mat-trans hummed to life, working their magic to clear the chamber of gas.

They were sitting in a different mat-trans chamber—its dimensions and design exactly like the one they had just left, the only difference being the color of its arma-glass walls, which was a sort of red-violet, Ricky thought.

Breathing through clenched teeth, he clutched his side, his eyes screwed up in pain. He still hadn't got used to the discorporation and reintegration of his molecules that was necessary for the mat-trans to shunt him to a new location, and the jarring only served to make the wound in his side feel worse. *"Madre—"* he muttered, doubling over in agony.

"Okay, Ricky," Mildred said, hurrying across the small room to the teen's side and opening her satchel of medical supplies. She moved a little unsteadily, still suffering from the aftereffects of the jump. Mildred was far more experienced in this than Ricky, but it could still catch her unawares sometimes, just the same way it caught everyone unawares sometimes. She usually had a concoction she called jump juice, which was helpful in settling the stomach, but she was all out.

As she moved, Mildred spotted the box. It loomed incongruously at the rear wall of the chamber, clicking to itself in a kind of constant hum. "Um…" Mildred began, stopping in her tracks. "Ryan? J.B.?"

Ryan was still recovering from the jump, but he moved to where Mildred had halted and scanned the device with his single blue eye. "Shit."

It was about the size of a shoebox, roughly a foot across and half as deep, and the top was open to reveal a mass of wires and a timer. The timer was analog, like an old oven timer, and it clicked quietly to itself as it counted down.

"What the hell is that?" J.B. said, peering past Ryan's shoulder. "Oh."

"Three minutes," Ryan said, reading the dial on the timer.

"Get everyone out of here," J.B. instructed, reaching into his pocket and pulling out a tiny pair of wire cutters no bigger than nail scissors. His instruction was unnecessary. Ryan was already rousing Krysty and the others, ushering them to the chamber door. "Triple red, everyone," Ryan ordered as he turned the door handle. They had less than three minutes. Ryan would wait. He knew why J.B. wanted to defuse the bomb—the importance of the mat-trans was impossible to put a value on. If they'd emerged in a hot zone or a settlement of crazies—or both, as they had in California—then this chamber may be their only means of escape.

J.B. had defused bombs before. They had three minutes, which meant they still had a chance.

Doc and Jak took out their blasters before they hurried through the doorway, while Krysty followed a little more slowly, still reeling from the blow of her post-Gaia comedown. Mildred helped Ricky through, glancing back at J.B. as the Armorer knelt to study the explosive device. A bomb inside the mat-trans meant someone had been in this redoubt, wherever it was.

Anyone with any brains would have gotten out double-quick as soon as they had placed the explosive, but Ryan wasn't taking any chances. He flipped the safety off his SIG Sauer blaster, left the chamber and anteroom and marched across the control room.

It was a redoubt like the one they had just exited, as most were—concrete walls, low ceilings, anteroom and control room, with winking and blinking lights and dials and comp monitors. The lights were on, but that didn't mean anything. Redoubt lights functioned automatically when a mat-trans fired to life, which meant that the bomber could be long gone by now. Or just around the corner.

There were several cracks that ran across one side of the room, up the walls and through the ceiling, wide enough to accommodate a person's arm. Something had struck the redoubt at some time, and struck it hard. Ryan's people fanned out swiftly. A layer of dust was sprinkled on the age-old com terminals, but Doc noticed immediately that several screens had been wiped clean.

"Someone tried to use these," Doc said. "Recently, too." Ryan waited while the rest of his friends made their way through the room. Jak keyed in the code to open the door, then they all filed into the corridor beyond. The albino youth scouted ahead, checking the immediate rooms of the redoubt, hunting for danger and for somewhere safe to position the group should the bomb go off.

While Ryan waited in the doorway, Doc helped a reluctant Krysty down the corridor.

"Ryan, come on," she urged. "We can't…"

"We have to try to save it," Ryan said, his single eye fixed on J.B.

"Get her to safety," he instructed Doc without turning. "Krysty, I'll see you outside."

The redheaded beauty wanted to say something else; she was his soul mate and she usually wouldn't leave him. But in her weakened state, leave was all she could do. And she knew that Ryan wouldn't leave J.B. alone, not if there was a chance they could defuse the bomb.

Doc guided Krysty down the corridor. "How are you feeling, my dear?" he asked.

Krysty smiled, her usually vibrant hair hanging limply around her face. "Still kind of woozy," she admitted, flashing him a half smile.

"Lean against me," Doc instructed. "I may be old but I'm still good for that much, at least."

While J.B. and Ryan dealt with the bomb, Jak employed his own natural talents to lead the rest of the group out of the redoubt as swiftly as he could.

While they had landed in an unknown redoubt, these military bases roughly followed the same basic design. Jak followed the widest corridor, turning each time it split and choosing the widest corridor again. The overhead lights flickered to life at each junction Jak stepped into, brought to life by motion sensors, filling in the void ahead with each step.

The others followed as fast as they were able—Doc

helping Krysty along at his side, Mildred watching Ricky carefully as the lad struggled with his wounded side.

Mildred looked worriedly at Ricky. She glanced back at the open door to the control room—not to check on J.B. but merely to see how far they were from the potential blast. Mildred had feelings for J.B.—they were lovers—but she remained professional and focused during times like this. She had seen too many mistakes caused by people not paying attention, and as a doctor her first concern had to be her patient.

Mildred could see that Ricky wouldn't make it to the outside in the two minutes they had left. He was slowing even now, not quite limping but certainly dragging his heels. His face was looking paler, too: blood loss.

"Jak, we're going to have to stop," Mildred called.

Without slowing his pace, Jak glanced over his shoulder and nodded. "We go. No point all dying."

It was a harsh truth, Mildred knew. She turned back to Ricky, indicating an open doorway. "Stop here," she instructed.

"But Ryan said…" Ricky began.

Mildred shot him a look. "I need to look at that wound," she said. "In here." She led him through the open doorway into what appeared to be a television monitoring room. The room contained two swivel chairs and a bank of television screens that dominated one wall in a gentle curve.

Ricky looked around with evident concern. "Lot of glass here if the bomb goes off."

Mildred ignored him. "Lift up your arms," she said, and Ricky did so.

RYAN STOOD IN the doorway to the control room, wondering how long they had.

"J.B.?"

Inside the chamber, J.B. crouched by the device, warily eyeballing it. The timer was attached to a chemical mix with an explosive and an accelerant to increase the blast. When it went off, it would appear to be a single explosion, but in fact there would be two in very quick succession, the first triggering the full payload of the device. The Armorer judged the size of the device.

"The armaglass will hold the explosion," he called back to Ryan.

"What about defusing it?" Ryan asked.

J.B. shook his head, still holding the wire cutters in front of him. "This bastard's wired up six ways to Sunday. I'd need hours to figure it out," he admitted.

"How long do we have?"

"Thirty seconds," J.B. replied, slipping his wire cutters back into his jacket pocket. Then he got up from his crouch, knowing better than to rush. Rushing only made a person careless; the one time in a million that a person would slip on the floor of a chamber and earn a concussion. Thirty seconds was plenty of time to get out.

Ryan was waiting for J.B. at the door to the control room. If the bomb went off early, they were dead, but Ryan wouldn't leave J.B.—they had been brothers in arms for too long for him to do that.

J.B. made his way swiftly to the chamber door and pulled it closed behind him. Once the door was closed, the mat-trans chamber was designed to be airtight to ensure a clean jump when in use. J.B. trusted that to help protect them from the blast. There were fifteen seconds left now before the bomb went off.

J.B. turned, checking his pockets nervously as he hurried from the room. He still had the M-4000 and the Mini-Uzi he habitually carried; it wouldn't do to escape the explosion only to find himself weaponless.

Ryan watched as J.B. strode toward him.

"What are you still doing here?" J.B. asked, irritated.

"You think I'm letting you get blown up on your own?" Ryan snapped back. "Too much water under the bridge for that."

J.B. nodded. "Ten seconds," he said as he followed Ryan into the stark corridor.

Then the two men started to run, hurrying for the nearest doorway, which was cracked open. They pried it open wider to accommodate their size and slipped inside.

"Four…three…two…one," J.B. intoned. When he got to "two," both men turned away from the direction of the blast and placed their hands over their ears.

A moment later a dull sound like a thump reverberated through the redoubt, followed by a much louder boom accompanied almost instantaneously by the tinkling sound of shattering glass. Ryan and J.B. fell to the floor as the shockwave rocked through the redoubt.

JAK WAS WITH Doc and Krysty when the bomb exploded. They were standing in a garage area of the redoubt, close to the surface and far enough away that they heard the explosion as a kind of distant cough. Still, they all knew exactly what it was and for a moment a solemn hush seemed to pass over them.

Krysty tensed. "Ryan…"

Doc held on to her, pulling her close. "Relax, Krysty, my girl," he said, trying to calm her. "We don't know what has happened yet."

"I want to go back," Krysty told him.

"Going back would only serve to place us in more danger," Doc said reasonably. "They will come to us when they are ready."

A few paces ahead of them, Jak had adopted a semi-

crouch as he walked toward the door to the redoubt. The
door lay on one side of the wide, garage-like area within
which a few military vehicles still remained. The vehicles
had been stripped down to shells, their components and
armament long gone, tires removed along with anything
else that anyone might be able to put to use. Worryingly,
the door to the redoubt was open and showed about four
feet of blue sky along with the scrappy dirt of an overgrown track.

Jak's Colt Python had materialized in his hand once
more. He didn't like the fact that the door was open. It
meant someone had been inside, which the bomb had already indicated, and that maybe they hadn't had time to
close it again, which meant they could still be nearby. Jak's
pale hand flicked at the Colt's trigger guard absently as he
approached the opening, padding toward it on silent feet.

Jak stopped for a moment at the open door and listened, isolating the sounds coming from outside. There
were birds chirruping, the buzz of insects…and a being,
moving amid the undergrowth, feet shuffling on leaves
and grass. A moment later Jak heard another sound—more
figures approaching, moving in unison with military pre-
cision, moving fast.

Blaster poised in front of him, Jak stepped through the
open door of the redoubt.

Chapter Three

The redoubt door had been propped open using a web of sawed-down tree limbs and pieces of metal, Jak noted as he stepped through the opening. The construction was well planned and solid, raised on a scaffold-type arrangement. In addition, attention had been paid to the meeting point where the door slid into the wall. There was no exposed hinge or mechanism there, but someone had gone to a lot of trouble to bend the thick titanium door so that it would not snap back. Someone who wanted to get in and get out again.

There were trees all around, and it took a moment for Jak to zone out the noises of the local fauna and locate the sound of shuffling feet he had first noted from inside the redoubt. *There. To the left.*

A dirt track led to the redoubt entrance with a scrubby grass border to either side, wide enough to carry a wag. The scarred remains of a tarmac road had all but disintegrated, leaving black chunks of broken tarmac dotted amid the dirt. Jak stepped over the path and onto the grass, where he could ensure his passage would remain silent. The grass shone with dew, catching the morning sunlight in sparkling spots like glitter.

The sounds of marching feet were getting closer, and they were moving fast. Jak guessed at least three people were among the group, but it was hard to tell from the way the footsteps echoed. There could be three or three hundred moving in step.

Crouching, his blaster held in one hand, Jak scrambled across the scrub, weaving swiftly between stubby trees. His keen eyes spotted the figure crouching behind a bush, tiny red berries arrayed across it like beads of blood. It was a man, mid-thirties with a little gray clouding his dark beard, wearing cotton clothes, light and simple and remarkably clean. His hands were dirty, though, and there was a streak of what looked like either oil or dirt on his face. He was breathing heavy, fearful. Jak slowed as he spotted the blaster in the man's hand. It was a Smith & Wesson, not much more than seven inches in length, its once-gleaming surface pitted and blackened with age.

The man turned at the albino youth's approach, as much sensing him as hearing him. Jak was still twenty feet from the man. Even from that distance, Jak could see the man's blue eyes were wide with anxiousness, and he brought the Smith & Wesson around to target Jak at the same time as he turned. But when he saw Jak, something seemed to change in his expression—first surprise, then relief.

"Thank heaven," the man said in a breathless whisper. "I thought you were…"

He stopped, alert like a dog, his head turning to locate the sound of the marching feet.

Jak spotted the figures moving through the trees for the first time. Dressed in white robes, they were easy to see. They didn't walk together but had spread out, taking different routes down the slope, but still marching in time. Jak counted five of them wending through the trees above, fluid and almost mist-like in their movements. It wasn't like watching soldiers, it was like watching dancers.

Crouched by the bush, the bearded man glanced back

at Jak, his eyes pleading. "Did the bomb go off?" he whispered. "You can't let them—"

His words were cut short by a woman's voice coming from upslope. "William! Will? What are you doing?"

The man—presumably William—turned back, raised his blaster and fired. The discharge sounded loud in the stillness of the woods, its thundering echo accompanied by the frightened cries of birds taking flight in its wake.

Jak ducked back, dipping behind the nearest tree and using its trunk for cover. It was a birch, and the trunk was too narrow to give adequate protection, even for Jak's small frame. But there was no time to find better, not now that bullets were flying.

William had clearly missed his target, and he blasted again, firing another shot into the trees. Upslope, one of the figures in white moved, stepping swiftly behind a tree as the bullet struck a branch.

Jak watched the figure slip out from cover and he could discern that it was a woman—perhaps the same one who had called to William.

"Help me," the man called, his voice raised now in panic. He glanced back to where Jak was hiding, his brow furrowing as he saw that Jak had disappeared. "Please, you know what they'll do…"

Jak almost gasped as the white-clad figures emerged from the trees, converging on the armed man in a flurry of fluttering robes. All five were women, young and tall and svelte with long limbs and long hair styled atop their heads in some kind of elaborate braid or plait. The robes were made of a light, gauzy material, pure white like predark summer clouds, covering each woman from her neck all the way down to her ankles. There were wide pleats within the design of the robes that made the skirts and sleeves billow around them like mist, making it hard to determine where their bodies ended and the robes began. They were beautiful, angelic.

Jak watched as the women converged on the lone man. William rose from his crouch and shouted, "Die! Damn you all!" before blasting wildly at the women, again and again, shifting his aim to shoot the next and the next and the next.

Still gliding toward the man, the women moved gracefully but swiftly, sidestepping the shots with breathtaking ease. Jak watched, incredulous, as one of the women, honey-red hair piled on her head, leaped from the ground and kicked out at a tree, using it to lever herself higher as a bullet whizzed beneath her. It was an exceptional move, both in terms of speed and agility, and the timing was nothing less than perfect.

The woman landed back on the ground in a swish of billowing robes, now just three feet from the man with the blaster. He depressed the trigger again, sending another .45 slug at the woman's face from almost point-blank range. The woman darted aside at the same time, and a combination of her speed and the man's fear sent the bullet wide.

Then the woman grabbed the barrel of the man's blaster in her right hand, yanking it aside as he fired again. All around them, the other figures had converged on this spot and stood just a few feet away, surrounding the two combatants as the unarmed woman overpowered her blaster-wielding foe.

Jak winced as the weapon blasted again, sending another bullet toward the woman's shoulder. It missed her but it was close, and Jak saw the wide shoulder strap of her dress shred as the bullet breezed past, a trace of red kicking into the air as the bullet clipped her skin.

The man was shouting in nonsensical sentence fragments now. Something about stopping them… Something about love… Jak could see the man's trigger finger squeezing again and again, but there was no ammo left in his blaster.

The white-robed women converged on him. What happened next, Jak couldn't see. All he saw was the billowing robes circling the spot where the man had gone down, fluttering there like waves.

MILDRED AND RICKY waited in the redoubt monitoring room as the explosion shook the walls. Dust escaped from the ceiling fixtures and a great cloud tumbled down from the bank of television screens that dominated one wall.

"You think…" Ricky began.

But Mildred was too focused on her task to respond. She was crouched beside him, her face close to the bloody mess that dominated the left side of Ricky's shirt. "Ready?" she asked, and Ricky nodded. She lifted his shirt in a single, swift gesture and Ricky yelped in pain. "Okay," Mildred soothed. "You're okay."

The blood made it look worse than it was, the way it had spread across Ricky's skin. But it had started clotting and had dried with Ricky's shirt, sticking flesh to material. That was why it had hurt so much when Mildred had ripped his shirt away.

Mildred prodded at the wound. You had to move quickly in the Deathlands, and field medicine like this was often the only option. Keeping the companions patched up was Mildred's job, and she was damn good at it, too. "How does it look?" Ricky asked, breathing through clenched teeth.

"Nasty," Mildred told him, taking an inch-high bottle of ammonia from her supplies. "You've lost a lot of skin, but we'll clean that out and get you bandaged up. You'll live."

Ricky winced, holding back the tears. "Hurts bastard bad," he said as Mildred knelt to clean the wound.

The physician arched a brow. "Boy, you listen too closely to J.B. and Ryan's turns of phrase."

DEBRIS LITTERED THE floor of the corridor and a coating of dust covered the two figures that lay inside the door.

Ryan moved first, pulling himself up to a sitting position and brushing plaster dust from his dark hair. Beside him, J.B. stirred and flinched at the movement, turning to Ryan with a coating of dust on the lenses of his spectacles.

Ryan looked at him and smiled. "You still alive?" he said.

"Hundred percent," J.B. confirmed, rubbing at one ear to stop the ringing. "Let's go check on the damage."

Warily, the two men entered corridor. It was a mess, but just surface mess—nothing a dustpan and brush couldn't smarten up in a few minutes. There was a hairline crack running up the wall beside the door to the control room, as thin as a spider's web. Ryan gestured to it as he passed. "Could have been your skull," he said.

J.B. laughed and rapped his knuckles on the wall. "Nah, my skull's thicker than this," he responded.

Moving quietly, Ryan and J.B. returned to the control room and surveyed the damage. The control area itself had barely sustained any damage other than a coating of plaster dust, but the mat-trans chamber was billowing with dark smoke and two-thirds of the toughened-glass walls that surrounded it had shattered, leaving a carpet of twinkling shards that spread out from the chamber like projectile vomit.

The chamber's fans were whirring loudly as they worked to clear the smoke while ancient, ceiling-mounted water sprinklers made a hissing, fizzing sound though nothing came out of their pipes. Presumably, in the hundred years since this facility had been built, the contents of their supply tanks had either leaked or evaporated, leaving just the sound of the taps as they opened and closed, opened and closed.

When Ryan and J.B. entered the anteroom, they could see fire within the hexagonal chamber of the mat-trans itself, spots of flame licking at what was left of the walls and burning in patches on the tiled floor. Black smoke poured from the smeared remains of the crate-like device that had once abutted the back wall, but almost nothing remained of the device itself other than the basic shape of the box that had held it, now seared into the floor in a black rectangle.

Ryan shook his head, waving smoke out of his eye. "We won't be using this again in a hurry," he said grimly.

J.B. nodded solemnly. He left the anteroom and peered around the control room before spying the fire extinguishers. He strode over to them and reached for the boxy cabinet that clung to the wall above them, removing the fire blanket that was strapped there. The fire blanket had waited a century for someone to use it, and it smelled of mildew.

The Armorer strode back to the mat-trans and shook the blanket, throwing it across the flaming scar of the explosive, his feet tramping in the shattered armaglass. "Could be our only way out," he reminded Ryan as they watched the blanket smother the flames. "Best do what we can to contain the damage."

Ryan eyed the damaged floor tiles and the missing armaglass with concern. "You think this is repairable?"

"If it has to be," J.B. told him. "Mebbe it won't come to that."

They waited a moment for the flames to stop burning and watched the smoke ease to a wispy trail in the air like a squirrel's tail.

Ryan watched the smoke dissipate, voicing the question that neither of them could answer. "Who did this and why?"

J.B. just shook his head. "For now, I guess we should be grateful we didn't arrive three minutes after we did," he said dourly.

ON THE SLOPE outside the redoubt, the white-clad women stepped away from the figure they had surrounded and Jak saw that the man was dead. His neck had been snapped and his head was poised at an awkward angle as he lay on the dirt, his eyes wide-open and staring into nothingness.

As one, the women turned at a noise. Jak heard it, too. It was coming from the redoubt.

Still in his hiding place, Jak saw Krysty and Doc emerging through the doors, their blasters held loosely in their hands. Krysty looked more able to stand on her own now, which was something.

As they stepped out onto the path, the women in the white robes moved through the trees toward them. Jak stepped out from cover, holding his blaster loosely, pointed straight up to the sky. "Wait," he said. "Mean no harm."

The women stopped, their white robes fluttering around them as they caught the breeze.

"Who are you?" the closest woman demanded. She had blond hair so pale it was almost white, and her eyes were a luminous green.

"Jak Lauren," Jak said before indicating the redoubt entrance with an incline of his head. "Friends. Not hurting."

Behind the blonde, another woman, this one with dark skin like Mildred's, smiled tentatively as she spoke. "He speaks like a child," she said. "It's sweet."

"His blaster isn't sweet," the blonde replied, her emerald eyes fixed on the weapon in Jak's hand.

Jak took his cue and, holding out his empty hand in a placating gesture, he lowered himself to place his Colt Python on the ground. Jak didn't like being weaponless—well, he was hardly that, as every sleeve and pocket contained a leaf-bladed throwing knife, though these strangers were not to know that—but he saw the necessity to act peaceably while the lives of his friends were at stake.

"Jak?" Doc's voice carried up the slope. "Where are you, lad?"

The blonde fixed Jak with a look. "You had better reply, Jak," she said. "Tell them to put down their blasters if, truly, they and you mean us no harm."

Jak did just that, raising his voice and explaining the situation in his clipped manner. "Put away blasters, no danger," he called back to Doc. "Five new friends here." He was careful to state the number, so that Doc and Krysty would know how many they faced should it come to a firefight.

Down by the redoubt entrance, Doc and Krysty reluctantly placed their blasters in their holsters. The white-robed women watched, and the blonde—their leader? Jak wondered—nodded agreeably.

"Now," said the blonde, "tell them to wait there."

Jak did, and a few seconds later he was being led by the group back to the redoubt entrance.

"Well, well," Doc said, appreciably eyeing the long-limbed beauties who accompanied Jak. "I see you have made some charming new acquaintances."

Then Doc bent at the waist in a slight bow. "My name is Dr. Theophilus Tanner," he introduced himself, "and my companion here is Krysty Wroth. You've already met young Jak here." Doc made no mention of their other companions, still inside the redoubt. It didn't do to reveal all your cards too early in the game.

"Doctor," the blond spokeswoman said, the hint of a smile crossing her thin lips. "This is private territory. Would you care to explain how you came to be here?"

Doc fingered the handle of his sword cane for a moment as he thought. "We...um...arrived via a miraculous machine."

"The mat-trans," a brunette said from the back of the group. "You worked it?"

Krysty gasped at her casual comment.

Doc had not intended to be quite so transparent in his explanation, but caught unawares all he could do was reply truthfully. "Yes, the mat-trans," he said. "We ran into a spot of bother out—" he gestured vaguely "—yonder and made the jump here, wherever here is. I am afraid it was all rather rushed."

The women stepped forward, concern on their features. "And how is the mat-trans?" the dark-skinned woman asked.

"They survived the jump," the brunette pointed out before Doc could reply. "Obviously, it's operational."

"Ah, no," Doc replied before the women could continue. "There was an explosive device inside the unit that..."

"Exploded," Krysty suggested, seeing Doc struggling.

"Quite, yes," Doc acknowledged.

"William placed a bomb?" the honey-haired woman said in alarm.

"Deirdre thought as much," the blonde confirmed before turning back to Doc.

Jak listened to all of this in silence, piecing together the story in his mind. William was the man he had come across in the woods, who had engaged in the firefight with these mysterious women before being chilled by them. William had said something to Jak before that fight began, something that might have been important. Jak thought back, recalling that the man had asked about the bomb. "You can't let them…" was all he had said. Can't let them…what?

"We should go check," the dark-skinned woman said and the others agreed.

"Darn it, if William has blown up the mat-trans…" the brunette said, bitterly shaking her head.

"And it had to be now," the honey-haired woman agreed, "right when these travelers could have…"

The blonde hushed them both with a look. "Melissas."

"Melissas," the honey-blonde replied, lowering her head, and her companion did the same.

The five women ushered Doc, Krysty and Jak back inside the redoubt. Doc wondered when would be the most appropriate time to mention that they had more companions waiting within.

Chapter Four

"I don't like losing the mat-trans," J.B. stated as he and Ryan moved through the redoubt. "Makes me edgy."

"I don't like it any more than you do," Ryan agreed. "The mat-trans have been our little secret for a long time, and I don't revel in losing our escape hatch like this if we are in a hostile place. Otherwise, it means a hike overland to wherever the next redoubt is."

As the two men trotted past the monitoring room, Mildred's head poked out, calling them back.

"Hey, guys!" They joined Mildred in the monitoring room, where Ricky was just fixing his shirt over the bandage that Mildred had affixed around his belly and ribs. J.B. touched Mildred's face briefly, leaving what he wanted to say unvoiced.

"What happened?" Ricky asked, looking from Ryan to J.B.

"Bomb went off," Ryan said, "ruining the mat-trans."

"Damn," Ricky cursed.

J.B. made a show of looking at the youth's bloody shirt. "How are you feeling? You okay, kid?" he asked.

Ricky shrugged. "*De nada.* I've had worse in Nuestra Señora."

He was bluffing, J.B. knew. That musket shell had scored blood and had to have hurt like hell, but the kid was proud and he didn't like to show weakness in front of the companions.

"I only heard one explosion," Mildred was saying as she put her extra bandage in her medical satchel.

Ryan nodded. "We were lucky," he agreed. "There were no other bombs. A military base like this could've been stuffed full of ordnance that might have been rigged remotely to go off when the bomb went off."

"You said the mat-trans was wrecked," Mildred said, phrasing it like a question.

"Yeah, for now anyway," J.B. confirmed. "We might be able to do something with it, given time, but we'd be better off finding another mat-trans if we need one."

"Let's hope it doesn't come to that," Mildred said, "but, assuming it does, how far would we have to go?"

J.B. shrugged. "Till we know where we are, I won't have clue one, Millie," he said.

"Then I guess we'd better start figuring out where we are," Mildred said, and Ryan agreed.

Checking that Ricky was okay to move—he was—Ryan led the way back out into the corridor and the foursome headed toward the outside door.

Doc looked surreptitiously at the five angelic women who accompanied them as he, Krysty and Jak were led back through the redoubt they just exited. Each of these women was young with flawless skin. Doc guessed not one of them was over twenty-one. The blonde led the way confidently, and she seemed to know which paths to take. Doc guessed that she was leading them to the mat-trans chamber to survey the damage that the bomb had wrought, and he wondered if Ryan and the others had survived the blast.

"So," Doc began uncertainly, "Melissa, is it? You seem to know your way around this...facility."

The blonde looked at Doc after a moment, confusion turning to understanding as she realized that he was addressing her. She smiled then, indulging him. "It's not Melissa," she said, "and yes, we've been here many times before."

"Ah," Doc said. "Please accept my apologies, I thought I heard your companions call you Melissa. I must have become muddled."

"They did," the blonde replied as she led them down a stairwell with concrete steps and reinforced-glass banisters dividing each level. "But that's not my name, it's a designation. We're all Melissas."

"I see," Doc said, though he didn't.

"I'm Phyllida. This is Linda, Nancy, Charm and Adele," she said, indicating the others.

"All pretty names," Doc said. "So you say you have been in here on other occasions?" Doc added, raising his voice a little in the hope Ryan would hear—if he was still here.

The Melissa called Phyllida looked back at him and smiled, her teeth white and flawless, much like Doc's own. "The mat-trans you came in was damaged a long time ago in the quake," she explained. "We've been examining its workings, trying to repair it."

"Our engineers," the dark-skinned Melissa, who was called Adele, elaborated.

"We noticed some quake damage when we came in," Krysty said from within the huddle.

"The unit's only been operational—what?—two days," the brunette called Linda said.

"Not even that long," Phyllida said. "They were still testing it yesterday evening."

"Then it seems we arrived bang on time," Doc said, wincing at his rather unfortunate choice of words. "Forgive the unintentional pun."

"Yes, you—"

"Nobody make a sudden move!" Ryan said, stepping from the cover of an open doorway with his SIG Sauer raised in a two-handed grip. "Hands in the air."

J.B. and Mildred stepped out of the shadows behind Ryan, their own weapons raised to target the group of robed women. Behind them both, Ricky waited in the shadow of the doorway, his De Lisle carbine clutched in both hands, the pain of his patched flank making him stand a little hunched over.

The Melissas tensed, moving automatically back so that they were close to the concrete walls.

Doc found himself front and center of the sudden negotiation.

"What's the state of play, Doc?" Ryan growled, his weapon fixed on blond-haired Phyllida where she stood behind the old man.

Doc took a deep, steadying breath, his hands surreptitiously twisting the silver lion's-head grip of his swordstick to release the blade within. "These people are unarmed, Ryan," he stated, "and they have shown no inclination to harm us. It is my understanding that their sole interest is in the mat-trans, which they have been working on for some time."

"Did they plant the bomb?" J.B. asked, running the shotgun over the group in warning.

"No," Doc explained. "I am led to understand that they opposed the individual who did that, and that they had hoped to stop it."

He turned to Phyllida. "Is this correct?"

Phyllida nodded. "Yes. You didn't mention that there were more of you," she said.

Doc raised his eyebrows. "You did not ask."

Phyllida looked from Doc to Ryan and the others who

had their drawn blasters pointed at them. "Your friend is quite correct," she said at last. "We won't hurt you."

"My name is Phyllida," the blond-haired woman continued. "We of the Trai have a strict 'no blasters' policy, and we would be grateful if you would adhere to that while on our property."

She waited while Ryan watched her, his lone eye scanning carefully over her companions as he weighed them up. Finally he said, "And your people are unarmed?"

"Precisely so," Phyllida confirmed.

Ryan searched Doc's face for some sign of deceit and saw none. It paid to be cautious in the Deathlands, but a standoff had to be resolved, one way or the other, and Ricky couldn't keep fighting without recovering. Slowly, Ryan brought his SIG Sauer down and holstered it, and his people did the same. Ryan knew just what J.B. was thinking as the Armorer slung his shotgun—it was the same thing that they were all thinking. Can these people be trusted?

"I'm Ryan," the one-eyed man said, though he made no move to meet Phyllida.

Instead she came to him, her pure-white robes fluttering behind her like mist, one delicate, pale hand outstretched in greeting. "Pleased to meet you, Ryan."

Ryan took the woman's hand. Her grip was firm, stronger than he would expect for her build. He released her hand after a moment.

"I guess you weren't inside when the bomb hit," Ryan said.

"What makes you say that?" Phyllida asked.

"Your clothes," Ryan said. "They're clean."

"You're right," Phyllida replied. "We were outside this structure, tracking down the violator who planted the device. I understand it went off."

"Yeah," Ryan said.

"Then I'm sorry we didn't get here sooner," Phyllida told him. She sounded genuine, her voice tinged with regret.

J.B. spoke up from behind Ryan's shoulder, his eyes watching the strangely garbed women carefully. "You use the mat-trans often?" he asked.

"No, never," Phyllida told him. "But we had hoped to, as stories had been passed down for generations regarding its purpose. As I was telling your companion here, the device was out of commission for a very long time. Our people only achieved functionality again barely a day ago."

"Then someone blew it up," J.B. said drily. "That's mighty inconvenient."

One of the other Melissas spoke up, the honey-haired one called Charm. "William was a fool." She spit. "He should have been driven out of Heaven months ago."

"Heaven?" Doc asked with obvious surprise. These women dressed like angels, but surely…

Phyllida turned back to him and smiled. "Heaven Falls," she said. "Where we live. We'll show you, if you like, once we've assessed the damage to the mat-trans. It won't take long."

"Heaven Falls." Doc rolled the name around in his mind. "It sounds, well… It sounds heavenly. Does it not, Ryan?"

The one-eyed man looked from Doc to Krysty and the others, judging their expressions. When he met with Mildred's chocolate-brown eyes he saw her nod subtly. She wanted somewhere to check Ricky over more fully. A ville could be it.

"I think we'd like that," Ryan said finally.

Together, the group made its way back through the redoubt to its heart, where the operations room and the mat-trans waited in their state of disarray.

"The bomb was set here," Ryan said. "My friend tried to disarm it, but we ran out of time."

"Placed the fire blanket over it to douse the flames," J.B. said, as if in consolation.

Kneeling, Phyllida lifted the soot-streaked blanket and swept her hand through the mess underneath. It was still hot, but she didn't seem to be bothered. Behind her, two of her companions were lamenting the shattered arma-glass walls, while the other two checked the equipment in the control room.

"No signs of additional damage," Adele said as she worked one of the consoles.

"All clear here," black-haired Nancy confirmed, running a boot-up sequence on another console on the far side of the room.

Ryan and his companions watched in silence, and he felt almost violated by seeing other people operating the mat-trans controls. The companions had no clue as to how the system worked, but seeing strangers working the equipment felt threatening and very wrong.

After a few moments Phyllida straightened from the smoke-blackened tiles of the mat-trans floor and stood at her full height in front of Ryan. She was a beautiful woman, statuesque with the flawless skin of youth. Women like this didn't usually exist in the Deathlands; it was a demanding environment, one that wore away at people, and at women most of all. Seeing these Melissas, as they called themselves, made Ryan feel uneasy, as if he was being tricked somehow.

"Thanks for everything you did to stop the fire," Phyllida said.

"J.B. here—" Ryan began, but Phyllida interrupted him.

"You're all to join us at the Home," she said. "I'm sure

that the Regina will want to thank you personally when she hears of your heroics."

With that, the Melissas ushered the group from the control room and out into the corridor. Within minutes they were outside, following the dirt track that led from the redoubt door.

IT WAS BEGINNING to warm up outside. They were in a wooded area, lush grass lining the steep slope that led toward a blue, cloudless sky. Surprisingly, the usual chem clouds were absent here.

Though she had been outside briefly, Krysty wore a broad smile as she stepped into the sunlight again. She looped her arm through Ryan's and pulled him into a sunny spot that was brightly illuminated on the dirt-and-tarmac path. "It feels good to be alive," she told him, and Ryan knew what she meant. She had had no chance to express her concern for him in front of all these strangers, and her comment now was a veiled reference to how pleased she was that he had survived the bomb blast. Giving away too much about relationships, or much of anything else, wasn't smart when you were around strangers.

"Your friend likes the sunlight," the honey-haired Melissa observed.

Krysty remained on the path, twirling joyfully with her arms outstretched, a few feet from the redoubt's entrance.

"She does at that," Doc agreed, "and her name is Krysty, though forgive me if I have already forgotten yours, foolish old man that I am."

"Charm," the woman replied, flashing Doc her perfect smile.

"How very appropriate," Doc replied.

The companions were allowed to keep their weapons, which boded well. In fact, *allowed* was too strong a word for it—the Melissas simply showed no interest in discussing their blasters just as long as they kept them holstered. Jak retrieved his Colt Python from where he had dropped it close to the redoubt entrance, and that was the only occasion where blasters were ever mentioned in conversation, wherein Linda instructed him to keep the weapon out of sight at all times. That was also when the subject of the late William came up.

"I'm sorry that you had to witness that," Phyllida told Jak.

"Not see much," Jak told her.

"The man was a violator," Phyllida explained sorrowfully. It seemed that she regretted not that Jak had seen it so much as that their society had deviants at all.

"Violation is a disease," she added. "It eats away at our love, fracturing the world we try to build. I'm proud of what I do for the Home, even though my contribution is small."

"What is it you do?" Ryan asked her.

Phyllida thrust her shoulders back proudly, like a soldier showing earned medals, and gestured to her white-robed companions. "We are Melissas," she said. "We protect the Home from factions that would destroy it, both from outside and within."

"Then you're sec women?" J.B. queried.

Phyllida looked at him and shrugged. "I haven't heard that term," she said, then remained silent, unsure of how to explain it to these strangely garbed outlanders.

Ryan and his companions followed as the white-robed Melissas led them up through the trees, following some unseen route they knew only from familiarity. There were flowers dotted here and there, more of them as they moved closer to their destination, brightening the surroundings with little oases of color: here a patch of magenta, there a line of red and white and blue. Occasionally, J.B. caught Phyllida and the others looking up at the sun, and he guessed that they were using it to navigate, the same way he did when he arrived at a new location.

Not far into the journey, Ricky stumbled and Mildred was forced to stop the group while she rechecked his wound. When he lifted his shirt, Mildred saw that the wound was still weeping blood; a darkness that was almost black had spread across the gauze she had used to patch him.

"Is your young friend going to be all right?" Adele asked with evident concern.

"He'll be okay," Mildred said, but there was worry in her tone.

Linda spoke swiftly, almost cheerfully. "We have a medical faculty at Home. Perhaps your companion could…" She trailed off, looking to the group's leader for confirmation.

"Of course," Phyllida said. "We would be only too happy to help."

"Thanks," Mildred said, but she sounded unconvinced. What kind of medical faculty? she wondered as Ricky replaced his shirt over the wound.

The group moved slower after that, with Ricky leaning alternately against Mildred and Jak as they trekked the path to Heaven Falls.

They were following a dead-straight path through the trees. Ryan sensed something familiar about the place; the foliage reminding him of Front Royal, where he had grown up. That was in Virginia, and he wondered if they had landed close. He caught Phyllida's attention and asked her.

"Where exactly are we?" he asked.

"Almost home," Phyllida replied, unintentionally cryptic. "You'll see in a few minutes."

And see they did. About six minutes later the group reached the summit of a rise and the trees parted to reveal a great mountain range towering over the grassy plains. Ryan's breath caught in his throat as he looked out over those familiar mountains, while the others stopped and stared. It was Virginia, he was almost sure of it. They were looking out over the Blue Ridge Mountains.

"Is it much farther to this ville of yours?" J.B. asked, his dour voice bringing Ryan back to earth.

"Through there," Phyllida told J.B., pointing down a little ways through the crags.

J.B. and the others looked, and they saw lush green grass dotted by wooden, boxlike constructions that stood to roughly shoulder height. The boxy constructions featured latticed sides and stood atop what looked like table legs, and each had been painted white.

"Are those beehives?" Mildred asked, surprised.

"We farm honey here," Phyllida told her in reply. "The bees like the coolness of the mountain air. They thrive in high environments."

"I did not know that," Mildred admitted.

Phyllida led the way through the rows of manmade beehives and deeper into the gorge between mountains. The beehives buzzed with a constant low hum, and Doc ducked his head as a bee flew close by.

"They won't hurt you," Charm told Doc, having somewhat attached herself to him during the journey over. "They just want to get to the pollen."

Embarrassed, Doc laughed. "I told you I was an old fool," he said.

There was an overhang of trees up ahead, creating a natural gateway leading into a sloping path. Beyond that stood a wide depression between the mountains within which lay the home of the Trai people.

And what a home it was!

There, in the wide plain that rested in the depression between mountains, stood a structure like nothing they had ever seen before. Like most villes the companions had encountered, it was surrounded by a high gated wall on which was located a sentry tower where sec men—or in this case, women—watched the surroundings, night and day. Behind that, white towers gleamed in the sunlight, arranged in a great circle that rose up into the sky, each building an almost perfectly circular tower. Tiny figures moved among the towers, striding across high walkways like acrobats in a circus act.

It was left to Doc to express what they were all thinking, albeit in his own inimitable style.

"By the Three Kennedys!"

Chapter Five

The companions followed Phyllida and the other Melissas onto the path that led into the gorge and, from there, to the gates themselves. As they approached, it became clear that the miraculous buildings were not quite circular. Subtle lines worked around their edges to form a soft hexagonal shape, utilizing the space perfectly. Arranged together like that, the buildings reminded Mildred of the pipes of her late father's old church organ, but even those pipes had never gleamed so vibrantly as the buildings she now saw. While it reminded Mildred of the church organ, it also reminded her of something else—a fictitious city she had seen in an old movie serial back when she and her brother had just been kids.

"Mongo," she muttered, shaking her head. "We've just walked to freaking Mongo."

The others didn't hear her; they were too wrapped up in the incredible sight in front of them.

"Welcome to Heaven Falls," Phyllida announced, leading the companions to the gates of this incredible ville.

The gates to Heaven Falls were tall and well secured, fifteen feet in height with great metal rivets and hinges, two alert sentries watching from a tower that loomed over them to the left-hand side. The sentries were women, dressed in the same white robes as the party of Melissas who had found Ryan and his companions. The sentry tower was like a wooden box on stilts, with barred sides and no glass, making it difficult to shoot into but also preventing the additional danger of shattering glass should a bullet find a path through the bars.

Ryan thought of those things as he approached, wondering how far he would need to be to get a good shot from his Steyr Scout into the sentry box. Such were the thoughts of a man who had been shaped by the Deathlands, where every stranger had to be presumed to be an enemy. At least these strangers hadn't disarmed them, and that counted for a lot as far as trust went. But Ryan was still conscious that he might be leading his friends into a trap.

It was a twenty-minute walk to the redoubt, but that had been with Ricky's wounded flank slowing them. Ryan estimated he could march it in under fifteen minutes, sprint it in maybe seven. But with the mat-trans out of commission, that knowledge would serve them little good.

The sentries recognized Phyllida and her group, and the towering gates began to withdraw on a great winch mechanism. The winch squeaked loudly as it moved the heavy gates, granting Ryan and the companions their first proper view of the ville that lay beyond.

A main track led into the heart of the ville, with other roads peeling away at regular intervals. The streets were wide and unpaved, with farming machinery, including plows and mowers, waiting at the edge of the thoroughfare. The pale-colored buildings visible over the walls were clustered close to the center, with a lot of the land to each side given over to animal farming. It didn't surprise Ryan that the animals were kept behind the gates—there was a lot to lose in animal farming. Rustlers could move in quickly and leave a ville starving in just a few hours.

Accompanied by the Melissas, Ryan and the companions entered. While the ville incorporated the central white towers, there were also other, lower buildings spread around, with plenty of wide-open space between them. Ryan's first impression was that the ville might cover as much as a square mile, with the walls giving way to the towering slopes of the surrounding mountains—natural protection. Grass grew everywhere, a vibrant green carpet running all through the ville, and as one looked away from the main cluster of buildings one could see the grass borders segue into rolling fields where just two or three hut-like lodges had been built.

The ville was very clean. The roads themselves were marked by borders of flowers running in great sweeping lines all the way through the ville in strict flower types, making the roads seem almost as if they had been color-coded like a landing strip. Phyllida and her companions pointed out several interesting features, including a grand meeting hall that was circular in design and covered enough ground to house a battleship. The women were clearly proud of their ville, and they were open and upbeat in welcoming these outlanders to their home.

Ryan listened without comment, nodding as social protocol demanded, but adding little insight of his own. He was too busy taking in everything: the towering buildings that reached six or seven stories into the air; the covered drainage system that ran along the sides of the streets; the series of water pumps erected at regular intervals in the gated community. There were people, too, all of them dressed well, and happy. A lot of children under five ran up and down the street, herded by women in formal-looking attire, their hair pinned back neatly.

One child ran over to take in the companions, stopping fearlessly in front of Ryan and staring openly at him. The child had black hair that had grown a little long so that it was hard to tell if it was a boy or a girl.

"You're dirty," the child said cheerfully.

Ryan looked from the child to his clothes and realized that, at least by the standards of the ville's other occupants, he and his companions were pretty dirty at that. He smiled at the child. "We're hoping to get cleaned up," he told him, "if we're allowed to stick around."

Phyllida turned back to Ryan, her blond hair catching the morning sun in a shimmer of gold. "That won't be a problem, Ryan," she assured him. "We have facilities here for bathing and for cleaning clothes."

Ryan nodded once in acknowledgment. "We'd be grateful, ma'am."

The dark-haired child was being called by one of the neatly dressed women, but didn't seem to notice. "Patrick! Patrick, come back here," she cried, trotting briskly over on low-heeled shoes. Finally the child turned when the woman was almost at arm's length.

"That man's got a blaster," Patrick told her without a hint of fear in his voice.

The woman looked at Ryan and smiled. She was young and pretty, with red hair a little darker than Krysty's. "Sorry," she said to Ryan before turning back to her charge.

"I'm sure he won't use it," she explained, taking little Patrick's hand. "While you need to get to school before the bell goes, otherwise you won't learn anything."

Patrick seemed reluctant to go for a moment. "Are you going to teach us about blasters, miss?" he asked.

"Well," said the woman, evidently Patrick's teacher, "you'll only find out when you get to school."

This seemed to satisfy the child, who'd probably have forgotten the conversation by the time he got to school anyway. The redhead turned back to Ryan just once as she departed with Patrick. She looked apologetic, but Ryan thought he detected something else there, too—she was eyeing his weapons, the handblaster at his hip and the Scout longblaster slung across his back like the Grim Reaper's scythe.

"Kid seemed surprised by my blasters," Ryan said to Phyllida. "Don't you have weapons here?"

"We have no need of them," Phyllida replied, "though we do understand that things are somewhat different outside these walls."

"Yeah," J.B. observed dourly. "You could say that."

What struck Ryan, however, was not the lack of weapons but the educational program that was apparently in place. Growing up as the son of a wealthy baron, his life had been one of privilege. Ryan had learned to read and to write and he had had a good schooling in history and other subjects, despite the mess the world at large was still in following the nukecaust of 2001. Ryan was one of the lucky ones, and his travels around the Deathlands had made him very aware of that.

Most of the people in the land that had once been called the United States of America scratched their living day-to-day, feeding on what scraps they could find and preying on one another. The strong used, abused and chilled the weak to satisfy their whims, and there was little opportunity for formal education or for the sharing and exploration of ideas. But what they saw here, with the children being herded to school like sheep in a pen, told Ryan something that no discussion would have—that this settlement, Heaven Falls, was progressive. It was a society with its eyes on the future, on building and on betterment. In short, it was the very thing that he and his companions had sought for so long as they'd traveled the broken roads of the Deathlands—the sprouting buds of new civilization.

THE GROUP SOON reached the complex of tall towers. Each stood as wide as a house and five or six stories in height, with gently curving sides in a hexagonal design. The cluster of towers was arranged in a circular pattern, six on the outside with a single, broader tower in the middle. As she looked at it, once again Mildred was put in mind of church organ pipes.

Despite the beauty of their surroundings, however, Mildred was conscious that Ricky was in pain. She called to the closest Melissa, the black-haired girl called Nancy. "Is there anywhere here that I can look over my friend without being disturbed? He took a hit and I'm trained in medical matters."

Nancy smiled warmly. "Of course," she said, and after a brief exchange with Phyllida, she led Mildred and Ricky to one of the towers that surrounded the central spire.

"Mildred," Ryan called, and she turned. "Why don't you take Jak with you?"

Jak nodded, taking his cue and bounding after Mildred and Ricky.

Phyllida's brow furrowed as she watched the albino charge away. Ryan saw that, and he offered a reassuring smile.

"Who knows how long she'll be," Ryan explained. "You have a smart-looking ville here and Jak's our best tracker—he'll make sure they don't get lost or lose us."

Phyllida seemed reassured at that. "You call it a ville?" she asked.

"Yeah," Ryan replied. "Like a village."

The Melissas laughed, and one of the others spoke up— the honey-haired one who seemed to have attached herself to Doc. "We call it Home," she said. "You may, too."

"Thanks," Ryan said uncertainly. Despite the friendly atmosphere, he was not quite sure whether he could trust these people. Ryan and his companions had seen a lot of bloodshed and a lot of duplicity over their travels.

MILDRED, RICKY AND Jak followed Nancy across the flower-lined path between the towers toward an entryway. The entrance was broad, with a rounded arch completing its design, and no door. "This place is beautiful," Mildred said, gazing at the gleaming buildings.

"One should be able to take pride in one's home," Nancy said, escorting the three of them into the tower.

The floor was paved, and it echoed their footsteps as they walked inside. Mildred smiled as she saw the entry room. It was spotlessly clean and featured a high ceiling that had to have taken up three floors of this lobby area, at which point the walls gradually began to angle inward as if they were inside some kind of conical pyramid. The grand lobby featured Impressionist-type art on the walls, great murals of swirling colors and abstract shapes. The place was lit by some trick of the wall structure itself, allowing sunlight to penetrate at regular intervals despite there being no visible windows either outside or within. Instead, it seemed that the walls were thinner in places, or perhaps constructed of some specific material that allowed light to pass through it unobscured.

Mildred shook her head incredulously. *Mongo.*

Nancy led them into an unoccupied room featuring two beds, a sink and several chairs.

THE REST OF Ryan's group was accompanied through a free-standing arch into an open-air courtyard, beyond which stood the largest and centermost of the white towers.

"If you would be so kind as to wait here," Phyllida said, "I'll speak with the Regina regarding your arrival."

That didn't sound good, but Ryan accepted it, taking up a position on one of the crescent-shaped benches that lined the courtyard. His companions joined him, weary from their travels, while Phyllida and Adele disappeared inside the tower.

Ryan's lone eye flicked up to watch the remaining sec women for a few moments. The woman with the honey-blond hair—Charm—was engaged in conversation with Doc. The old man had an eye for a pretty woman, and he could be a witty conversationalist. The other Melissa—Linda—paced across the courtyard before assuming a position beside the freestanding arch.

"You trust these people?" J.B. asked Ryan, keeping his voice low.

"Sec force," Ryan replied with a shrug. "What's to trust?"

A peal of laughter erupted from a nearby bench. Doc was showing Charm some kind of old-fashioned dance that involved using his stick as a cane, and they were in the middle of muddling into each other as he tried to demonstrate the steps.

"Doc seems at home already," J.B. observed.

Ryan shook his head. "Doc doesn't know what year it is half the time and he spends the other half wishing he didn't know."

J.B. continued to watch Doc as he showed the younger woman the dance. "Seeing him happy like that reminds me of how he was with Lori," he said.

One of the dance moves seemed to involve turning one's back on one's partner and bumping rear ends. The woman called Charm blushed fiercely when Doc showed her, and, still laughing, she patted Doc's hand.

"Yeah, a lot like Lori," Ryan agreed.

Remembering what had happened to Lori Quint, Ryan wasn't sure that this was such a good thing. She had died shortly after betraying Ryan's group.

JAK WAS PACING the room like a caged tiger. "Not like place," he said to no one in particular. "Too clean."

He halted by the open door, peering out into the lobby area that waited beyond where Nancy had retreated to get help. He could see people moving there, men, women and children, same as in the streets beyond. They were quiet and ordered and clean. It seemed a world away from the life he was used to.

Standing over the bed, Mildred bit her lip in thought. "I'm not going to pull punches, Ricky," she said. "Internal bleeding would be bad. But we can check for that. This seems to be a sterile environment."

Jak hissed in warning. Nancy was returning, accompanied by another woman, this one older, with short, nut-brown hair and wearing a simple jacket-and-pants ensemble of very light blue material. Unseen by the pair, Jak slipped back from the door, gliding across the room until he was standing in the far corner from which he could observe everything. A moment later Nancy and the other woman entered, solemn expressions on their faces.

"Mildred, Ricky, Jak…" Nancy began. "This is Petra, one of our medical experts. Petra, this is Mildred, whom I told you about."

Mildred looked up from where she was checking Ricky's wound, and she showed her hands in slight embarrassment. "Just washed them," she explained to prevent any awkward moment of being expected to shake this new woman's hand.

"That's a nasty-looking wound your patient has suffered," Petra said, stepping closer to the bed. "Nancy said you were all caught up in a bomb blast. None of the rest of you suffered any—"

"No," Mildred said, "we're all fine, barring a little dust in our hair." She was glad that Nancy had informed the woman about the bomb, and that both had assumed that was where Ricky had sustained the wound. It saved her having to explain the fraught circumstances in which they had arrived.

Petra introduced herself to Ricky and began to examine his wound, first with her eyes and then by gently running her fingers over it, careful not to cause the patient too much distress. "There's some grit in the wound," she said.

"I had to patch him in a hurry," Mildred admitted. "I cleaned the wound with ammonia—"

"Which stung like hell," Ricky declared.

"—but there was a lot of dust floating around after the bomb burst," Mildred finished.

"That's understandable," Petra concurred, placating. "I can assure you that this is a sanitary environment. We'll clean out the wound properly with a sterile irrigant, then take a look at treating it with a salve."

Mildred was surprised. "Do you think that will be enough? It's pretty nasty."

"We've been developing some remedies here," Petra told her, "that we've found to be very successful. I think you—and your patient—will be pleasantly surprised."

OUTSIDE THE CENTRAL tower, Krysty joined Ryan on one of the crescent-shaped benches. "I was devastated when I heard the bomb go off," she whispered.

Ryan ran his fingers across her hand, working them along the webbing at the base of hers. "We found somewhere safe," he said. "Those old redoubts are built to withstand a lot."

"So are we," Krysty said, and she raised an eyebrow and smiled.

Before they could say anything further, Phyllida and Adele appeared at the doorway to the grand tower.

"Ryan," Phyllida began, "you and your friends have been granted an audience with the Regina. You may follow us to the meeting suite."

Thanking her, Ryan stood, adjusting the longblaster he carried across his back. Krysty, J.B. and Doc also stood, and together the group was escorted into the towering building.

Chapter Six

The Melissas took up positions to either side of the companions as they strode out of the morning sunshine and into the tower. A broad archway granted entry, with bent sides that worked outward to symmetrical points, and a horizontal apex in mirror to the ground. The entrance was wide enough to drive a couple wags through, shoulder to shoulder, and it served to dwarf any visitor.

Beyond that arch, the interior was almost as bright as the direct sunlight that washed the courtyard. The opening space was a grand reception area that featured a number of smaller, six-sided arches leading from it. The whole place was painted white, with hints of very light grays and blues to highlight certain features such as the grand columns that held the ceiling in place. The floor was covered with large tiles, each one as long as a man was tall, shaped in hexagons so that they could be easily slotted together. The tiles were colored lightly in subtly different off-white shades, creating a clean feel to the room. The ceiling stretched at least four stories overhead, with walkways crisscrossing high above the companions' heads, and a grand balcony stretched along each level where a few people puttered around on errands. Six chandelier-type fixtures hung at regular intervals from beams that crossed the vast area. They were delicately designed from an amber-like substance to create splashes of color in the air, like liquid gold caught in the freeze-frame of the camera shutter. The clear amber jewels caught and spread the light, casting spots of golden orange around the chamber that moved slowly with the breeze. Despite the high ceilings and open space, the room was remarkably quiet, with barely a hint of sound echoing from its other occupants.

Doc was taken with the whole place immediately. "What a wonderful room," he said. "Quite, quite exquisite."

Ryan, however, looked at the room with indifference. As ever, his mind was focused on their destination, not the journey.

Despite the vast proportions of the room, it felt pleasantly warm—even tropical—to Ryan, and he suspected some hidden system of heating was in play.

The group was led through another arch, down a corridor that had been painted a very pale yellow, to a set of closed, wooden double doors that featured an elaborate floral design carved upon their surface. Phyllida waited while Charm and Linda hurried ahead to open the doors. The floral design split perfectly in the middle when the doors opened, reconnecting seamlessly when it was closed. Once the doors were opened, the two white-robed Melissas waited to the side as Phyllida led the way inside.

Beyond the doors lay a grand room, almost circular in design with a low ceiling that loaned it a more intimate feel than the lobby. The walls were carved of wood, with elaborate designs notched into the panels, similar to the one on the doors. A long, straight table dominated the center of the room. The table was forty feet in length and could have seated twelve people easily on each side. A woman sat at the far end of the table on its shortest side, reclining in a seat whose back towered grandly above her to at least double her height.

Chairs were set around the table at regular intervals, and

Ryan and his companions were invited to sit. The woman
at the head of the table looked about thirty-five to Ryan,
and she reclined sideways in the grand chair, her legs dangling over one arm, her feet bare. She was slim and had
flawless skin that had bronzed with the sun. She had luxu-
rious blond hair that shone like gold, wide, appealing blue
eyes and a generous mouth. The clothing she wore was a
vibrant red in color, and though the blouse and pants were
separate they matched exactly. Her clothes were loose, the
top open well past the neck, with billowing sleeves, and
pantaloons that ended high in the calf. She acknowledged
the visitors with a casual nod and a closed-lip smile.

"This is our Regina," Phyllida explained as the companions took their seats. Then she bowed to the Regina
and said two words. "All love."

A heartbeat later the other Melissas mimicked the gesture.

Once this ritual had been performed, the four white-
clad Melissas stepped back to take up discreet positions
around the room, with Phyllida taking a spot close to the
Regina. The Regina surveyed the newcomers in silence.

Sitting beside Ryan, Doc leaned to him and J.B. and explained in a low voice that *Regina* meant *queen* in Latin.
"One of the old languages that was dead before I was
born," Doc clarified before Ryan could ask.

Nodding, Ryan addressed the woman in the red robes.
"Thank you for seeing us, Regina," Ryan began. "My
name's Ryan Cawdor and this is J.B., Krysty and Doc. I
understand that you have some rules in your ville, and I'd
like to apologize if we've offended you in any way, with
our ignorance."

The Regina's mouth opened in a wonderfully warm
smile, her line of teeth straight and dazzlingly white. "Your
blasters have no place being in this room," she said, though

her words sounded nonjudgmental, "but I understand that things are different outside these walls, so that's something you'll get used to in time."

J.B. had removed his hat, and he fiddled with it in front of him as he spoke. "We're just passing through, ma'am. We didn't plan on staying."

The Regina sighed. "How often we've heard those words, Mr.... J.B."

"It's just J.B.," the Armorer told her. "J. B. Dix."

"Yes, J.B.," the Regina continued, "we've seen a few travelers since we established Heaven Falls here in the mountains. It's not easy to get here, and most journeymen are exhausted by the time they find us—those who survive. Though I am led to understand that you did not cross the mountains, but rather arrived via the matter-transfer unit."

"That's right," Ryan told her. "Your people said they'd only just got the thing working not two days before."

"Only for someone to blow a hole in it," J.B. grumbled dourly.

"William," the Regina said wistfully. "He always seemed...ill at ease. Still, one would never have imagined he would become so afflicted that he would be driven to such an extreme act of defiance."

"Defiance?" Doc repeated, surprised.

"Every Home must have rules," the Regina told them all. "Otherwise, order loses and chaos reigns. Without order, we'd have no civilization."

"And from what little we've seen, that's something you have here in spades," Ryan said, annoyed at Doc's interjection. "It's admirable."

"Thank you," the Regina replied. "When we all work together, it's amazing what can be achieved."

"I know the words," J.B. said. "I guess having a look around will help me understand the context."

The Regina indulged him with her brilliant smile before turning back to Ryan. "I suspect that you and your friends are hungry, Ryan. Could I interest you in a small repast?"

Ryan said that she could, and the companions waited in place while one of the Melissas left the room to fetch the serving staff who would prepare their meal. There was something here, Ryan felt, just beneath the surface. The place was too ordered, too military. It seemed—for want of a better word—inhuman.

IN THE MEDICAL tower, Petra worked with Mildred on Ricky's wound while Jak and Nancy looked on.

Petra's work was efficient and painstaking, with an attention to detail that Mildred couldn't fault. Once the wound was clean, she'd instructed Nancy to retrieve something from a supply room, and the dark-haired woman departed. While they waited, Mildred asked Petra about her training.

"We pool our knowledge here in Heaven Falls," Petra told her. "It's a simple principle—the more we learn, the more we all discover and can put to use."

"Your work with Ricky is very good," Mildred said, trying not to sound patronizing.

"I studied in the house of learning," Petra explained, "where all knowledge can be shared. They showed me the parts of the human body, and how it can be repaired and kept in good working order."

Mildred snorted. "You make it sound like a machine," she said.

"It's a structure, if that's what you mean," Petra said with no sense of irony. "And one that can be improved upon, given the right input, the right tools."

Mildred was intrigued by that. "You…improve?"

"You'll find there's very little illness here in the Home," Petra told her. "We've found ways to keep ourselves healthier."

Now Mildred was really intrigued, but before she could say anything, the Melissa called Nancy returned pushing a wheeled trolley on which were various bottles of liquid, creams and jars of unguent. Petra showed Mildred several of them while Jak watched sullenly from the corner of the room. Jak didn't like this woman. In fact, he didn't like any of the people he had met here so far. If it wasn't for Ricky's wound, he would be insisting to Mildred and Ryan that they get out of here, triple fast. There was something not quite right about the place, but he couldn't put his finger on it yet.

RYAN AND THE companions were served cakes and honey water in the Regina's meeting room. The cakes were light and delicious, while the honey water tasted subtly sweet and was wonderfully refreshing after their long trek.

"You have really outdone yourself as a host," Doc said in toast as he took a bite from his third scone.

The Regina held her cup up in acknowledgment to him. "We treat outlanders as we would wish to be treated," she said.

"That's one heck of an enlightened attitude, ma'am," J.B. remarked, wiping at his lips with a napkin. He found the honey water a little too sweet for his tastes, and suspected that the honey was used in part as a preservative to prevent stagnation or to perhaps mask the bitter taste of mineral content. When civilization had fallen apart, preserving food and drink had become a challenge.

"We hope that one day our kindness will be repaid, when we find a community that welcomes us with open arms," the Regina told her audience.

J.B. laughed. "In our experience, open arms is the usual response—though the other kind," he told her, mimicking a blaster being fired.

"You've traveled far, then?" the Regina asked.

Ryan nodded, swallowing a mouthful of delicious sponge cake. "We've been on the road a long time," he said, "moving from place to place. The screw-up at the mat-trans coupled with our companion's wound is what brought us here."

"Do you ever think of settling down?" the Regina asked before taking another sip from her cup.

"Sometimes," Ryan admitted.

"It's a lovely dream," Krysty added, her eyes meeting with Ryan's for a drawn-out moment.

The Regina nodded in understanding. "We should all harbor dreams," she told the companions. "They're what make us strive and force us to grow. Without dreams we can never better ourselves, and so life remains static. You're very welcome to stay," she offered.

"That's a mighty generous proposition," Ryan responded.

"We have food to spare, and there are several empty properties—certainly enough to house all of you if you don't mind sharing."

Ryan looked at Krysty as he replied. "We don't mind that in the slightest, Regina," he said. "If it's no trouble, that is."

IT WAS ALMOST an hour later when Ryan and his companions were ushered from the Regina's presence, accompanied once more by Phyllida and her three associates. Charm stuck close to Doc, who seemed more talkative than usual—if such a thing was possible—and had a new swagger in his step.

The sun was higher in the sky as they entered the court-yard beyond the tower door, slowly notching toward mid-day. Waiting there on one of the crescent-shaped benches were Mildred and Jak. Mildred sat, rummaging in her backpack as she reordered her supplies, while Jak was crouching with his feet up on the bench, his head down, his eyes narrowed as he watched the surroundings. Jak looked incongruous in the tranquil surroundings, like a cat ready to pounce on an unsuspecting bird.

Mildred looked up as the group approached. "Hey, guys, what kept you?" she asked cheerfully.

"Tea and scones with the queen," Doc replied, delight on his aged features.

Mildred glared at him before turning to the others. "Anyone else care to elaborate?" she asked.

Ryan ignored the question, instead asking one of his own. "What's the news on Ricky?"

"He's fine," Mildred told him, "but a few days of bed rest would do him good. We left him at the…hospital, I guess you'd call it." She pointed to the white-walled tower. "They've made some interesting medical developments there that I think are worth looking into, if we have the time." She was clearly excited by the prospect.

"We have the time," Ryan told her. "The baron of this ville just invited us to stay."

Mildred looked suddenly wary.

"Is there a problem?" Mildred asked, her eyes flick-ing to the Melissa guards who stood at a discreet distance from the talking companions.

The companions had been forced to stay in places be-fore, often at the mercy of a sadistic baron who wanted to use them either as slave labor or something even more reprehensible.

"No problem," Ryan told her. Not yet anyway.

Call him suspicious, but Ryan didn't trust this place. It was too friendly, too welcoming. They'd been asked to stay, but it was really a soft sell, with the offer of abundant food and a place to sleep. People in the Deathlands didn't give without expecting to get. Plus there was the issue of the bomber and just why he had found it necessary to plant a bomb in a mat-trans that had only just been made operational. There had to be a reason for that, and Ryan wanted to know what it was. But he knew better than to ask straight-out; that was a quick way to alienate themselves and maybe get chilled for the inquiry. Sticking around a few days and observing the goings-on in this strangely peaceful ville might just yield the answers he was looking for.

Chapter Seven

Life in the Deathlands was all about "take" with very little "give." That was the sole reason that Ryan and his companions distrusted what they had found there in the mountains. But when they left the central towers of Heaven Falls and followed the Melissas to their new lodgings, their anxieties began to diminish.

The land the Trai had acquired massed several acres within a valley. It was ideally placed, set within the declivity in the mountains to provide natural protection that was as effective as any wall. Two mountain peaks soared high above to either side, leaving in their wake sharp, craggy walls that towered to the left and right of the Trai's land. These walls were wide spaced, leaving enough land between them for farming but creating almost vertical plummets from above, making it difficult to reach the settlement from that direction. The chances of a sneak attack from above were remote, but the vast space that was left for the valley gathered plenty of sunlight, allowing crops to flourish. People worked at those fields, tilling them and sowing seeds in the midmorning sun, as Ryan and the companions followed a rough path down into the valley.

Jak sniffed the air and smiled. There was sweetness here from wildflowers that dotted the slopes and from the blossoms in the trees.

"How many people do you have here?" Ryan asked.

Phyllida smiled, pushing her hair back from her slender

neck. "Almost one hundred and eighty adults at the last census," she said, "and expanding all the time."

Doc nodded in comprehension. "You have security and an organized food supply, from the looks of things," he said. "Little wonder that this young ville is growing. Long may it continue."

"Thank you," Phyllida replied, leading the way down a roughly marked path that led toward a cluster of cabins.

The cabins were simple wooden structures, single story with no walls or fences to stake any boundaries around them. The land was the Trai's shared garden; individuals needed no parcel of land to call their own. There were approximately thirty dwellings in total, and they were widely spaced on a gentle slope that gradually rolled away toward a natural step in the ground, beyond which three additional wooden lodges waited.

At first glance, the placement of the cabins seemed haphazard because of the slope, but Ryan realized that they were placed in lines, albeit far apart from one another. The buildings followed a single basic design, with a door to one side and a window in the center of the front, more windows along the sides and a chimney on top. Puffs of smoke emanated from a few of the chimneys where the occupants were cooking, for it was too warm in the sunlight to need to heat them. Teams of carpenters worked at two new structures in varying states of construction, their component parts laid out on the grass around them as they toiled.

"You know," Doc said, "this reminds me a lot of home. A whole community working together like this."

"Lot of building," J.B. said.

"One does not make a community without giving them someplace to live," Doc reminded him. It was clear that the old man was taken with what he saw.

Ryan halted a moment, holding his hand up against the strong sunlight. The line of lodges ended abruptly just a little way ahead. "What is that?" he muttered almost to himself.

"What?" Krysty asked.

Ryan pointed. "There. The lodges just stop, looks like the ground…"

Seeing where he was pointing, Phyllida turned to Ryan and explained. "We think a quake hit this area at some point," she said. "It left a crevasse that's not wide but it is deep. Makes it hard to cross."

"And hard to sneak up on the ville," Ryan said in realization, seeing the potential that the Trai's land had for protection.

"No one's going to sneak up on you, Mr. Cawdor," Phyllida assured him. "I understand how fraught things have been for you out there, but you're quite safe here. I promise that."

Ryan smiled uncomfortably. Promises were easy to make, but keeping people alive took more than words.

THE COMPANIONS WERE escorted to three wooden lodges scattered along the slope. The cabins were set apart, with several similar dwellings between them that, the Melissas regretfully informed them, already had occupants.

"That's okay," Ryan said. "We don't all need to be holding hands when we sleep."

J.B. and Mildred took the first cottage, and Ryan and Krysty took the second, which left Doc and Jak as housemates in the last dwelling. Each group was shown inside by one of the beautiful Melissas, with Charm remaining close to Doc as she led him and Jak to the farthest cottage.

Inside, the cottages were simple structures featuring a main room off which was a spacious kitchen area, whose hob used the same central chimney as the fireplace. The buildings featured a large bedroom along with a smaller box room within which a crib or single bed could be placed. The buildings contained little furniture, but were newly built and looked sturdy. Doc guessed that any carpentry skills would be highly prized here. There was also a wet room at the back of each building where washing could be left to dry. Like the town area, there were several wells dotted along the slopes that could be used to draw water for washing and bathing, although the companions were informed that there were better facilities in the main part of the town where they had met the Regina.

Each lodge contained a single box set in one corner of the main room, about the size of a trunk. The box was affixed to the wall and floor and featured a simple sliding lock so that it could be sealed. The Melissas explained that this could be used to store important items, and they requested that the companions store their blasters in them for the duration of their stay. While some were reluctant—especially Jak and J.B.—the companions agreed to that as a rule of the ville.

Doc actually seemed rather keen on the idea. "While I shall miss carrying this hog leg around with me," he told Jak as he placed his LeMat in the box, "it is rather appealing to think that we are in a place where one does not need to go armed at all times."

Jak eyed him suspiciously. He would place his Colt Python in the box while Charm was here watching over them, but his cache of throwing knives would remain hidden around his person, and he made sure he could operate the lock on the box.

"Your weapons are not going anywhere," Charm promised with a flash of her warm, friendly smile. "You can retrieve them at any time. No one else will touch them."

IT TOOK J.B. several minutes to place his weapons in the lock box. He took great pains to ensure each was in prime working condition and selected its placement carefully so that it would not be damaged. Adele, the Melissa who had accompanied him and Mildred to this lodge, departed during this time to retrieve blankets and other essentials from either a central store or one of the other properties that had more than it needed. J.B. and Mildred were struck by how trusting that move showed the locals to be—this was not a prison where they were being disarmed, it really was about the general safety of the locals.

Even so, J.B. didn't like it, and he grumbled to Mildred once Adele had gone. "It's not right, making a man strip off his essentials. Not right at all."

Mildred was struck then by how different her life had been from J.B.'s. She came from the twentieth century where, while guns were part of life, the overt carrying of them was unusual for the general populace. J.B., by contrast, expected people to be armed and to wear his or her blaster on show in warning to anyone who might attack them.

Watching J.B. place his armament into the box, Mildred shook her head. Besides his shotgun and Mini-Uzi and their respective ammunition, J.B. had spare parts for several smaller blasters, at least a dozen different gauges of extra ammo, several knives, including a Tekna combat knife and a standard pocket type, a clutch of grenades, detonators, bottles of ignition fluid and what looked like a wad of plas ex, plus strings, ropes and other useful items that he continued to remove from various pockets hidden within his coat long after he had placed his satchel down.

"How do you carry all that stuff and not keel over?" Mildred asked.

J.B. shrugged. "A man gets used to staying alive," he

said grimly. Then he smiled mischievously. "Plus I don't go swimming in the coat," he added, indicating a man drowning as he sunk from the weight.

Mildred laughed hard at that. It was the break in tension that both of them needed.

THE MELISSAS RETRIEVED blankets and other basic items like pots and mirrors that they brought to the companions' new dwellings, after which they were left alone to settle in. Shortly after that, the other companions exited their assigned cabins and gathered at Ryan and Krysty's dwelling. They met on the stoop, as the sounds of wood being sawed and fields being worked carried across tranquil plains.

"We've been invited to join Phyllida and her friends for lunch," Krysty told everyone, "until we get ourselves properly set up here."

Jak snorted, and Ryan turned to him.

"Is that going to be a problem, Jak?" the one-eyed man asked. He had known Jak a long time and knew to trust the albino's instincts—that faith had saved Ryan's life more than once.

"Not like," Jak said, pulling his arms around his chest. "No blaster."

Ryan nodded. "Yeah, that's an interesting turn of events, but I think we're all going to have to trust these Trai folks for now. I haven't seen anyone here carrying, so there's that. And you've got your knives, I bet."

"A blaster's easy enough to hide," J.B. pointed out reasonably. "All of us know that."

Silence reigned for a moment while the companions considered that. Finally, Doc spoke up, his rich voice full of cheer.

"Well, I for one like the place, and the people," he said.

Mildred began to laugh, shaking her head.

"What is it?" the old man asked. "Did I say something to amuse?"

"No, it's just…" Mildred began. "Well, you're a hound dog, Doc."

Doc was taken aback. "I am a…what?"

On seeing Doc's expression, Mildred began laughing again, so hard that she couldn't speak.

"What is it?" Doc asked the others, irked.

Ryan took up the explanation. "I think what Mildred's trying to say is that you seem to be getting on well with Miss Charming," he said.

"Charm," Doc corrected automatically, and then he began to blush. "Well, perhaps you are right at that. But there is nothing unusual about a man enjoying the attentions of a pretty woman. She happens to be knowledgeable and friendly. In fact, she invited us all to a dance this evening."

"A dance?" Krysty asked in surprise.

"Yes," Doc explained. "It seems that the people of Heaven Falls like to get together once the workday is done. I think it is rather delightful."

"Sounds quaint," Mildred said, having finally recovered from her laughing fit.

"It's kooky is what it is," J.B. muttered, shaking his head. He had a hand in his pocket and was bringing out a sheaf of folded maps along with his mini-sextant. "I haven't heard of anything like that in a long while."

Ryan held up a hand for calm. "Let's put aside Doc's dance for now," he said, "and figure out where we are. J.B.?"

Aligning the mini-sextant with the sun, J.B. took its reading and compared it with the maps he had produced. The maps were aged and scarred, with crease lines down their folds where they had been refolded too many times.

After about a minute, J.B. looked up at Ryan and smiled. "You were right," he said. "We're in Virginia. Smack dab in the Blue Ridge Mountains."

Krysty looked at Ryan with wide eyes. "You're home, Ryan."

"Not quite," J.B. corrected. "Still a good hundred and twenty miles from Front Royal, give or take. You've never heard tell of this place, Ryan?"

"It's a big mountain range," Ryan stated.

J.B. traced his index finger across the map. "Putting Front Royal out of the mix, we have a few redoubts we could access, but none real close."

"How far?" Ryan asked.

"Two days' walk," J.B. estimated, "depending on terrain. Mebbe three, given how impassable some of this territory looks."

"What about repairing the one we used to get here?" Krysty asked.

"Maybe can be done," J.B. said, "but it'd take time."

"It rather sounded that the Trai people were planning to work on that very issue," Doc said helpfully, "which makes me inclined to stick around a while and see what life is like here in Heaven Falls. After all, food and shelter do not often come this easy."

Ryan looked from one companion's face to the next, judging their expressions. Apart from Jak, they seemed by and large okay with Doc's proposition.

"I think you're right, Doc," Ryan decided. "Anyone disagree? Jak?"

Jak looked sour but said nothing.

"Anyone else?" Ryan asked.

"It would be good for Ricky's recovery to stay in one place for a few days," Mildred said.

"I don't like being somewhere without a back door,"

J.B. pointed out reasonably, "but the promise of regular meals and no mutie attacks is something we haven't had in a long while."

"Then we'll stay," Ryan said. For now, he added mentally. At least until he could find out more about why someone had wanted to plant a bomb in an operational mat-trans unit.

Chapter Eight

Phyllida was waiting on a moon-shaped bench at the edge of the town center, looking out at the path that led to the companions' lodgings. She had changed clothes and was now wearing a short dress in a burnt umber color. She had also untied her hair and, freed of its bindings, her blond tresses cascaded to the small of her back like a golden waterfall. Phyllida smiled when she saw Ryan leading the companions up the slope.

"You found your way back," Phyllida said, rising from the bench.

Ryan tipped two fingers to an imaginary hat brim. "Without a single wrong turn," he boasted.

Having met them, Phyllida led the companions into one of the towers. It was cool inside, and a meal of cold cuts and freshly baked bread had been laid out in a buffet, allowing the visitors to take whatever they wished. The room featured lattice-style walls that created gridded panels to split the ground floor of the tower into smaller rooms in a semi–open plan style. Two of the other Melissas joined them, Linda and Charm, and while the former was still in her white robes, which Ryan realized had to signify some kind of uniform. Charm had switched to a loose cotton dress in a sunny yellow, which she had augmented with several bangles, leaving her shoulders and knees exposed. Charm smiled when she saw Doc and hurried over to him, pulling Linda behind her.

"Charm tells me you know how to dance," Linda said boldly.

"Some," he admitted, "though I am a little rusty. There is not much need for dancing when one lives life on the road, I am afraid."

Small plates were provided, and the companions were invited to take as much as they wanted from the spread. Krysty was impressed.

"You must have an abundance of food here to be so generous," she remarked as she added a slice of honey-roasted ham to her plate.

Phyllida shook her head indulgently. "We have enough to share," she said. "Cooperation is at the heart of our Home, and through that we've produced high yields."

Krysty nodded. "There's not much cooperation outside these walls," she said. "It makes a refreshing change."

Finger bowls had been placed on the table and together the companions and the three Melissa warriors sat to eat. Sweetened water was provided along with four flagons of amber-colored mead, which were brought in by serving men who silently delivered them to the table and filled a goblet for each diner. The men were young and hardy, dressed in simple, toga-like robes that had been dyed different colors to differentiate them. The clothing was very different from that worn by the people the companions had seen working the farms and building the cabins, as if each task had its own dress code.

The atmosphere was casual and friendly. Ryan was surprised at how easily everyone seemed to be getting along. Often when two groups met in the Deathlands, differences would result in combat, yet here the Trai were friendly and accommodating and seemed to be tolerant of others' differences. Even Jak's eccentricities seemed unremarkable to their hosts, and at one point Charm moved to a seat beside Jak to patiently answer his questions about the meats and how they had been preserved.

"Place like this must have taken some time to build," Ryan said, clearly impressed.

"We work together," Phyllida told him.

Picking up on this, Krysty asked what would be expected of the companions if they were to stay.

"We're assigned roles by the Regina," Phyllida explained as she tore into a crisp lettuce leaf. "Everyone is asked to perform that role to the best of her ability. *His* or her," she corrected as Ryan began to query.

"So I'd be given a sec man role and—" Ryan said.

"No," Charm said from two places down the table. "Only women can guard the Home."

"Is that right?" J.B. asked, swallowing the mouthful of mead he had just taken. He was clearly surprised.

Phyllida picked up the point. "Strict organization is at the heart of Heaven Falls," she explained, "with a clear delineation of roles."

"Well, I guess we can't argue with the results, can we, J.B.?" Ryan said, fixing his oldest companion with a stare.

J.B. shook his head after a moment. "Guess not," he said. He knew that look from Ryan—it meant that now was not the time to rock the boat; better to play it safe and hold their cards close to their chest.

The conversation continued amiably for more than an hour, during which time the goblets were refilled and the companions were invited to help themselves to seconds— and, in Jak's case, thirds.

While J.B. found the meal a little sweet for his tastes, Mildred felt oddly wistful—the sweetness reminded her of the food she had been used to in twentieth-century America, with its added sugars and sweeteners, feeding that cultural sweet tooth that seemed to come with civilization. Idly she wondered whether the same was true here, if somehow organization brought with it a taste for sweeter food.

At the end of the meal, a tray of cakes was brought in by one of the serving men, who bowed respectfully to Phyllida after placing the tray down before leaving the room. Linda excused herself at that point, explaining that she was expected back on patrol.

"What kind of patrols do you run here?" Ryan asked as the brunette left. He tried to make the question sound casual, but was thinking once more of the bomber who had targeted the redoubt.

Phyllida seemed all too happy to share. "Heaven Falls is very secure," she told him, "so you shouldn't expect trouble. However, there are occasional sightings of animals and, very seldom, people like you who appear in our region. We like to keep abreast of who's approaching and why."

"That's reasonable," Ryan said, nodding.

Phyllida brought the tray of cakes around the large table, and as the companions were making their selections, the doors opened and Nancy strode in, pulling her black hair free from its clips. "Sorry I'm late," she said in apology. "I was held up by my sister and lost track of time."

Phyllida encouraged the dark-haired woman to help herself to what was left of the buffet, and Ryan took the opportunity to pour her a goblet of the amber mead. When Nancy joined them at the table, Mildred asked about Ricky.

"Your friend was sleeping when I left him," Nancy said, conscious that the other conversations had petered out as the companions listened to her reply. "He appeared to be in no danger, just tired."

"When can we see him?" J.B. asked.

"Whenever you wish," Nancy said, taking in the whole table with a sweep of her head. "And, Mildred—Petra asked me to extend a welcome to you if you would like to tour the medical faculty."

Mildred was surprised. "I'd like that a lot," she said, a broad smile appearing on her face.

Once again, Ryan was struck by how friendly everyone here seemed. In fact, it was beginning to wear down even his ingrained skepticism.

AFTER THE LONG lunch, the companions trekked to the nearby tower where Mildred and Jak had left Ricky to rest. The lunch had put everyone in a happier mood. The companions were accompanied by Nancy, who informed them that she was pleased to stay but had no official position here. Phyllida's words came back to Ryan at that point, of how the society of the Trai was rigidly organized.

Ricky had been moved to an upstairs room in the six-story building, and the companions followed a winding ramp up there. They found him as the sole occupant of a white-walled room, lying fast asleep in a freshly laundered bed. The room was of modest size, and it took a little maneuvering for all of Ryan's crew to fit in all at once, with Nancy watching from the doorway. The room was clean and sparsely decorated, with a single small window that let in a little direct light and air. Most of the light, however, seemed to ebb through a translucent exterior wall, illuminating the room without glare.

After a few seconds J.B. nodded, satisfied. "Looks like the kid's doing all right," he said, turning to Mildred for confirmation.

"Yes, he is," Mildred said, and she could hear the surprise in her own voice. Not that she had expected Ricky not to pull through—though painful, his wound was superficial and barring internal bleeding he should recover quickly. But what surprised her was how well he had been taken care of in her absence. Despite the outward differences, this place reminded her of a twentieth-century hospital, something she didn't think she'd ever experience again.

Just then, Ricky started to stir, no doubt roused by all the movement in the room, and after a moment his eyes flickered open. Like anyone waking when ill, he looked younger somehow, innocent and more boyish. "Hey... guys," he said weakly.

"Ricky," Ryan said, stepping close to the bed. "How are you feeling?"

"Like...I could take on a mutie army..." Ricky began, but Ryan looked at him firmly.

"Really, how are you feeling?" he asked. "Straight up this time."

Chastised, Ricky looked away for a moment. "My side's numb," he said, "but kind of hurts, too. And my head feels light, not quite there."

"That's the anesthetic they used to numb the pain," Mildred reassured him. "What you're feeling is quite normal."

Ricky smiled, the handsome rogue once more. "Did you do this, Mildred?" he asked. "Thanks."

"Not me," Mildred told him. "I had some help from the locals. You're going to be in here for a few days, just to rest up until you're back to normal."

"We're staying, too," Ryan told him.

"Thanks," Ricky said, visibly relieved. The kid had not been on the road long, and it was obvious he feared being abandoned as deadweight. "You, too, J.B.?"

J.B. nodded. "All of us," he said, "until you're on your feet. No one's leaving without you."

Ricky idolized J.B. and J.B. accepted the kid, seeing in him the potential of a knowledgeable weaponsmith. Occasionally the kid made a mistake, as most kids did, but here in the Deathlands it could get a body chilled. It had been close this time, the way he had waved that freaking flare around in the predawn as the deranged scalies had chased them down the overgrown road in California. This time Ricky had taken a shot and survived it. But next time? J.B. thought. Yeah, the kid needed a firm hand if he was going to reach his seventeenth birthday in one piece.

WHILE THE OTHERS waited at Ricky's bedside, Mildred left them, and she and Nancy went to find Petra. They walked amiably down near-empty corridors, which featured more of the lattice-like walls to differentiate the individual rooms without closing them off entirely. The design allowed for a lot of light to pass through the building, although it cut down on privacy.

"This floor is dedicated to people recovering from physical trauma," Nancy said, "like your companion."

Mildred couldn't resist peering into a few of the rooms as they passed, and she soon noticed that most of them were empty. That was encouraging anyway—it either meant that Heaven Falls was a pretty safe place, or that their medical expertise encouraged a quick turnaround in cases, helping patients to recover quickly.

"Petra's on the next floor," Nancy explained as she guided Mildred to a ramp.

Together, they strode up the ramp and onto the next level, which once again featured the lattice-style dividers between rooms. Walking the sterile corridor, Mildred couldn't help but think of this place as a hospital. What was it they'd called it? A medical faculty, she recalled. The term *faculty* reminded her of high school, and she began to wonder if this was what she would have called a teaching hospital?

They arrived at a small room where Petra was labeling cylindrical clay containers with color-coded stickers. The room was full of such containers, each with its own color label, lined up on shelves that ran floor to ceiling along all four walls with two further freestanding aisles down the center. The containers were arranged in color-coded sequence. Reading was a luxury in the Deathlands, and while Heaven Falls appeared to have an educational program in place, it was little surprise to Mildred that they relied on a more primitive system to identify their stock. Mildred wondered where they got their supplies.

"Mildred, I'm so pleased to see you again," Petra said, greeting Mildred with a warm smile. "If you have a few minutes, I'd like to show you around."

"That sounds good to me," Mildred said. And it did. Imagine, Mildred Wyeth back in a hospital after all this time.

BY THE LATE afternoon Ricky had fallen back to sleep and, confident that he was in safe hands, the companions left the medical faculty and returned to their lodgings. On the walk back past the fields, Mildred told J.B. excitedly about her tour of the tower. "They're serious about making people well," she declared enthusiastically. "You have no idea how amazing this place is."

"I've been to a few quacks in my time, Millie," J.B. told her. "I can see the appeal of docs who take their job serious."

Laborers were still working at the construction of the two new wooden buildings. With the insight that Phyllida had given him, Ryan noticed that the laborers were all men, but that they were being given commands by women. That could just be coincidence, he knew—come back tomorrow and a new crew with a new male boss might be doing the job—but still it made him wonder.

With everyone exhausted from their fraught all-nighter in mutie-filled California, the friends agreed to split up and return to their own shacks for rest and a cleanup. As Ryan and Krysty walked toward their dwelling, Krysty turned to him and he noticed the joy in her face.

"What?" he asked.

"I was just thinking—it's a nice place," Krysty said, reaching for Ryan's hand and taking it in her own. "It feels like home."

Krysty's original ville in Colorado had been ravaged by bandits, but Krysty always thought of Harmony fondly.

"I'm not sure," Ryan said, his free hand unconsciously reaching for his holster and finding it empty.

They stopped at the stoop to their cabin and Krysty looked out at the trees, grass and flowers. "The people here have something special, Ryan," she said. "They've learned to trust, and I think they try to see the good in people."

"Yeah, mebbe they do," Ryan agreed, reaching his arm around Krysty's shoulder to pull her close.

Krysty turned then, and her emerald eyes shone as she looked at Ryan's ruggedly handsome features. "Perhaps this is it," she told him quietly. "Mebbe this is what we've been looking for all this time. A place we can settle and call home."

"I don't know," Ryan admitted hesitantly. "But we'll stay long enough to find out why one of their own wanted to blow up the mat-trans. Because that is bothering the shit out of me."

Together they went into their cabin, closing the door behind them.

Chapter Nine

J.B. dreamed about scalies. In his dream, he was on a beach at night, a thin sliver of orange peel on the horizon where the sun was starting to rise, the ocean at his back. The surf rolled in and breakers crashed down with the same timbre as his M-4000 shotgun blasting, but he didn't have the weapon in his hand. Instead he had the Mini-Uzi, with its fast action ideal for holding off a crowd.

The Armorer stood alone, but he could hear the scalies approaching, a hundred feet moving in unison, tromping closer and closer as they strode across the sand.

The first head appeared over one of the undulating sand dunes, silhouetted by the thin streak of sun. It was hairless and scarred, the face of an acid victim, and its eyes glowed an eerie silver like the moon's reflection on a lake. J.B. raised the Uzi and squeezed the trigger, and nothing happened.

"Dark night!" J.B. cursed, feeling along the length of the Uzi to detect the problem. Knowing the weapon by touch, he kept his eyes on the scalie at the ridge. The magazine wasn't attached properly, or maybe it had come loose.

J.B. looked down and tried adjusting the ammo feed, but the damn thing wouldn't lock, and in moments he was fumbling with the black magazine and watching in horror as it slipped from his hands and dropped into the sand. The scalie had been joined by others, those of the hundred footsteps moving in unison, a line of heads silhouetted against the horizon as they peered over the sand.

The scalies were closer now, surrounding him on three sides, blocking any escape.

J.B. raised the empty Uzi. "Stay back!" he shouted, bringing the muzzle around in an arc to encompass the circling muties. "Help me!" The cry was sharp and sudden, a child's voice.

J.B. turned, locating the source in an instant. Out in the dark water, twenty feet from the shore, he could see a figure waving its arms in fear. He knew who it was right away.

"Ricky!"

"J.B., help me!" Ricky cried. His hair was stuck to his head and his arms were waving, splashing the dark water as they batted against it.

J.B. stomped determinedly toward the water, the useless Uzi still in his right hand. He tossed the blaster aside as he stepped into the rippling, oil-dark mass of the ocean, striding out into the water as the scalies closed in behind him. Up ahead he saw Ricky splashing fearfully, and then he saw hands grasping at Ricky from below, callused hands reaching up the lad's chest, pulling him down.

"Hold on, kid!" J.B. shouted. "I'm coming!"

One arm over the other, J.B. began to swim, great strokes eating up the distance. Up ahead, Ricky was struggling to stay afloat as the scaled hands dragged him beneath the surface. And then he was gone, and J.B. was swimming in empty water.

"Ricky?" J.B. shouted, spitting out a mouthful of salt water. "Ricky?"

A shadow moved beneath the surface where Ricky had been, like a dark balloon bobbing against the ceiling that was the ocean surface. Knowing that it was Ricky, J.B. swam.

J.B.'s jacket was heavy with water now; he could feel its weight increase with every stroke. Ricky's head crowned the water surface ahead, just the top of his head like the first push of a baby being born, but J.B. couldn't reach him—he was struggling to stay afloat himself.

J.B. dropped beneath the dark surface for a moment, a second under the water, two seconds, *three,* and then he was up again and gasping for air.

"Rick—" J.B. began, but the current caught him and dragged him under a second time.

It was cold beneath the surface, and everything was cast in a gray the shade of a rainstorm cloud in those seconds before a downpour. J.B. could see Ricky's legs waggling in the water, his body struggling as long arms dragged him down. He wasn't far ahead, maybe six or seven feet.

J.B. struggled to surface once again. His shoulders ached from the weight of his jacket, and he could barely pull himself away from the almost magnetic drag of the ocean bed. He did it, one arm plunging ahead after the other, cupping at the water and almost physically pulling himself up and out of it.

J.B. emerged with lungs aching and muscles burning. Ricky's face appeared inches in front of his, eyes closed and water pouring from his mouth. Then his lips pulled back in a snarl that mocked his charming smile, and his eyes opened to show silvery, mirrorlike orbs. J.B. saw then that the kid's face was scarred and callused like a burn victim's, and he realized that he was too late—that Ricky was one of them now, a scalie like the others.

Ricky's hands reached toward him, grabbed the top of J.B.'s head and shoved him under the water once more.

Bubbles. Darkness.

HE AWOKE REACHING for his blaster and swore harshly when his hands grasped nothing where the gun should have been.

"J.B.?" Mildred asked, looking across at him where he was huddled in a chair in the main room of the shack.

The long day had caught up with J.B. awhile back and, almost as soon as he and Mildred had returned to their cabin, the Armorer had reclined in the chair and dropped straight off to sleep. Now rich orange sunlight filtered through the window behind Mildred as afternoon turned to evening.

Staring at Mildred and the window and the bare wood walls of the cottage, it took J.B. a few seconds to remember where he was.

"J.B.?" Mildred asked again, padding across the room from where she had been standing staring out the window. There was a mug of water in her hand, and she offered it to him as he recovered himself. "You okay?"

The Armorer nodded, brushing the mug aside, not quite feeling awake. The dream had been vivid and cruel, like the hallucinatory jump dreams that were sometimes initiated when they used a mat-trans.

He struggled to move, looked down and saw how his jacket had tangled around him. "Damn it," he cursed, extricating himself from the coat and standing. His head swam a little when he did, and he tottered in place for a moment.

Mildred grabbed his arm, steadying him. "Bad dream?"

"Long day," J.B. answered, sitting again. He looked from Mildred to the sealed wooden box in the corner of the room and nodded. "Don't feel right, not having a blaster, Millie," he said. "Makes me edgy."

Mildred shrugged. "Rules of the game in these parts," she said. "Either we go along with it or we get out."

"Yeah," J.B. said, reaching for his battered fedora where

it had dropped on the floor as he'd slept. "Doesn't mean I've got to feel happy about it."

"Come on," she said after a moment. "We ought to get ready. We promised Doc we'd attend this dance he got us all invited to."

J.B. sighed. A dance. In less than a day his life had gone from blasting scalies to hell to kicking up his heels.

Chapter Ten

As the sun disappeared below the mountains, Ryan and his companions made their way back into the center of Heaven Falls. People were already gathering and making their way toward the cluster of towers. From the size of the milling crowd, it appeared that everyone had come, including children, who were running around the dirt street, giggling and playing.

"It feels like Christmas," Mildred said, astonished.

Doc agreed. "There's something rejuvenating about the sound of children's laughter," he said, striding purposefully toward the towers.

The towers had been lit by freestanding sconces that stood seven feet high like streetlamps, with flames burning at their top. One of the seven towers was assigned solely for ville meetings, and it had been given over this night to recreation.

The companions traipsed after Doc as he led the way to the tower, following the crowds. Some of them, like Mildred and Krysty, were excited to see what was happening here—the sounds of laughter and happiness spoke to them of the lives they had led prior to becoming nomads on the Deathlands' roads.

Ryan was more wary, but he felt a sense of familiarity to the event. He had grown up the son of a wealthy baron and had attended social gatherings from an early age.

Jak looked less pleased to be there, and he hung back

as the companions crossed beneath the towering arch that led inside. Jak was naturally an outsider, and he could be uncomfortable around big crowds such as this, with too many variables involved, too many people to watch.

At the back of the group, J.B. noticed Jak's trepidation and he hung back to speak with him. "Dancing isn't really my bag, either, Jak, but we do what's expected of us at times like this, same as we chill animals so we can eat."

Jak understood, and he paced through the arch with J.B., hurrying to catch up to their friends.

They found themselves in a grand hall with equidistant wooden columns that held an impressive bowed ceiling aloft. The ceiling featured an elaborately carved criss-cross pattern that captured the light of the flaming lamps and candles in its angles, flickering almost as if it was aflame itself.

The room was filling with people, and it was warm from their body heat and from the burning flames that had been used to illuminate it. The room could hold two hundred people comfortably, and Ryan assumed it had been built with the foresight that the ville's population would expand.

A raised stage was located to one side of the room, where a quintet made up of men and women was using homemade stringed and wind instruments to create ambient music.

At the opposite side to the band, a long table had been set up over which a cover had been placed.

Looking around, Mildred noticed how young everyone looked, with most people in their twenties or younger, and no one much over forty. That in itself was unremarkable—the Deathlands life was a harsh one, the average lifespan had dropped considerably since the days of civilization. But what struck Mildred was not simply the youthfulness of the crowd, but how healthy they all appeared. The men were tanned and muscular, the women strong and poised, with the undeniable beauty that youth granted and age stole slowly but relentlessly away. It reminded her of high school in that way—all those bright eyes and quick smiles.

Here is a population that lives well, Mildred thought as her eyes roved over the pretty faces in the crowd.

There were some familiar faces there, too. Four of the Melissas who had met the companions at the redoubt were present, wearing vibrantly colored dresses that swept the floor, their hair simply but gracefully styled.

Still standing by the door, Ryan took a step back and spoke in a low voice to J.B. "Your assessment?"

"First impression—friendly enough," the Armorer replied. "You?"

Ryan inclined his head in agreement. "Odd, though," he said quietly, "seeing this many people and not a blaster in sight."

J.B. nodded. "Yeah, that takes a little getting used to."

Then Krysty hooked an arm through Ryan's, pulling him away from J.B. and deeper into the room. "Come on, lover," she insisted joyfully, "this is no place for a war council."

Taking Krysty and Ryan's lead, Doc and Mildred filtered into the crowd to speak with people they knew. Mildred gravitated toward Petra while Charm spotted Doc and found her way toward him accompanied by another beautiful young woman whom Doc didn't recognize. Charm had dressed in a long, floaty dress dyed violet, and she offered Doc a huge smile as she caught up with him.

J.B. watched his companions fitting in, and he looked back toward the doorway where Jak was hovering uncomfortably. "Come on, Jak," he called, "let's see if there's anything to eat at this social."

As they strode across the room, the music came to a halt and a hush ran through the crowd. All attention turned to the raised platform where the band was set up, and after a half minute of silence a figure strode through the crowd toward the stage surrounded by four women, all of them dressed in the same white robes the Melissas had worn when they'd first met Ryan's team. The woman in the center was the Regina. She had changed her appearance and now wore a long, silky dress, sleeveless and with a train that followed five feet behind her on the floor, ending in a point. The dress was a vibrant yellow and had been accented with black-belted accessories that swirled around it like stripes.

Gracefully, the Regina stepped onto the raised stage, taking up a position in front of the band while the other members of her entourage took up places to either side of the stage at floor level. The Melissas surveyed the crowd with watchful eyes as the Regina raised both arms.

The Regina held her arms outstretched for a moment, her hands open to silence the crowd, though she need not have bothered—a deathly hush had already fallen on the hall as the people of Heaven Falls awaited their leader's words.

"People of the Trai," the Regina announced, a broad smile materializing on her face, "it brings us all great pleasure to come together like this.

"Within us lie the seeds of tomorrow. And it is a glorious tomorrow—one that will be free from the blight of the past, and the darkness that wrought across this once beautiful land. By working together we shall bring hope, we shall illuminate the darkest corners and drive back the fear that grips this land. We shall bring change and prosperity and *life*."

The Regina lowered her arms then and spontaneous

applause rippled through the audience. Doc joined in, too, as did Mildred, used to obeying social convention. A moment after that, Ryan and Krysty began to clap, too, though Ryan watched the crowd, studying their faces surreptitiously.

J.B. remained a little farther back from the stage with Jak, and put his hands together as if applauding, holding them there as he studied the crowd.

"S'pose clap?" Jak asked quietly.

"I didn't hear an order," J.B. whispered in reply. While it may have sounded flippant, he realized there was something to his statement. Too many times in similar situations, force would be used to get an unwilling audience to kowtow to a baron's ego when they gave a speech like that. While the Regina didn't call herself a baron, the Armorer recognized that that was just what she was—a leader of a walled ville that kept itself protected from outlanders. The fact that the Trai had welcomed J.B. and the others didn't guarantee that they trusted them, or that they would extend that same hand of friendship to the next group of travelers who happened upon this hidden enclave.

Gradually, the applause began to peter out. The Regina remained on stage, smiling broadly and clearly enjoying the adulation. "Continue to build togetherness," she said, raising her voice over the last smattering of applause, "for in togetherness we shall build the new world."

A second round of applause took the room, during which the Regina turned to say something to the band before stepping down from the stage. Then she made her way back through the crowd, accompanied by her four guards.

Ryan was deep in thought as he watched the woman walk to the covered table on the far side of the room. He and his companions had witnessed similar rallies like this before, where occupants of a walled ville were gathered to pledge fealty to a baron. If anything, this one seemed remarkable only in how benign it was. These people seemed to genuinely believe in a better tomorrow, one they could build for themselves. It was a refreshing discovery.

The covers on the long table were removed to reveal an impressive spread of food and drink. Two huge barrels lay at either end of the spread with tap nozzles protruding from their sides. One of the Melissas—this one a redhead—took a golden goblet from the side of the table and handed it to the Regina, bowing at the waist and lowering her head in supplication.

The Regina took the goblet and held it up to the watching crowd who waited in anticipation. Then she stepped across to the barrel at the far right of the table and worked the tap, pouring amber liquid into the goblet. Once filled, she raised the goblet in a toast to the crowd before drinking—just a little.

"All love!" the Regina announced.

The phrase "All love" was repeated by the room's participants, and Ryan and his allies joined in, too. This was clearly the signal for the party to begin, and the band struck up the first chords of a punchy tune.

People offered Ryan and his companions drinks and food, and within a few minutes the center of the hall had filled with dancing bodies as more than half of the attendees took up the dance.

Standing to the side of the dance floor, Krysty turned to Ryan and showed a bright smile that illuminated her whole face. "When was the last time we went dancing?" she asked.

"If I remember correctly, would it get me out of doing it again now?" Ryan teased.

Krysty laughed, putting her empty plate down on a clear

patch of the food table. "No," she said, grabbing Ryan's hand and tugging him toward the dance floor.

Ryan had been taught to dance as a child, though it was a talent he rarely had cause to call upon. The last time, he remembered now, had been during their adventure in Canada.

This night, with Krysty's body close to his, he was happy to revisit those old steps once more.

As THE NIGHT wore on, Doc, too, joined in the dance, taking pains to imitate the steps that Charm and her friend showed him. He was clearly delighted by the whole event, and looked as if a great burden had been removed from his soul, especially in those moments when he made a wrong step and his partners simply laughed.

At some point in the evening Charm left Doc in the company of her friend—a young woman called Bella—and made her way to the food table. When she got there she recognized Jak piling cured meats onto a small plate—indeed, it was hard to miss his striking albino appearance.

"It's Jak, isn't it?" Charm said, stepping close behind him. "The healer's friend."

Jak turned warily and looked at her through narrowed eyes.

"I'm Charm," the woman said, extending her hand toward him. "We met at the bunker."

Charm smiled as the pale-faced young man took her hand and shook it. "You have a strong grip," she said. "Would you care to dance?"

Jak shook his head. "No."

"Come on, it'll be fun," Charm insisted.

Jak looked the woman up and down uncertainly, and, under his inquiring gaze, Charm brushed a stray lock of honey-gold hair from her eyes, blushing a furious shade of red.

"What? Aren't you able to have fun," Charm challenged Jak, "because of your color?"

J.B. stepped in and introduced himself to the woman with a tip of his hat before speaking with Jak. "I figure the lady isn't the type to take no for an answer," he said, "so why don't you go have a bit of fun out there with the other lunatics?"

"No," Jak said, shaking his head. "Check Ricky."

J.B. held up a hand. "*I'll* check on Ricky," he insisted. "You go on and be young with this pretty woman."

Reluctantly, Jak put down his plate—gobbling up another slice of honeyed ham as he did so—and followed Charm to the edge of the dance area.

As the music played on, J.B. maneuvered and excuse-me'd his way through the crowd to the hall's exit. He had kind of promised Jak that he would check on Ricky, and with Mildred busy chatting to her new friends and no danger of a pretty girl asking a worn-out old bastard like him to dance, he figured there was no time like the present. Besides, he wanted to look around the ville without being disturbed, and doing so now, while most everyone in town was attending the social, made a lot of sense.

INSIDE THE MEDICAL tower, it was quiet after the hubbub of the dance hall. J.B. went to Ricky's room without incident. A few women—nurses maybe?—greeted the Armorer in a friendly manner as he passed, but no one questioned or tried to stop him. Hell, why would they? J.B. thought. Seems everyone's your friend here in Heaven Falls.

The white corridors were lit with flickering candles under glass, but Ricky's room was kept in darkness. Inside, Ricky was fast asleep in the bed, snoring gently. J.B. had heard the snoring ten feet away and he smiled when he realized that the noise was coming from his companion.

"Keep it up, kid," he said quietly, standing just inside the doorway. "Your body needs all the recovery time it can get."

Oblivious, Ricky continued to snore.

J.B. stayed there almost an hour, standing in the doorway, leaning on the frame, glad to escape the claustrophobia of the crowded dance hall. The walls to the room were of that same lattice design he had seen elsewhere, and it allowed the flickering light of the corridor candles to filter into the room. The light was just enough that J.B. could watch the youth sleeping, and he took a certain comfort in knowing that the kid was safe.

What had happened out in California had not been J.B.'s fault—the mat-trans jump had dropped them there, and no one could account for the random factor. But still, the kid's bravery was maybe a little on J.B., if he was honest with himself. Sure, Ricky was brave already—didn't need J.B. or Ryan or anyone else to prod him into a dangerous situation if it was what was needed. But Ricky idolized J.B.; he'd mentioned that the Armorer reminded him a little of his uncle Benito, also a weaponsmith back in his home ville of Nuestra Señora. And it was that that made him reckless sometimes, in his desire to impress J.B. and show he was worthy of sticking with Ryan's band of survivalists.

J.B. shook his head. No good ever came from blaming yourself, he thought.

In the bed, Ricky snuffled a moment and rolled over. His brow furrowed momentarily as he wrenched the wound in his side, but he didn't awaken.

The kid'll be all right, J.B. told himself, turning to leave.

THE ALCOHOL HAD been flowing for a while now. Inside the dance hall, the atmosphere was warmer as a new tune began. From their thrilled reactions, it was clear to Ryan and his partners that it was a dance favored by the locals. They took their positions during the opening strains, women in line down the center of the room, men to either side a few feet back, all of them moving in time to the rhythm.

Ryan and Krysty stepped to the edge of the group, where they could watch without interrupting. Then the music began in earnest and the patrons swayed seductively in time with it, stepping into the music, following its beats. The women swayed their hips suggestively, while the men watched appreciatively. The Regina stepped among them, weaving in and out of the writhing women touching their faces in the briefest of strokes as she passed, her dress a swirl of yellow and black.

Doc was among the throng, lined up with the other men, copying them step for step, albeit a beat behind. He faced the woman called Bella, with whom he seemed to have partnered for the night.

Watching, Krysty reached her hands behind Ryan's neck and pulled him close. Her eyes shone with joy, and this close Ryan could smell the sweetness of her breath from the mead she had drunk.

"This is it, Ryan," she whispered, her lips brushing against his ear. "This is the normal life we've waited for. A normal life full of wonders and miracles."

For that moment at least, Ryan liked to think that Krysty was right. And perhaps she was.

JAK COULD BE almost balletic in combat, and he was unarguably in touch with his primal side, but dancing, for all that its proponents insisted that it was about "feeling the music" and "letting go," remained too much of a social construct for Jak to comfortably engage in.

Charm smiled sympathetically at Jak's discomfort, and plied him with more of the sweet-tasting, fermented beverage that filled the barrels. "It's an old recipe, dating back hundreds of years," she explained as they supped at their drinks at the side of the hall where things were quieter. "It's called mead."

"Taste sweet," Jak said, smiling. He liked it, but then Jak liked most things he could eat or drink, because of the privations he had suffered as a youth.

In the center of the room, the dance with the Regina was continuing, the music getting faster as the women shook their butts at the men, flirtatiously peering over the shoulders with each erotically charged thrust. Without warning, Charm reached over to take Jak's empty goblet, and her hand touched his.

"Let me show you the dance," Charm said, stepping out in front of him.

Jak began to shake his head but Charm pressed her finger to her lips and hushed him.

"You don't need to do anything," she promised, "but watch." With that she began to sway her hips in time with the music, turning slowly as she raised her hands high above her head, stretching her back and pushing out her backside as she rotated in front of Jak's eyes.

Feet away, the dancers continued their own interpretation, each one moving in perfect time.

THE MOON WAS higher in the sky when J.B. exited the medical faculty, and the streets were still empty. He stood for a moment, listening to the music as it carried from the dance, drifting on the breeze with the same ebb and flow of the ocean. There was laughter and voices, too: the sounds of human happiness. He could waste a while yet; no one had come looking for him.

Thrusting his hands into his jacket pockets for warmth, the Armorer took a slow stroll around the towers and beyond, up along the main thoroughfare toward the gates through which they had entered the ville that morning. There was no one around, and once he was beyond the circle of towers there was barely any light to see by. J.B. walked slowly, trusting that the darkness would hide him from casual observers just as much as it hid them from him.

The water pumps that were spaced along the sides of the long thoroughfare glistened slightly as they caught what little illumination the tiny sliver of moon cast. As he got closer, J.B. saw that same sliver of moon lit the metalwork that crisscrossed the ville's gates. The gates were closed and, up close, J.B. could see the sentry box poised at the top of the high wall beside them. He stepped back into the shadows, eyeing the sentry box for thirty seconds without moving, checking to see who was inside. For a moment he thought that perhaps it was empty, that everyone in town had gone to the dance, but then he spotted the black shapes in the windows. There were two of them, he concluded, their ink silhouettes catching the moonlight as they performed the watch.

I wonder what shifts this place has? J.B. pondered. And whether anyone's allowed out of the gates at night? Come to that, can just anyone go out in the daytime, or are there rules to that the way there is to other stuff?

Maybe now wasn't the right time to find out. Skulking in the darkness was one sure way to arouse suspicion. Better then to keep an eye on the comings and goings and figure out the pattern from a distance. He'd do that the next day, and see if maybe he could slip out and take another look at the redoubt and that wrecked mat-trans.

AFTER THE DANCE ended, the companions returned to their cabins with conflicting thoughts.

For Ryan and Krysty, the night had only begun. As soon as they closed the door of their wood cabin on the outside world, they made furious love, with the urgency of lovers parted for too long.

Afterward, as they lay in the darkness, their bodies glistening with sweat, Krysty asked Ryan if they might stay here.

"Mebbe we could," Ryan replied, his words swimming around the room in the darkness. Then he rolled over and kissed Krysty, and their lovemaking resumed.

DOC FOUND JAK with Charm, but he said nothing. The two men returned to the shack they shared in silence.

Doc knew he was a fool to be jealous. Charm was young and pretty and he was just an old, worn-out thing; old before his time but old all the same.

Jak was silent for his own reasons. He was remembering the transitory happiness he had had with Christina, and how it had been snatched away from him. If it should come to it, could he build a life again? Was he capable?

The two men retired to separate rooms, exchanging just the briefest of words as they parted for sleep.

MILDRED'S BRAIN WAS racing with thoughts of the medical faculty and the invitation that Petra had extended for her to join them. She bubbled with excitement, telling J.B. all about what she had seen and been told.

J.B. only half listened, wrapped up as he was in his own thoughts about the sec of the ville and the nature of its regime. There was nothing wrong here, not in any obvious way, and yet he was uncomfortable for reasons he couldn't put his finger on. Maybe it was something about him, and not the ville, that was nagging at him, that he was a weaponsmith in a ville that had outlawed weapons. He went to sleep wondering what the future held for a fighter who could no longer carry a blaster.

Chapter Eleven

Morning arrived in a blaze of streaming sunlight through drapeless windows. The alcohol of the night before hung inside the head of each companion like a wet cloth. All, that was, except for J.B., who had spent little time at the actual dance. As such, it was J.B. who answered the polite but insistent knock at the door to the cabin he shared with Mildred.

"I'm comin', I'm comin'," he said as he tripped across the floor in bare feet, pulling his pants on over his underwear in an ungainly, hop-skip-sway maneuver. A moment later, pants on and an open shirt over his undershirt, the Armorer pulled the front door open.

Phyllida stood on the stoop. She looked immaculate in her white robe, and her blond hair was once again elaborately pinned back from her face. "Mr. Dix," she said, favoring him with her bright smile.

Behind her, the sunlight was filtering through the trees, casting dazzling streaks across the ground. J.B. noticed people out there in the distance carrying great wooden beams and bags of tools: a work crew.

"Miss…Phyllida," J.B. said, uncertain how to address the woman.

"It's a new day," Phyllida told him.

J.B. rubbed at his face, adjusting the glasses he wore. "It surely is." Almost as an afterthought, he began to button his shirt and force its tail down into the waistband of his pants.

"You heard the Regina's words last night," the white-robed Melissa said. "Within us lie the seeds for the future. But only by working together can we…"

"Yeah, I remember," J.B. grumbled. "You, er, have anything you wanted?"

"New day, new future," Phyllida said cheerily. She had apparently missed or chosen to ignore J.B.'s sour response. "We shall all work together in our ways to build our better tomorrow. You, the Regina sees, as a carpenter."

Aha. Now J.B. saw where this was going. If he and his companions were to stay in the ville, they would be expected to pull their weight. He shrugged. "I've worked a little with my hands. I'd be willing to give it a go. Ryan, too, I imagine," he added almost as an afterthought. He wanted to speak to Ryan about what he was sensing here, see if, as his oldest friend, Ryan was also sensing something out of step.

"That's perfect," Phyllida said, her smile never wavering. "The Regina has assigned Ryan to a construction team just like you."

"Together, I hope?" J.B. said.

"We all work together in Heaven Falls, Mr. Dix," Phyllida replied. "No point in a hundred and eighty people building a hundred and eighty different tomorrows."

That wasn't what J.B. had meant, but he let the matter slide.

Mildred had been awakened by the sound of voices at the door, and she wandered into the main room to see what was going on. Phyllida seemed heartened to see the woman, and she gave Mildred her assignment, which Mildred agreed to gleefully. She was to train in the medical tower, where she would get to see how the Trai were advancing their medical knowledge. It suited Mildred perfectly.

THE OTHERS WERE also given assignments, delivered by one of the white-robed Melissas.

For Krysty, her day would be spent in the ville's kindergarten, where the under fives were brought while their parents were at work in the fields or patrolling the mountains.

Ryan was assigned to a construction team, as J.B. had been told, though his role was to move the heavy wood around a construction site.

Jak was given a role in the fields as a farmhand, while Doc—apparently something of a novelty to the people of Heaven Falls because of his advanced age—was instructed to join the beekeepers who collected honey from the hives located in and around the ville walls.

The efficiency with which roles were assigned gave some insight into how the advances here had been achieved. With everyone assigned a role, the companions barely saw one another, working hard through the day. Everyone in Heaven Falls was open and friendly, and the companions made new friends with their particular work buddies. Even Jak, whose natural inclination was to be a loner, seemed at home tilling the fields where the work was hard, though much of it remained at a distance from his colleagues.

Every worker was provided with an ample lunch consisting of dried breads and fruit, more mead—which J.B. swore away from given the way his colleagues' heads were pounding—and sweetened honey water. Lunch was eaten mostly where one worked, with a full ninety minutes given over to not just its consumption but also some general, easygoing socializing.

Someone at Ryan's construction site produced a ball and the workers had a little kick-around on a patch of newly cleared forest just beyond the fields. In a few weeks, Ryan was told, this space would be inhabited by three new cabins—but for now they could use it for recreation. Ryan was grateful. He was used to constantly moving while on the road, but building houses—or at least lugging around hunks of wood—proved demanding on even his fit body, utilizing muscles he wasn't used to punishing so much.

By THE TIME the sun set, all of the companions felt that they had contributed to the upkeep of Heaven Falls, and if it had bothered any of them before, they no longer felt that they were abusing their hosts' generosity without giving something back.

J.B. caught up with Ryan on the path home.

"So what did they have you doing in the end?" J.B. began.

Ryan stretched his arms, easing out the kinks in his back. "Mostly carrying planks and bricks," he told the Armorer. "Feels like I carried a whole house."

J.B. guffawed. "Mebbe you did," he said. "They sure do like to work you hard around here."

"A little hard work never hurt anyone. Keeps a man honest."

"I guess it does at that," J.B. agreed, smiling.

As they reached the door to the cottage that J.B. shared with Mildred, the Armorer held up his hands and showed Ryan. There were a couple fresh scabs there, newly dried.

"You been getting in fights?" Ryan asked.

"No, just working hard," J.B. said. "Chisel," he said, indicating one scab. "Nail." He pointed at the other.

Ryan laughed. "I take back what I said. Mebbe in your case a little hard work does hurt."

For a few seconds the two old friends laughed at that. Then J.B. said what was really on his mind.

"You think this place is okay?" he asked. "On the up-and-up?"

"I haven't seen anything to make me think otherwise," Ryan said pragmatically.

"Me, neither," J.B. admitted before adding in a low voice, "and that worries me."

Ryan raised his eyebrows in surprise. He stepped closer to J.B., and the Armorer was suddenly conscious of how Ryan towered over him. "These people have opened their doors to us, J.B. Krysty's happy here."

"What about you?" J.B. asked.

"Krysty's happy," Ryan repeated. "I haven't seen that as much as I'd have liked. It's worth clinging to."

J.B. looked at the taller man, an unspoken challenge in his eyes.

"They're good people," Ryan told him. "Honest people. They have shown us more kindness than a hundred other villes we've stumbled upon. Don't overthink that."

"And what about the bomb?" J.B. asked. "Is that the work of good people, of honest people?"

"Someone did that to them…" Ryan began.

"One of their own," J.B. reminded him. "I haven't seen any signs of dissent, have you?"

Ryan shook his head.

"Then why would someone do that?" J.B. persisted.

"The guy was…disturbed," Ryan said. "Not in his right mind."

"Mebbe," J.B. allowed. "But planting a bomb takes planning. You don't pull something like that out of thin air."

Ryan reached out with his hand and pressed it firmly on J.B.'s shoulder, adding just enough pressure that J.B.

knew he meant it. "Don't ruin this, J.B. Live and enjoy what we've been given—a second chance."

Then Ryan turned, and J.B. was left alone on the stoop watching the bigger man go. "I don't know that I can do that," he muttered to himself. "I'm not a house builder or a farmer. Spent too long on the road to do that now."

WHEN MILDRED ARRIVED home later that same evening, she found J.B. in the main room of the cabin with the wooden box unlocked, its lid open. He had its contents arrayed around him and was sitting in a chair oiling his shotgun.

"Problem?" she asked as she closed the door.

"No problem," he told her. "Just figure it pays to keep our weapons in working order. Never know when we might need them."

Mildred watched him for a few seconds, not knowing what to say. "Just make sure no one sees you with those things," was all she could think of.

"Sure," J.B. replied, already lost in his work cleaning the blaster.

As he said it, Mildred saw the new cuts on J.B.'s hands. One of the scabs had torn open as he worked, and Mildred's doctor instinct kicked in. She trotted across the small room and crouched in front of him. "You're hurt," she said. "Let me look at that."

Reluctantly, J.B. showed her the cut on his right hand. It wasn't deep and the scab would dry in a while, if he would only stop what he was doing long enough to let it.

Mildred reached into her satchel and brought out a little pot, not much taller than her thumb joint. She unscrewed the lid and, inside, J.B. saw a hard, greasy-looking substance of a dull yellow color.

"What's that?" J.B. asked.

"Something I picked up at the medical faculty," Mildred said, scooping a little of the jar's contents onto her fingers. "It'll help it heal."

J.B. wondered what was in it, but he didn't ask. He trusted Mildred—she was the doctor of the group, and she had patched them all up more than once. He sat there, one hand out and the shotgun resting in his lap as Mildred rubbed the salve into his cuts.

Chapter Twelve

On the second day Charm found Jak just before lunch. The sun was shining, and she came wandering up the aisle between potato crops in her white robes, her hair pinned back the same way it had been when he had first met her.

"You must be hungry," she said, stopping where Jak was digging a drainage ditch. "Do you want some lunch?"

Jak looked up, shielding his eyes from the sun. With the sunlight playing through the veil of her dress, Charm looked beautiful—almost angelic to his eyes. She was holding a simple, short-handled wicker basket that had a cloth wrapped over its contents. Jak's sensitive nose could smell the food beneath.

"Yeah," Jak agreed. "Hungry. Worked hard."

The woman did something unexpected then—she reached down and let Jak take her hands, then helped pull him up. It pleased Jak to notice that she was strong.

"Came far?" Jak asked as the couple walked along the narrow strip between crops.

"I'm still on shift," Charm told him, "but my patrol brought me out this way and I saw you in the field. You're kind of hard to miss."

Jak shrugged. He guessed he was. "Patrollin'?" he asked.

Charm smiled, trying to make sense out of Jak's abbreviated phrasing. "You mean 'where'? All around. The Melissas take turns checking that walls are secure, and that we don't get any interference from anyone or anything else. There are a lot of wild animals in the mountains."

Jak nodded in understanding as they walked toward a towering pine tree that stood at the field's edge.

A sec woman, he thought. What a strange role for a woman to take when there were clearly stronger men working the fields. Maybe they wanted that strength to feed the ville, he thought, rather than to guard it. But if you didn't guard it properly, no amount of food was worth shit to you.

Charm placed the basket down and sat in the shade of the tree, patting the ground next to her in invitation to Jak. "The grass is dry," she said.

Jak sat and together they ate a small lunch of sweet, fresh bread with honey, along with a small flagon of mead, and pieces of fruit soaked in sweet syrup to finish the meal. They sat there awhile in companionable silence, listening to the insects buzz as they pollinated the flowers all around them. It was tranquil there, as if they were light-years from the ongoing slaughter and barbarism of the Deathlands.

DOC HAD SPENT his first working day being shown around the various beehives, and on the second day he was invited to pitch in.

"Honey plays a big part of our lives," a friendly beekeeper called Jon explained. Jon was a handsome blond-haired man, whose tanned looks belied his years. As Doc spoke with him that first day, he began to realize that Jon was older than he initially appeared, and he pegged the man as being in his forties despite having near flawless skin—particularly unusual in someone who labored outdoors under the full intensity of the sun.

The "honey poachers" worked in two- or three-man teams running in strict and constant rotation through the hives. Jon was happy to have Doc on his squad, which included another man called Thomas who had so much brown curly hair that it looked like a wig. Thomas kept largely to himself, working at other hives in their vicinity while Jon meticulously showed Doc the ropes. As such, the men were never out of eyesight of one another, and the companionship tripped over into their designated lunch period when they gathered to eat fruit and fresh bread, washed down with a mug of mead.

The man-made beehives were spaced at frequent intervals around the edges of the ville walls, with further hives dotted on the landscape just beyond the gates. The hives were wooden, slatted constructions that looked a little like boxes on legs, and all of them were painted white or a very pale cream.

Bees from the hives pollinated the flora within and around the ville, which ensured hearty plant growth and helped to bolster the ville's food supply. That, however, was a fortunate side effect of the beekeeping operation, which was primarily concerned with harvesting the honey they produced.

To access the honey, the bees would be smoked into dopey submission using a little controlled fire, such as a slow-burning, oil-soaked rag. Once the hive was sedated, the wooden roof would be removed so that each section could be accessed, slotting in and out of the boxlike construction with ease.

Doc was initially concerned that the bees might sting him as he gathered honey, but Jon assured him that that was rare.

"We keep them docile while we gather their crop," Jon told him, "and we wear protective gloves just in case."

Before long he had been given his own set of oversize gloves made from thick material weaved into multiple, padded layers that reached up well past his elbows.

On his first couple attempts, Doc was nervous from the buzzing coming from the hives. It sounded angry to him and he said as much to Jon.

"Buzzing doesn't mean they're angry," Jon said. "You know how honeybees talk, Doc?"

Doc was too intensely focused on lifting the hive lid to answer.

"They dance," Jon said. "Waggle their butts at one another like they're on fire. I'll show you, once you get your sea legs."

Once gathered, the honey was stored in clay vessels, cylindrical in shape and standing almost up to Doc's hip. Full, these vessels were too heavy for one person to lift, but their narrow shape and dark exterior ensured that their contents remained cool until they could be taken to a storage facility.

Under Jon's scrutiny, Doc became a competent beekeeper, albeit a slow and wary one.

ON THE SECOND afternoon, the beekeepers' rounds took them back into the heart of Heaven Falls where the seven towers were located. The group brought with them the great storage canisters of honey that they had gathered, placed in a small cart that was little more than a wheelbarrow and which had been delivered at one of the hive sites without any fuss. Another group was responsible for delivering these carts, leaving them at assigned spots around the ville on gathering days. It was all very regimented and efficient.

Jon led the way, assisting as necessary while Thomas wheeled the cart along the path until they reached the entrance to one of the towers. Doc had not been inside this one before and, unlike the others he had been in, he noticed that it had a proper door with a thick bolt so that it could be locked, though it was open right now. Two women in white robes waited just inside the doorway, out of the sun. They were dressed in the same manner as the Melissas, and Doc guessed they performed a similar role here, working as sec for the store.

After the briefest of discussions between Jon and one of the white-robed women, the group was ushered inside. It was dark and cool within the tower, with the interior arranged in boxy compartments between which ran narrow aisles just wide enough to wheel the cart through. Indefinable but heavy sounds could be heard inside, things being moved or dropped or stacked.

Jon had been given some information at the doors, and he led the way through to a specific area located several floors up within the six-story structure. To reach this, Doc and his companions utilized a wall-mounted ladder that ran in the center of the hexagonal tower, while the barrow they had brought was placed on a flatbed made of wood that was connected to a pulley system a little like a dumbwaiter. Once they had ascended to the correct level, Thomas walked over to a point directly in line with the flatbed and used the winch system to pull their cart up.

Pulling the cart with them, the trio paced a compartment simply identified by an eight-inch circle of pale blue that had been painted on the floor of the open doorway. The circle was well placed, a single strand of pinprick light illuminating its center from high above. Jon stepped through, ducking his head a little because the doorway was only about five feet high, and then reached back for Doc, encouraging him to join him.

When Doc was through the doorway, he stood inside a squat room, almost circular in design, with broad shelves running the entire length of its walls, including above the low doorway. The shelves stood four feet from the walls and were arranged close to one another, leaving a space of perhaps ten inches between them. That was the ideal height to hold the clay canisters when laid down, leaving just enough space to maneuver them. Already the shelves were about one-third full, the tiny pinpricks of light allowing Doc to see just enough to make out the shadowlike mounds of full canisters.

"We need to pile our crop neatly," Jon explained while Tom maneuvered the cart so that it abutted the doorway.

Doc was a little overwhelmed. "How much honey do you have here?" he asked.

Jon shook his head. "The store isn't full yet, and we keep using it," he said. "So not enough!"

Doc smiled at that logic, displaying neat rows of perfect teeth. "And this whole silo is just…"

"Honey," Jon confirmed. "Sweet, sweet honey."

LATER THAT SAME day, once their harvesting shift had ended, Doc was shown another building that was used for brewing mead. He was also issued for the first time two jars of honey for his own consumption. With no money or barter system, food was rationed. But the rationing was clearly generous and no one seemed to go without. There was no hunger nor any noteworthy signs of excess, Doc observed. He had seen no obese people among the population who had attended the dance.

Shortly thereafter, the other companions were placed on the rationing system, which equated to a food bank from which all produce was allocated. This system may have seemed strange, but it appeared to be effective enough. There was no squabbling, and the process was very orderly. Furthermore, the population looked markedly healthy, although Mildred suggested that this was also due to the top-notch medical care that the ville supplied as a matter of course. Most important, people were happy—genuinely happy. That was the real revelation of Heaven Falls, the one thing that marked it out from so much that Ryan and his companions had seen before.

J.B. REMAINED HESITANT to embrace the community they had stumbled upon, however. He was a natural loner in many respects, despite being a long-serving member of Ryan Cawdor's group of survivalists and, before that, a member of Trader's wag crew. The Armorer trusted few people, and he gave that trust none too easily. Being in a ville with plentiful food and no obvious signs of conflict wasn't enough to reassure him. His mind kept coming back to that bomber—William, the Regina had called him—who had felt it necessary to destroy the mat-trans just hours after it had started working.

On the third day, knowing the routine of his work now, J.B. took a stroll during his lunch break.

J.B. made his way to the ville wall where the gates were located, coming at them from a side angle rather than past the towers and along the main thoroughfare. He made the walk look ambling and casual, stopping now and then as if to survey the flowers that colored the grass in pretty clusters, occasionally flat out changing direction as if he had settled on going somewhere else in midstride. For that, J.B. took inspiration from his early days with Doc, whose involuntary trip through time had left his mind addled for a long period, making him frustratingly unpredictable.

Eventually the Armorer reached the ville gates. They were closed. Adjusting the brim of his hat, J.B. gave a quick up-from-under look and checked the sentry post. Lookouts were posted; this time three of the white-robed women were within, though one sat with her legs out the open door, hanging down the side of the wall beside the ladder she would have used to climb there.

J.B. strode closer to the gates, doing his best to look both lost and as though he had every right to be there, not meeting anyone's gaze.

Eventually the woman who was sunning her legs from the sentry post door craned her neck and called to J.B. "You look awful lost," she said. "You expected somewhere?"

"Just, er…" J.B. waved a hand vaguely "…stretchin' my legs before my shift starts up again."

The white-robed woman leaned forward, and J.B. saw she was young and pretty with hair so blond it was almost white. "It's a mighty fine day for that," she said agreeably.

"Any way I can get out without disturbing you all up there?" he asked.

"Nope."

"Well, I didn't want to make work for you…"

"Work's nothing to shy away from," the blonde replied. J.B. thought that was ironic, given that he had found her topping up her tan while the rest of the ville was sweating to build houses, plow fields and whatnot.

"In which case," J.B. said, tipping his fingers to the brim of his hat, "can I disturb you for the gate and see where my legs take me?"

The Melissa looked regretful, her lips forming a little moue. "Not unless you have business outside," she said. "But you knew that."

J.B. nodded. "Yeah, I guess I did," he said, filing the information away. "I'll just have to take my roaming off back that away." He thumbed vaguely in the direction behind him. "You keep watching the…er, watch."

"All love," the blonde called as J.B. turned.

"Yeah," J.B. called back as he turned to walk away. "All love to you, too."

Well, that was a bust. But it had told J.B. something. In fact, it had told him a whole handful of somethings.

First, no one was going outside without permission, which meant that permission could be gotten, and presumably from the Regina who acted as the baron of this ville.

Second, someone was getting out and probably quite a few someones because Phyllida had mentioned that the mat-trans had been brought up to working order by the ville's engineers. Furthermore, she had stated that they would shortly repair the damage done by the bomb.

With this latter fact in mind, it wasn't too huge a stretch of the imagination to assume that an engineering posse had visited the redoubt since the bomb blew up. Given the damage that bomb had done, any repair would involve significant man hours to complete. Which meant that someone may quite possibly be there now.

J.B. pondered all that as he walked back through the open fields toward the construction projects. Around him, pigs were snuffling in the dirt or cowering in their little wooden homes to keep the sun off, with no comprehension that they could end up as honey-roasted ham in tomorrow's sandwiches.

"But then, pigs aren't smart enough to realize when they're in a prison," J.B. muttered to himself. He wondered if his companions were.

Chapter Thirteen

On the fourth day, J.B. got up before dawn. He had disciplined his mind to awaken him, though it had resulted in a restless sleep. He dressed in darkness and crept from the bedroom in silence. It was J.B.'s good fortune that Mildred had come home late from her role at the medical faculty and had taken the other bedroom so as not to disturb him. Now she was sound asleep, and J.B. stood at her door for a few moments, listening to her breathing.

Then he pressed one hand against the door to the cabin and pulled with the other, inching the door open as quietly as he could.

A moment after that, J.B. had slipped out into the darkness. It was a few minutes before dawn, and the purple blackness of the predawn brushed the sky through the trees. J.B. had no blaster, but he was not unarmed. The previous night when he had returned to his shack, he had gone to the weapons cache and removed his Tekna knife. The six-inch combat blade was small enough to be concealed and, if it was found on his person, J.B. was reasonably confident he could bluff that it was part of the toolkit he was amassing for his construction work.

Outside, the ville was almost silent, only the sounds of a few overdue nocturnal creatures scurrying back to their burrows and the occasional flapping of wings overhead to accompany the noise of the wind stroking the leaves.

With the streets empty, J.B. felt confident enough to

take a direct path to the ville gates, though he kept to the shadows, and didn't walk on the flower-lined thorough-fare that he thought of as Main Street. It took ten minutes to reach the exterior wall and bring the gates within sight. By then, that first surge of adrenaline had passed, and J.B. could feel the cold in the air. The sun was rising now, and droplets of dew clung to the grass and the plants, like a little distillation of moonlight stolen from the sky.

In the lee of a boxy building, hidden by its shadow, J.B. looked up at the guard tower. There were figures within, the same as there always were. No matter how free a so-ciety might seem in the Deathlands, no settlement lasted long without constant vigilance. Anyone could attack, be they norm or mutie, because those who had nothing had nothing to lose in such an attack. Even the remote location of Heaven Falls wouldn't be enough alone to keep it safe from an army of scalies or stickies or outlanders armed and determined.

Moving in a crouch, J.B. hurried to an outcropping he had made a note of the preceding afternoon. The tallest rock came up to J.B.'s collar, which meant he could crouch behind it and still observe the watchtower and the gate without being seen. By and large, sec men didn't watch the inside of a ville, J.B. knew, and he counted on that to save him from chance detection.

Then J.B. hunkered down and waited.

It took close to an hour and a half, by J.B.'s chron, until the group came marching along the main street toward the gates. It was made up of five women, two of whom were dressed in the white robes of the Melissas. The women carried bags and cases with them, nothing big—probably just something to carry their lunch in and maybe some tools, J.B. figured. One of the women said something to the sentries that J.B. didn't catch, but the gates were already being pulled back to allow them passage out of the ville. J.B. watched them go, and then the gates were winched closed after them, sealing the ville from the outside world.

"Women," J.B. muttered. That made it awkward. He couldn't just sneak out with the group, not unless their make-up changed day by day, shift by shift. If it didn't, he'd stand out like a sore thumb.

J.B. pegged them for the engineering party that was traveling to the redoubt to repair the mat-trans. He couldn't be certain, but it was hard to think of many reasons for going outside a self-sufficient ville like this, other than to fix the damage that had been inflicted by that bomb, or maybe to hunt wild animals—but they weren't armed for that.

Even as he thought it, J.B. stopped himself, recalling something. When he had first come to this ville, he had seen beehives lining the approach. *Man-made* beehives, which meant someone was going out to gather the honey.

Doc!

Yeah, the old man had been assigned beekeeping duties, something a little less strenuous than house building or sod busting for his old bones. And if Doc was allowed out of the ville, then…

The plan began to take shape in the Armorer's keen mind, slotting together in his brain the same way as a field-stripped Colt M-16. He just needed the right ammo before pulling the trigger.

Unnoticed, J.B. sauntered away from the outcropping and made his way back to the construction site he had been assigned. He would be a bit late, but he could make his excuses, tell the foreperson he'd slept late. Just as long as no one figured out where he had really been while the rest of the ville was asleep.

MILDRED LOVED GOING to work, simply loved it. As she
strode through the arched doorway into the medical tower,
she had a spring in her step and was actually whistling
to herself.

One of the assistants—for everyone who helped out
in a role here was called an assistant—looked up at the
sound before returning to her duties, pushing a cart laden
with "medicine" across the clean, sterile floor. The term
medicine was relative, of course, but Mildred had been impressed with the medical acumen the Trai showed.

It was all down to honey. That sounded stupid, when
Mildred said it out loud. But Petra and another assistant
called Collette had showed her the core materials that were
used on her first day here, and she had been learning about
their derivatives ever since. The health benefits of honey
were well documented in Mildred's time. Manuka honey
was highly prized—and highly priced—in the natural
health aisle of many a twentieth-century supermarket. The
nutraceutical benefit—which is to say, the positive long-
term health effects—of honey was no secret, in much the
same way aspirin was employed as a kind of catch-all to
stave off many long-term illnesses.

Even so, the way the Trai employed honey in the medication here, refining it, mixing it, turning it into a salve
and crude capsule and what her grandmother would have
called a potion, now *that* was truly remarkable. And yet,
despite Mildred's initial skepticism, the honey-based medication was effective. No, more than effective—miraculous. Well, now, wasn't that a word to be weighed carefully
before employing?

Mildred made her way to Ricky's room, stopping to
help one of the other assistants when her cart toppled over,
sending its contents rolling comically down the ramp. Everyone helped here, no matter their place in the hierarchy.

"Hey, Mildred," Ricky said when he saw her. His voice was quiet and gravelly, as though it hadn't been used in a while. It hadn't. He'd been mostly asleep the past three and a half days.

"Ricardo, you're awake," Mildred said, smiling. "I'm so pleased. Oh, I'm so pleased." Her words came in a rush. Ricky was no longer a patient; he was her companion, her ally, her *friend*. "How are you feeling?"

"I'm—" Ricky coughed, his left hand flicking around to his side and clutching it as he did so. After a moment, the fit passed and he tried again, quieter this time. "I'm okay. Did I…did I wrestle with a bull at some point?"

Mildred shook her head.

"Feels like I got on the wrong end of a stampede," Ricky said.

Mildred leaned down and reached for the dressing over Ricky's wound. "Lie still, let me take a look," she instructed.

Ricky winced as Mildred plucked away the bandage on his side. Beneath, the wound looked as though it had healed. In fact, the skin showed no sign that it had been broken; there was no redness and no scarring. The only noteworthy thing was that it looked a little paler than the skin around it.

Mildred reached her fingers out and gently touched the piece of skin where the musket ball had struck. In the back of his throat, Ricky gasped.

"Tender?" Mildred asked.

"Yeah," Ricky said. "Little…yeah. Tickles."

"The healing is remarkable," Mildred said. "You were lucky. The wound wasn't too deep, but even a wound like that— I thought it might leave a scar. Anyway, you must be starving."

"I could eat, for sure," Ricky agreed. "When are we leaving?"

Mildred shook her head slowly, as if deep in thought. "I don't know. Ryan and Krysty and the others seem to be settling in pretty well. We all are."

They spoke a little more and then Mildred left the room to try to, as she put it, "rustle up something to clear the echoes out of your belly."

Chapter Fourteen

Jak was working a hoe over a field when the bear showed up. It appeared without warning, galloping through the undergrowth, its dark fur ideal camouflage for the shadows cast by the trees at the edge of the farmland.

Jak was part of a three-man crew that had been tasked with turning the woodland into something farmable, which meant a lot of clearing and raking and sifting to get the surface free from clutter in preparation for sowing. His colleagues continued working the field when Jak stopped, his ears pricking up. Jak had heightened senses, not beyond human, perhaps, but certainly at the human animal's very upper limit. He sensed the bear like a change in the wind direction, something shifting just beyond his field of vision.

His body tensing, Jak eyed their surroundings, his gaze working meticulously over the dark patch of tall trees that ran in a semicircle around two and a half sides of the would-be farm.

"Jak? You okay?" asked Sylvio, one of Jak's colleagues.

Jak said nothing for a moment, his head swaying ever so slightly as he tried to locate the source of the disturbance in the trees. He had the point fixed, couldn't see the thing but could see the location where he knew it had to be. The hoe still in hand, Jak began to pace toward the trees.

"Jak?" Sylvio asked again. He had been sifting earth when he had first spoken, tossing the bigger stones into a barrow so that they could later be dumped. Now he stopped and held the circular sieve up like a tiny, ineffective shield.

"Trouble," Jak said without looking back. That was the old watchword; the code that told Jak's old companions that something big was about to happen and that they had best be prepared. Jak used it now, even though the old codes meant nothing to these farmers.

The other member of the crew, a bearded, dark-haired man named Paul, with fearsome shoulders and the reach of a prizefighter, paused, his foot on the crossbar of the shovel he had been using to turn the earth.

"What's he seen?" Paul asked, his quiet voice belying his huge size.

"I don't know," Sylvio replied.

Both men had worked with Jak only a couple days, but they had already picked up that he was a strange one, with his own quirks and his own outlook. They'd taken him on board as part of the clearing crew because Jak was a good worker who toiled without complaint, and often without a word for hours on end. A little eccentricity could be overlooked when a man worked hard without complaining. But this—walking to the trees, all fired up—this was something new.

Then the bear crashed through the trees like a freight train, all muscle and blackness, looming over Jak like a collapsing mountain. It was huge. Up on its hind legs, the beast had to have been twice Jak's height, and at least as broad as Jak was tall. Its pelt was a velvety blackness that seemed to absorb the light around it, almost creating an absence where it moved.

Its arm was as broad as a tree trunk, swishing through the air as it emerged from the woodland, the round paw ending in pointed, black nails.

Jak sidestepped, bringing the haft of the hoe up until it covered his chest at a protective horizontal.

Behind Jak, Paul and Sylvio were voicing their astonishment. This area was considered safe. Melissas patrolled all of Heaven Falls, outside and in. The front of the settlement had the wall and gates to stave off human attack, but most of the Trai land enjoyed the natural protection of its inaccessibility. Human attackers were few, because it was so difficult to reach. Animals could occasionally slip past the patrols unnoticed and find a way to the settlement, drawn by the smell of food or by curiosity, or just plain old chance. Humankind had a tendency of thinking of places that they had settled as "theirs," but Mother Nature didn't make such delineations.

"Back!" Jak called as the bear began to explore the newly cleared field, trundling forward on all four paws. Its movements were ungraceful, a kind of up-and-down gallop that forced its head forward as it sniffed the air. It had seen them. Now it was thinking about its next move, whether attacking one or all three would be necessary to fill its empty belly.

"Don't antagonize it," Sylvio whispered.

Jak and his coworkers stood still, watching as the beast hunkered down, sniffing the freshly turned ground, then raising its head and scenting the air. Its eyes were bottomless black pools rimmed with red, its nose a twitching black smudge at the end of its snout. Two short, devil-pointed ears poked up from its head with the nubs of horns beside them—some kind of mutation brought about by the radiation that had been in the air since the nukecaust.

And then it moved, charging across the field—not at Jak, who was its nearest target, but at the two men who stood together in the field. Hoe clenched like a quarterstaff, Jak began to chase after it.

Chapter Fifteen

The mutie bear was standing in front of Paul and Sylvio in seconds, straining on its rear paws as it reached for them. The two farmhands scrambled away, running east and west to better split them as a target.

Paul was out of the bear's reach in a split second, but his companion was not so lucky. Sylvio was the smaller of the two men by some considerable measure, and doubtless the weaker of the two targets in the monster's mind.

The bear's paw swung for Sylvio, curved claws snatching at his shirt and tearing it from his back in a shredded mess. Gobs of Sylvio's skin came with the shirt as the bear's razor-sharp claws snagged his back, and he collapsed to the ground with a scream of pain.

The bear snuffled over Sylvio, flicking the remains of the man's shirt away. A moment later it was standing over him on all fours, its forepaws set to either side of his torso, hind legs spread out just beyond Sylvio's feet. Charging across the field, Jak swung the hoe in both hands, using his own momentum to power the makeshift weapon so that it struck the bear's back with a definite thud.

The bear stopped in what appeared to be surprise, then turned its head, piercing Jak with its black-eyed stare.

Jak swung the hoe again, this time raising it over his head before bringing it down, blade first, against the beast's skull. It struck with another thud, snapping the tool's shaft in two.

"We've got to keep it from the Home!" Paul shouted from somewhere behind Jak's back. "Beast like that will cause untold damage! We've got to protect our Regina!"

Jak wasn't worried about the Home. Right now, he figured they had more immediate concerns—like saving their own skins.

The bear lunged at Jak, swinging one mighty forepaw at his torso from where it stood like some strange table over Sylvio's fallen body. Jak reared back, his heels scrabbling against the freshly turned soil as he took himself out of the path of that mighty limb. Jak managed to slip—just barely—out of the bear's reach, but the soil remained loose where the ground had been turned and he went skidding over and crashed to the dirt.

Riled, the bear took a long step toward Jak, its dark form looming over him like a solar eclipse. Jak dodged as the bear thrust a paw at his head; the paw struck the ground, kicking up a shower of loosened earth that struck Jak's face.

The albino could taste earth in his mouth now, caught up in his saliva as he scrambled backward, elbows and butt and feet, as if comically imitating a beached swimmer doing the backstroke. The bear followed, stalking over Jak with its teeth bared, the distinct smells of plant sap and raw meat rank on its breath.

A shadow moved overhead, almost from nowhere, and suddenly the bear seemed to stop in place while Jak continued to scramble on his back. Jak looked up, saw Paul—the muscular farmhand—grab the bear by its leftmost hind leg, clinging on to it like a human ball-and-chain. For a moment the two figures were stuck in that weird embrace—the bear finding itself suddenly unable to propel forward, the man clinging to its leg, trying to secure a stronger hold on its slick pelt. Then the bear turned its head and saw what had happened, and it kicked out. Paul held on, shouting something that was hard to make out. It was something about the Regina, maybe a curse in her name, but due to the strain Paul was exerting Jak couldn't distinguish all the words.

During the brief respite, Jak got to his feet. He was aware of more movement behind him, as people in the other fields began to respond to the altercation. Then the bear flicked one of its forepaws at Paul's face, and the short claws that lined its stumpy digits extended from hidden sheaths, jutting like a handful of flick knives to turn the man's face into a crisscross of red.

Extending claws! Jak let that register for a half second, which was the time it took for Paul to let go of the monster's leg and slump to the ground, his hands going up to his ruined face. That was the trouble with mutation—it didn't work the same way twice. Sometimes there'd be gigantism and that would be the extent of the mutation, other times it was a new limb or a new kind of tail. Nature adapted things to survive.

Already, the bear had brought itself up to stand upright on its hind legs, and it snuffle-woofed in what Jak took to be a cry of victory. Standing upright like that, the bear was close to ten feet tall.

Jak reached into his sleeve, feeling the familiar handle of the leaf-bladed throwing knife he stored there. He had three on him, one in each sleeve and a third hidden in an ankle sheath. He had become too trusting in Heaven Falls, and in just four days he had sunk out of the habit of wearing the numerous hand-fashioned blades that had kept him alive during his time in the Deathlands. But this was no time for regrets; the bear was charging toward Jak across the field, trampling over the prone body of Sylvio.

Jak ran, scrambling over the turned soil, the throwing knife ready in his right hand.

The bear thundered on, a force of nature made solid.

Jak's right arm flicked forward, his hand moving up from under, moving with such rapidity and such grace that it looked as if he could bend the limb in a way that was impossible, as though his bones had become liquid. The knife left his hand as it reached a fraction of an inch above shoulder height, the point of the blade turned upward, taking it in a straight line at a twenty-degree angle, whistling as it cut the air.

The bear shook its head as Jak's blade struck, and a gout of optic fluid spurted from one eye where it had been split by the projectile. The reaction, momentary though it was, slowed the beast from its charge, changing its trajectory just fractionally as it tried to get away from the searing pain that was tearing through its eyeball. In that moment Jak leaped, running up the side of the bear, using its moving body like a cliff face, wedging his booted feet and grasping hands into nooks and creases in the flesh to bring himself up the ten feet that would put him level with the thing's broad face. By then, Jak had the second of his knives in his hand, slipped out from beside his left wrist, glinting silver as the sun reflected off it.

Jak was standing now, balanced perfectly against the bear's torso, one foot higher than the other, using nothing but momentum and the angle of his body to hold him there as the monster continued to charge.

"Night falls," Jak swore, pulling his hand back before plunging the blade into the bear's remaining eye with all his might.

The bear roared in surprise as Jak's blade cut deep, delivered with such power that it went in beyond the edge of the handle, the top of Jak's index finger and thumb disappearing into the monster's face.

Jak let go of the blade and sagged backward in the grip

of gravity. He fell away with arms outstretched before initiating a flawless twisting flip that sent him six feet away from and to the side of the charging juggernaut. The bear plowed blindly on, both eyes gushing blood, its teeth bared in agony.

Jak landed in a semicrouch, watching as the mutie bear charged past him. The thing was blind now, which wouldn't cut down the potential damage it was capable of, but it did mean that Jak could sneak up on it and maybe halt it. Jak or…

He turned, sensing the other people who had joined them at the edge of the field. Charm was running across the turned soil, straight hands cutting the air like blades, her legs pumping so fast they seemed to be a blur. She had come to meet him for lunch, Jak guessed, spotted the altercation from the distance and run all the way to help. Behind her, other locals were hurrying to help, carrying pitchforks, spades and long-handled hammers, the kind they used to knock nails into the ground.

"Stay back!" Charm shouted to Jak, authority in her tone.

That surprised Jak a little. Then he watched as the white-robed woman leaped up and over the charging bear. Once she was over it, Charm came down with her feet together, legs straight, driving her body into the beast's back like a nail being driven into the ground by one of those long-handled hammers. There was an audible crack and the bear continued to run, but it sagged at the back, its hind legs giving way even as it moved.

Charm flipped away, recovering her balance before leaping straight back into the fray unarmed. Jak was only now moving to help, two seconds passing in a snap. As he ran, he watched Charm leap at the sagging bear where it flailed at the ground. She had already broken its spine,

Jak realized, and now she was simply working at it with rapid punches and kicks, keeping it at bay the way a mongoose sparred with a snake.

The movements were so fast it was hard to follow. Though the bear had been wounded, crippled even, it still had plenty of fight left in it. Mother Nature's survival card in play once again, never easy to trump. The blade-like claws in the bear's forepaws swept at Charm, and she stepped out of their path with an inch to spare.

Jak leaped into the battle with his remaining knife, driving it at the bear's flank, jabbing here and there to distract the beast from attacking his friend. The bear snarled, aiming one of its flailing paws at him, its back legs twitching but no longer able to support it.

Charm arrowed a snap kick across the beast's snout as it went for Jak a second time, a crack of bone on bone as the two met. "I told you stay back," she called.

"Helped," Jak replied, ducking low as the bear swatted for him again.

The bear's extended claws swept up, scoring along Charm's left leg as she kicked out. She cried out as droplets of her blood winked red in the air, spattering across the ground like spilled rubies. Then Charm's foot struck the bear's throat dead center, heel driving deep.

Jak held his breath, watching as the beads of blood turned into tiny rivers that ran down the woman's bare leg. The bear trembled, and its writhing tongue emerged between its open jaws, flicking at the air as if to taste something. Charm remained in place, holding her leg straight; the foot plunged deeply into the beast's throat. It took thirty seconds, maybe forty, before the bear's body stopped trembling, then another thirty until the tongue's movements became less frantic, transforming from the tail of a beached fish into a leaf on the faint breeze, then stillness. The beast was dead.

"Must have broken a fence," one of the farmers was explaining as Jak came back to his senses from the place he had been where combat and survival had been everything.

There were other people in the field now, several of them massed around Paul and Sylvio as the two farmhands struggled to sit up. Paul was in a bad way, blood on his face and clothes. Sylvio looked better, just shaken and suffering where he had been struck.

"You okay?" a bearded farmhand asked, padding over to Jak and Charm.

Jak nodded.

Charm brushed at the blood running down her leg. "Yeah, it's just a scratch."

The farmhand took that as his cue, and turned to some of the others. "Let's get this carcass out of here," he called, jabbing his thumb in the direction of the mutie bear.

Jak looked at Charm, astonished. "Thank you," he said.

"Yeah, you, too," Charm replied, her breathing just a little labored. "Let's go have lunch. Maybe take the afternoon off. There won't be much to do here for a while, not until they get this beast out of the way."

Jak nodded slowly.

Charm and Jak left the cleanup to the others and meandered slowly through the neighboring fields, discussing what had happened and Jak explaining—in his own abbreviated way—how the bear had first attacked. Charm admired the way Jak had stepped up, brave and protective of his colleagues, and she told him so. Jak, for what it was worth, expressed similar sentiments in his own inimitable way.

"Like way you fight," he said with a roguish smile.

They made love for the first time in the shade of a tree,

away from prying eyes. And that evening, Charm invited Jak home with her for a meal of smoked meat and vegetables, washed down with mead. They made love twice more before they slept, Charm holding Jak close.

Chapter Sixteen

Doc was eating honey slathered on fresh bread for breakfast with a broad smile on his face. Jak hadn't come home the previous night, which was why he sat alone. He was missing his companion but was also optimistic about what the day might bring.

The first thing the day brought was an unexpected knock at the door.

"Jak?" Doc called as the unlocked door opened.

J.B. stood there, dressed in his battered jacket and fedora, his glasses catching the rays of the rising sun. "You don't need Jak's help, Doc," J.B. said, misinterpreting why the old man had called his companion's name, "it's just me."

"J.B....." Doc began, a little startled. "What brings you to these parts so early?"

"We're neighbors," J.B. reminded him, "so it wasn't a great hike. I've been meaning to discuss something with you, figured I'd catch you now before we're all expected back at work."

Doc smiled, taking another bite of his breakfast. "Ah, yes, they do run a rather orderly ship here, do they not?" he agreed. "Would you like some breakfast? This honey is delicious."

"I'll pass," J.B. said, holding up his hand. He took a chair opposite Doc, pulling it across the floor before sitting. "Perk of the job?" he asked as he sat.

"This? No, everyone is welcome. Have you not been granted your allotment yet?" Doc asked with a surprised raise of his eyebrows.

"Probably," J.B. admitted vaguely. "I've let Mildred deal with all that, seeing as she's the one who's in the ville center all day.

"But I didn't come here to talk about food. Well, kind of I did. You gather the honey, did I get that right?"

Doc sat a little straighter in his chair and puffed out his chest. "I am a beekeeper, yes," he said proudly.

"Great," J.B. said dismissively. "Do you know who tends the beehives that we saw when we were on the walk up to the ville gates a few days back?"

"Oh, yes—*I* do," Doc said. "Which is to say, it is a strict rotational system. Each group of beekeepers, which usually features three men to a team, is expected to tend to all the hives in turn, with four or six separate teams—I do not remember which—running the circuits at any given time. As such, there is not a hive inside or outside Heaven Falls that I won't have had my, if you'll excuse the pun, sticky fingers in." Doc finished the statement by spreading a dollop more honey on the crust of his bread before licking the excess from the spoon.

"Delicious," he said to himself.

"It's the outside I'm interested in," J.B. explained. "I want to check on the redoubt and see how our mat-trans is doing, but I can't get out there without giving a reason."

Doc shrugged. "Can you say that you plan to check on the work at the mat-trans?"

J.B. shook his head. "I get the feeling that might not be a popular thing to say after the whole bomb incident."

"I can see that," Doc agreed as he sealed the honey container. "But where do the hives fit in?"

"I want you to take me with your team," J.B. said, "the next time you go outside."

"That would take a lot of explaining on my part," Doc said reasonably.

"Say I'm interested in how you go about your job," J.B. suggested. "I might mebbe switch careers. I'm not much of a carpenter, not for building houses anyway. We being old pals, you're just trying to help me out by showing me my options."

"Is that true?" Doc asked. "About the carpentry?"

"Truthfully?" J.B. replied. "I don't know that settling in just one place is really for me."

"And that is why you want the mat-trans?" Doc asked.

"No, that's something for all of us. We've never been anywhere before where we didn't have a way figured to get out again, even if we got ourselves bastard sidetracked getting back to it. I'm just thinking of the group and keeping our options open."

"Very noble, I am quite sure," Doc said with a sliver of sarcasm. Then he got up and walked over to the kitchen area of the shack, where he placed the pot of honey on the shelf beside its unopened twin and slipped the dirty plate and spoon into the bowl of water he had already used that morning to shave with.

"So?" J.B. asked as Doc strode back into the main room.

"I shall ask," Doc told him. "After all, what are friends for if not to ask favors of?"

"Thanks, Doc," J.B. said, standing to leave. He was due down at the construction site in less than twenty minutes.

THE NURSERY WAS located in a single-story building on the main street. It was a simple wooden building that featured a line of windows along both sides, a few of which that had been painted with colorful animal designs using food dyes. Krysty had been working here for four days now, and with her fifth it was seeming like a home away from home.

"Good morning, Kryssie," said Christine, one of her coworkers, as she entered the doorway to the low building. Christine had raven-black hair that was trimmed short to her neck in a pixie cut. It was ironic that Christine, whose name was so similar to her own, always got Krysty's name wrong. So frequently, in fact, that already Krysty had stopped correcting her.

"Hey there," Krysty replied. She had pulled her hair back from her face in a long ponytail, better to keep it out of the reach of sticky hands as she took care of the troop of under fives who attended the kindergarten while their parents worked the fields.

It had taken three days just to get used to the noise of the kids as they played, but they were good-hearted kids and well behaved most of the time, which made it easier. There were some real characters among the twenty-strong group, too, and a couple of the girls had taken a real shine to Krysty.

Six of the children were still babies, four of them under a year old. Another woman called Andrea supervised them, but mostly they just slept in the cribs that the nursery had set up in a separate, smaller room. Sometimes you could hear one of the babies rouse and begin crying, which would set all the babies off for a little while, but mostly they were quiet.

The main room itself was a big, empty space encased by four walls, with plenty of room to run around indoors as well as a fenced-in area of cleared land where the kids could just go off supercharged and use up all their energy in the way kids did. There were some toys kept inside the nursery room, teeter-totters built by the Trai carpenters during their off hours, dolls sewed or knitted by the women. It was all voluntary, Krysty was told, but people wanted to help out and the kindergarten wasn't short of supporters.

"Everyone likes kids, don't they?" Christine had said on Krysty's very first day there.

Krysty had shrugged. It was a raw point between her and Ryan. Ryan had had a child, Dean, with another woman, and the one-eyed man had ended up with his heart gouged out when father and son had been separated. Krysty meanwhile had not conceived a child for Ryan—their lifestyle had been too unsettled, too dangerous for that.

"So what do you want me to do today?" Krysty asked as she walked with Christine into the nursery. It was quiet right now, but all that would change in a few minutes once the parents started arriving with their kids.

Christine laughed. "You make it sound so structured," she said, reaching for the cool jug of sweetened water that was stored in a pantry cupboard out of the light. "Drink?"

"Yes, please," Krysty agreed, taking up an empty mug.

Christine outlined their day as she poured the drinks. "Keep an eye on the little monsters and have fun," she said. "But if you can take a look at the windows, that would be great. The paint's looking a bit patchy in places. Do you know anything about plants?"

"A lot actually," Krysty told her. "My mother taught me the properties of many herbs and flowers."

"Can you paint?"

"On windows? I can try," Krysty said.

"Good. Maybe we can get some of the kids to help out on the lower windows."

Krysty laughed at the thought. "It's going to get messy."

"We'll use a stencil," Christine told her.

A THIRD ASSISTANT called Davina arrived at the nursery shortly thereafter, along with the first trickle of children. Krysty recognized them all now and knew most of them by name—although she had gotten Harry and Nate mixed up so many times now, despite the fact that one of them was blond and chubby while the other had brown hair and dusky skin—that she figured she would always get them muddled.

Krysty spent some of her morning cutting out flower stencils for the children to paint with while she sat out in the sun watching them run around the secure yard. Many of the kids had taken to Krysty on the first day, and two of the girls—called Kelsey and Hailey—had spent much of the first three days trying to copy Krysty's hairstyle while she pretended not to notice.

At some point in the morning, as the sun disappeared behind a bank of white clouds drifting lazily across the sky, Hailey came waddling over on her stubby legs and stood in front of Krysty as she sketched out another flower stencil.

"Whatcha doin'?" Hailey asked.

Krysty looked up and smiled. "Drawing flowers. Do you like flowers, Hailey?"

"Yes," Hailey decided, making the statement as if it was the most important fact she had ever been asked to recite. "Do you want to play Places?"

"Places?" Krysty repeated. "I don't think I know that game."

"We'll show you," Hailey said, boldly grabbing the fingers of Krysty's right hand and tugging.

Krysty got up from her stool, reaching up and carefully placing the stencil, blade and drawing nib out of the way on the low roof of the building, safe where children's hands could not reach. Then she followed Hailey across the scrubby yard to where two other girls, including blond-haired Kelsey, were already deep in the ritual of some elaborate game of pretend.

"Auntie Kryssie is playin', too," Hailey announced, and the other girls cheered.

All around, other child attendees were busy with their own games, chasing one another or scrabbling in the grass, prodding at bugs or whatever.

"Someone will have to show me how to play," Krysty said.

As if that were a cue, the girls stood side by side in a line while Hailey stood in front of them. "I'm the Regina," Hailey explained, "and you are my Mel-missas."

"Melissas," Krysty corrected with an indulgent smile.

"You have to stand, too," Kelsey whispered to Krysty, pointing to the spot next to her.

Krysty did so, clasping her hands behind her back and standing very erect. "What are your orders, Regina?" she asked.

"Today we're going to have a big dance," Hailey told everyone with mock seriousness. "So you have to find someone else to dance with and…that's it. All love."

"All love," the girls repeated automatically, and Krysty joined in, too.

The game wasn't "Places," Krysty realized. It was "Palaces." These girls were learning to be the next Regina should their leader ever step down.

MORNING TURNED TO afternoon, and a spell of persistent rain meant that the children were forced to play inside. The inside of the nursery became warmer with all those bodies running around, but there were no great fallings-out and the kids seemed to carry on without too much screaming or complaining.

Krysty took a little time to sort out her stencils and figure where best to place the flowers that would surround
the happy-looking animals that peered from the windows.
The children were excited to hear that they would be painting after lunch, but Christine reminded them all that lunch
came first, and no one was to skip it because they wouldn't
get to start painting early just because they had.

Like the other sites of work in Heaven Falls, the nursery
was supplied with fresh food that was delivered each day.
Just after the rain started, three women arrived laden with
baskets of freshly baked bread, pots of honey and some
salad, along with cool water for the kids to drink. There
were also a few cured meats for the adults, although feeding those to the children was generally discouraged because they were frequently quite rich. "Experience taught
us that you get toilet troubles in the afternoon if you feed
the kids too much meat," Davina had told Krysty on the
first day.

Lunch was taken together on three low tables where
the children were expected to sit quietly while the food
was served. Then one adult each would sit at the head of
the table and a few words of thanks were said to the Regina for the generous bounty. Most of the kids knew the
words by rote, and Krysty felt a little embarrassed as she
tried to keep up. The last words of the litany were *All love*.

The food arrangements impressed Krysty, and it made
her realize just how progressive the Trai were. The divi-
sion of labor and the organized food supply ensured that
no one went without, and it also ensured that people could
concentrate on their tasks without having to halt to fix a
meal. Furthermore, all food was fresh and the distribu-
tion meant that it was used in strict rotation with nothing
getting wasted or spoiled. Where other communities in
the Deathlands often struggled to feed their people, the

Trai had streamlined a process that ensured no one went hungry—and the net result was more productivity right across the board.

The food itself was excellent. Fresh ingredients, washed and lovingly prepared. It was good enough for a baron's table.

That afternoon, Krysty painted up her stencils and helped those children who were interested to fill in the flowers with the correct colors. Some of the boys thought it was a bit too sissy painting flowers, so Krysty relented by making some stencils of bugs that could be flying around pollinating the flowers. "Just not too many," she told the boys. Davina promised to keep an eye on what the boys did so that Krysty could get on with her task.

Hailey, Kelsey and their other playmate, Matilda, clung close to Krysty as she painted on the windows, copying her color choices and asking for frequent approval as they worked. While the girls filled in the purple petals on the violets, Davina brought Krysty a cup of sweetened honey water and encouraged her to take a break.

"Looks like you've made quite the impression," Davina said, indicating the girls.

Krysty rolled her eyes. "They're sweet girls," she said, keeping her voice low. "I never really saw myself doing this, you know."

"What? Painting windows?"

"Unarmed," Krysty replied.

Davina looked momentarily nervous at that, but she recovered. "It's safe here in Heaven Falls," she said. "Not like what people are used to out there. You'll get used to it."

"I think I already have," Krysty admitted.

"Auntie Kryssie?" Kelsey called.

"No rest for the wicked," Davina whispered.

Draining her cup, Krysty leaned down on her haunches to bring herself to Kelsey's level. "What is it, sweetie?"

"Do you think this color looks okay?"

Yellow.

"Yes, that's pretty," Krysty told her. "Like a buttercup."

It was strange. Krysty Wroth had been a warrior who worshipped the Earth Mother, Gaia. Now she found herself placed in the role of mother and it seemed to be a good fit. The children liked her and, what's more, she liked them. Maybe this wasn't such a bad life. Maybe Heaven Falls really was the thing that she and Ryan had been looking for all along.

THERE CAME A point late in the afternoon when Andrea asked Krysty to look in on the babies for a while. "I need to pop out," she explained, "but I won't be long." Andrea was a sweet young woman with strawberry-blond hair. She was twenty years old, with wide child-bearing hips and the start of a bump where her second child was on the way. Her firstborn, a girl called Amy, was almost two and had graduated into the full-time nursery just a few months before.

"Go," Krysty urged, "while things are quiet. I've got this."

Things were quiet. The kindergarten encouraged the kids to rest for an hour or so in the afternoons after either Christine or Davina had related a story to them to quiet them. Well fed and warm, most of the kids went to sleep without too much fuss, and those few who didn't were given quieter activities to do, like working on jigsaw puzzles or painting.

Krysty snuck out of the main room and sat in the smaller one where the half dozen babies were resting in their cribs. This room was kept darker, with light drapes drawn over the windows to keep out the direct sunlight. A cooling cupboard idled in one corner of the room where breast milk was stored, along with a little wood burner that could be used to heat it. There was a single stool at the side of the room on which Andrea generally sat if she wasn't wandering around checking on her charges, and a blanket had been laid over the stool to keep her warm.

Krysty walked past the stool and over to the windows, twitching back the drapes and listening to the rain. It was light rain, not much more than mist really, but she guessed Ryan would come home soaked through with his muscles aching. That didn't matter; he wouldn't complain.

As she stood there, Krysty heard the usual gurgles and snuffles of the babies. It was kind of musical in its way.

She turned and walked down the aisle of cribs, careful to keep her movements quiet. There were nine in total, although only six were in use right now, arranged along the walls with their short ends sticking out to create a single aisle down the center. Though roughly the same size and design, the cribs didn't match. They had been built by friends of the kindergarten, and one of them had yet to be painted. The six in use had mobiles hanging over them, simple things of stars and moons, birds and clouds, that spun in the lightest breeze.

Krysty looked at the mobiles, watching as they spun in her wake. She couldn't resist peeking into one of the cribs—though it wasn't as if there was some rule that said she shouldn't, far from it in fact—she was here to check on the children and make sure they were okay.

Inside the crib was a baby, fast asleep and wrapped in a blue blanket, its thumb rammed in its mouth in a glistening smear of drool.

A boy, Krysty thought. He looked so sweet; it made her want to hold him.

Krysty moved over to the next crib. This one held a girl with a fuzz of blond hair on her head that stood up like a wave, a little stuffed doll lying in the crib with her. The girl was coughing a little in her sleep, a kind of hiccupping movement, her chest going up and down.

"It's all right, sweetie," Krysty whispered. "You're safe here."

The next crib and the next, Krysty checked them all. In the fifth crib she noticed something that struck her as off. She couldn't really say why it struck her that way, but the little boy who lay there with his blanket draped over him looked like he was grimacing and maybe struggling to breathe. His snoring came in an irregular stutter, barely audible until Krysty leaned in close.

Though it was probably nothing, Krysty popped her head out of the nursery room and attracted Christine's attention, gesturing for the older woman to come over.

"I'm sorry, I don't know the babies' names," Krysty began. "I wonder if one of the boys looks all right to you."

Christine walked quietly with Krysty and peered into the crib she had indicated. "Oh, that's Geoffrey," she whispered. "He looks a little knocked out, poor lamb." She reached into the crib and, very gently, lifted him into her arms. "Feels floppy, too."

"Is that normal?" Krysty whispered. "I don't have much experience with babies."

"I'll take him outside and see if he perks up," Christine said. "You stay here, Kryssie, and keep an eye on the others. He'll be all right. You did the right thing."

Krysty watched as Christine took the slowly stirring Geoffrey through the main room and out the back door that led to the fenced-in yard. The rain had eased up and there was just a little water on the ground now. Krysty strode over to the window and watched as her colleague held the boy in her arms and tried to rouse him. He was alive, that was obvious, but he didn't seem to want to be roused. His head kept flopping away from Christine's touch and he seemed to have little energy.

After a while, Christine came back inside still holding the little boy. "I think he's all right," she told Krysty as they laid him back in his crib. "Just tired. Doesn't want to wake up."

"Is that normal?" Krysty whispered.

Christine shrugged. "Some kids need more sleep than others," she said. "We'll keep an eye on him."

Krysty did just that, and over the next few hours she made sure to drop in on the baby area even when Andrea was there. She also made a mental note to talk with Mildred about what she had seen.

Chapter Seventeen

The farmhands had been brought straight to the medical faculty tower after the incident with the bear. Mildred had attended to Sylvio, who had been in a state of shock but, other than a few scratches and bruises, had been unharmed.

Paul was a different matter. The guy had wrestled with that bear in a no-holds-barred match and had his face badly lacerated by a slash of those extending claws. He had been left in a bad way, holding the torn flesh of his face up where it should belong when he had arrived at the tower.

Petra and some of the other clinicians had swarmed on Paul, patching up his wounds and sedating him to keep him comfortable. Mildred had peeked in on that first day, but the guy had been sleeping and his wife and kids had arrived to hold vigil, which made her feel like she was intruding. Even from that little peek, however, Mildred had seen the awful wounds the farmer had sustained; the attack had left his face lopsided, as if his expression was trying to melt away the way wax will from a candle as it burns.

The next morning had been a busy one for Mildred, who was on a fast-track training program as she tried to memorize as much as she could about Heaven Falls' medicine for her projected jaunt back out into the Deathlands. She hadn't told anyone here about that yet, not even J.B. or the other companions, but it was something she kept mulling over each time she administered one of the honey-scented patches to a skin tear some carpenter or other had managed to snag during the routine construction of a new building.

It was close to the end of the day by the time Mildred checked on Ricky, and she decided she would drop in on Paul on the way there, while things were quiet. Paul's room was similar to Ricky's, a single bed raised high in its center with obscured lighting coming from the grillwork wall. A couple pieces of elegantly simple furniture and three chairs had been brought in for the family the afternoon before. The family wasn't there now; it was just Paul lying alone in the bed, knocked out on sedatives.

"Paul?" Mildred whispered as she stood in the doorway. "Are you okay? Do you need anything?"

The man in the bed didn't answer. He was just a silhouette with the light the way it was, and he didn't move other than the way his chest rose and fell. He was asleep. Good for him, Mildred thought. He needed it after what had happened.

Curiosity made her walk into the room. She had come here out of curiosity, too, though she had maybe told herself that it was medical duty, care, something like that. But now… Well, now it was pure curiosity. A man had had his faced ripped off by a mutie bear and the local doctors had patched him back together using primitive balms and salves and maybe a little needle and thread. A person had to be curious how that was going to wind up looking; it was human nature.

Mildred stepped over to the bed, her footsteps quiet. She stopped in front of the bed and looked at the man who lay there. He had dark hair and the scrappy remains of a beard. The docs had probably shaved him when they had worked on his face, so only a few tufts remained dotted around the scars. He was a handsome man, or had been, Mildred could tell.

Now his face showed three thick scrapes across it, plunging from above his left eyebrow down to the inside corner of his left eye, across his nose and into his mouth. His nose looked crooked, white bars striped across it where the claws had snagged. And he looked sad, his mouth downturned, his eyes closed as if downcast.

Mildred looked, her dark eyes roving across that face, drinking in the wounds. The patient looked remarkably normal. The wounds were there, the left eyebrow now two separate tufts with nothing to connect them. But he looked normal.

Standing there in the half-lit room, Mildred thought back to how the man had looked on arrival. Was it really as bad as she had imagined? It was hard to second-guess a memory seen when emotions were running high, something barely glanced at before she had been called to work on the man's colleague, Sylvio. Whatever she saw here and now, she knew it was a remarkable recovery. He was young and healthy; that could help with surgery. Maybe it had.

Mildred left the room, thinking about Paul as she made her way to see Ricky. The medical treatment here was effective and it was quickly employed. That had made a difference to the dark-haired farmhand. If she could bring this expertise to the field, out there in the Deathlands where people were dying every day, where it could genuinely do some good, well, that would be a goal worth pursuing.

Ricky was sitting on a chair next to his bed, eating a small bowl of dried apples that had been cut up like potato chips and glazed in honey. He looked a little pale, but otherwise in good health as Mildred walked in.

"Mildred, how are you?" Ricky asked.

"I should be asking *you* that."

"Ah, I'm fine," the lad said, crunching on another slice of apple. "Getting kinda bored, but the food's good."

"Yeah, the food's good all over," Mildred opined. "You want me to take a look at your wound?"

Ricky rolled his eyes. "Can't wait! It's the highlight of my day."

"Mine, too," Mildred said as she gestured for Ricky to remove his shirt.

"You want me to lie down?"

"No, you're good," Mildred told him as she crouched next to Ricky's chair. With his chest revealed, Mildred could see the spot where the musket ball had struck him. The skin was unmarked and there was no sign of bruising. Gently, Mildred pressed her fingers against Ricky's flank. "This hurt?"

"Nah," Ricky said around a slice of glazed apple.

"How about when you breathe? Or when they got you out of bed?"

"I got myself out of bed," Ricky told her. "And no, it didn't hurt. Nothing hurts. Doesn't even tickle anymore."

"That's good," Mildred said, suddenly thoughtful. "You know, maybe it's time we got you out of here, walking around."

"I'd like that," Ricky agreed, and he offered Mildred the half-empty bowl of apple cuts.

So together Ricky and Mildred left the room and paced up and down the clean corridors of the medical faculty, slow at first but speeding up as Ricky got his sea legs back.

"Anything hurting?" Mildred asked.

"Nada," Ricky told her. "I feel like new. Or old. Whichever it was I was before that scalie clipped me."

"Old," Mildred said. "You want to go home?"

Ricky looked up at Mildred, surprise in his wide eyes. "Home?"

"Well, out of here at any rate," Mildred said lightly. "I'm sure the Regina could allocate you a place to stay."

"What's the Regina?" Ricky asked.

"The baron of this place," Mildred said.

"And she let you stay and use this doctoring stuff?"

"Gave me a job here," Mildred told him. "Gave us all a job, as it happens."

"J.B. isn't a doctor," Ricky said, "unless they needed a doctor of blasters."

"Oh, yeah, he sure could do that," Mildred agreed, laughing. "But, no, J.B.'s been working with a construction crew. Ryan, too, while Jak's been helping out on a farm."

"And Krysty? Doc?"

"They have stuff to do, too," Mildred confirmed. "It's all…organized." It sounded strange to her to say that, as if it had only now struck her how easily they had fitted in. "They'll find something for you to do, something you'll enjoy."

"Then we're staying here?" Ricky asked. "Long-term?" He was concerned that he would have to give up searching for his sister, kidnapped by pirates from their hometown on Monster Island.

Mildred shrugged. She didn't know. "Let's see how we go about getting you discharged, and maybe you can stay with J.B. and me for a while, just so I can keep an eye on you, make sure you heal right."

"Sounds good to me, Mildred," Ricky agreed.

Judging by the way he had recovered, Mildred wouldn't need to keep an eye on Ricky very long.

WHEN HE WASN'T on shift, J.B. took to walking the limits of the ville. The fields and housing gave way to trees that, in turn, hit the cavernous sides of the mountains to either side the farther he walked.

J.B. had heard about the bear attack from Mildred, though neither he nor Mildred had spoken to Jak about it.

Their albino ally had all but disappeared, burying himself in his new life here and spending no time with his old companions. Even Doc had remarked that the lad had stopped returning home at night, and he suspected that Jak had found himself a woman with whom he shared a bed.

J.B. took some time scouring the fields with a set of miniature binoculars given to him by the owner of the Library Lounge, a place in a ville they'd recently visited. He'd got into the habit of carrying his satchel with him, even though it was no longer weighed down with spare ammo and detonators. He found Jak working one of the fields at the very edge of the settlement, where the trees still threatened to encroach. The albino was clearing the wilderness using a great scythe. It was backbreaking work, but necessary if the community of Heaven Falls was expected to expand.

There were two other men working in the field, clearing dead shrubbery and pulling up bindweed and creepers whose roots were buried deep. One of the men had a ponytail of hair and he walked with a limp, as though he was recovering from a fall.

"Hey, Jak," J.B. called as the albino worked the scythe through a clump of weeds. "How are things?"

Looking up, Jak nodded, his ruby eyes fixed on J.B.'s. "'Kay."

"Tough work that." J.B. indicated the scythe. "You must be tired. Why don't you take a break?"

Jak looked at J.B. and cut once more with the scythe. "No break," he said.

Stepping closer, J.B. spoke to Jak in a low voice, watching the other farmhands working the soil. "Look, Jak, I'm worried about some stuff I see here. I wanted to discuss things, make sure you're all right. Think you can take five minutes out for an old friend?"

Jak looked at him, his eyes narrowed. "Worried?"

"Yeah." J.B. nodded. "Five minutes, what do you say?"

Jak called over to his fellow workers and explained in his curt manner that he was taking his break early. The others okayed that, but told him not to stray far.

"What happen?" Jak asked as he and the Armorer walked close to the tree line.

"Nothing's happened," J.B. said. "Not yet anyway. Doc said you'd disappeared off the map and we were wondering where you got to. We haven't seen you around."

"New bed," Jak said, smiling.

"New bedmate?" J.B. asked. "Not that it's any of my business."

Jak shrugged. It didn't matter to him who knew his business. "Girl. Melissa. Name Charm. Nice to me."

"That's fine," J.B. said. "You want to tell me where you're staying in case we need you?"

Jak explained the location of Charm's lodge. It was over in the east of the settlement, on the other side to where J.B., Ryan and Doc had their cabins. J.B. figured he could find it if it came to it.

"Worried?" Jak prompted as they peered at the massing green at the edge of the fields.

J.B. nodded. "We're splitting up. We mebbe don't mean to, but it's happening all the same. And every time we got split apart before it led to bad things happening. To you most of all."

"Safe here," Jak told him, and he meant it.

"Yeah, that's what everyone tells me," J.B. said. "Safe, just like a prison cell."

Jak shook J.B.'s hand, reminding him that they were still friends, no matter what was happening here. Then he went back to the field, where he would put in another three hours of backbreaking work before sundown. J.B.

watched him go before turning back to the wilderness and trekking some way into the strip of forest.

The trees were dense, and there were a few critters living here, little mammals, the kind that he and the companions had lived on before now, when food had been scarce. That was one change that he appreciated here: food was plentiful.

The ground began to slope upward and before long J.B. was having to use the tree limbs to help steady himself and literally pull himself up. After a while he gave up. It was just as he had thought—the mountains were too steep to climb without gear, which meant no one was coming down, either. Secure. But as he had told Jak, that sec reminded him of a prison.

J.B. turned back and made his way across the settlement in the opposite direction until he came to a similar line of wilderness that stretched up into the mountains. He tried again to climb, but found it was almost as steep as the westerly edge, leaving him boxed in on two sides.

The south side was less overgrown, but a small fence had been erected there that marked the end of Heaven Falls. The fence was constructed of wooden slats and stood a little more than waist height. It took little effort for J.B. to scramble over it and drop down on the other side. Beyond was a border of scrubby grass and a few bushes, and twenty feet beyond that was a crack in the earth that was wide enough to drive a wag through. The far side of the crack was a lot lower, the depth of a couple of the shacks that J.B. had been building, stacked floor to roof. The gap looked natural and it ran the whole way around the ville until it met with the steep mountain slopes. J.B. didn't know if it had always been there or was something recent, something caused perhaps by an earth-shaker missile dropped here during the nukecaust. That didn't matter. What mattered was that here was another escape route blocked off, leaving only the front gates as a viable path from the ville, or perhaps that tough climb to the east.

"Come on, Doc," J.B. muttered as he made his way back to the low fence. "I'm relying on you here."

Doc was his out, his chance to take another look at the redoubt. Other options were dwindling as he investigated them, and J.B.'s mental checklist was getting shorter and shorter.

Chapter Eighteen

Charm had prepared the evening meal. Jak liked that. He could pull his weight, knew how to skin a rabbit and how to cook one, but he liked that she took care of him and had a meal ready when he came in from the field. The smell of herbs mixing in the pot was enough to make him smile as he walked into the shack they now shared.

Charm had not been working this day. The Melissas were rotated three days on and one day off, and this was her day off, though she cooked for him other times, too. He found her sitting on the back porch with the kitchen door open so she could hear if anything boiled over. The porch looked out over fields and the side of a mountain. It was a simple view, nothing special about it, but it looked good in the sunset.

"Missed you," Jak said as he walked through the house, through the kitchen and out to the back door.

Charm looked up. She was wearing a light dress colored the same yellow found at the center of a dandelion. It came down to her knees, leaving the bottoms of her legs and feet uncovered. She wore no shoes, and her honey-colored hair was loose. "Missed you, too," she said, smiling with her eyes.

Jak looked down at her, leaned in to kiss her. Expressions of closeness didn't always come easily to him; he had spent too long on the road, too long hiding and fighting for his survival. All this was new, or new enough after what had happened with Christina.

"Eat soon?" Jak asked after they had kissed.

"Yeah, not long," Charm told him, gazing out at the fields again. There was a low drone from the fields, and dark specks could be seen rushing in zigzags in the air as the last of the insects hurried to gather pollen before the sun disappeared.

"You okay?" Jak asked, watching the field.

Charm nodded. "Look at them go," she said, indicating the bees. "It must be frantic, being an insect, not really knowing how much time you have left before the sun sets and you're on your own. They always find their way home, though, don't they?"

Jak nodded, moving to sit beside her on the stoop. Charm moved over, letting him squeeze on, his arm around her.

"We're different from them," Charm told him. "We're not stunted by the sunset the way that they are. We're not scared by the dark."

"Not always," Jak said. His eyes moved from the field to look at Charm's legs, the way they stretched out in front of her. The right had been scratched by the bear but the wound had healed. She had not been to the medical faculty; she had just let it heal its own way. The cut had been deep but the skin looked unmarked now. If he hadn't seen the wound, Jak wouldn't know it had ever been there. What had it been? Two days? Two and a half? She was strong; he liked that.

"I should get serving dinner," Charm said suddenly, "or we won't eat."

Jak held her gently, pulling her close. "Can wait," he said.

Looking up, Charm kissed him on the mouth. Together

they made love there on the stoop, the last rays of the sun warming their bodies as it set.

RYAN AND KRYSTY meanwhile found themselves in the strange position of visiting friends for dinner. Ryan had switched from house building to farming after four days, and he wasn't sure which discipline he was better suited to. In essence, his strength was an asset wherever he was assigned, and so he had agreed to help out on a day-by-day basis wherever he was needed. It was his foreman at the farm project—a lettuce-and-tomato growing operation—who had suggested dinner.

"My lady insists we meet new people," Terrence told Ryan. "Make you feel welcome and us a little less boring, I guess."

Ryan laughed at that. "Yeah, things can get kind of routine, can't they?"

So a little after sunset, Ryan and Krysty strolled arm in arm from their cabin to the little hillside shack that Terrence shared with his wife and two kids. Krysty was as surprised by the offer as could be—she thought of Ryan as something of, if not a loner, then an individual. This was a glance into the life he had led before then, when he had been a baron's son in a privileged social world.

"We'll have to have these people over, you know," she told Ryan as they walked up to Terrence's door. "To return the favor."

Ryan looked at her and smiled. "I'm okay with that."

Krysty looked good to Ryan's eye, with her hair freshly washed in clean water and her clothes washed and mended where they'd needed to be.

The door opened and Terrence and his wife, a short woman called Bernadette—"Bernie, I insist"—stood there, welcoming Ryan and Krysty inside. Their two children were laying out the plates at the simple dinner table, and the youngest smiled broadly when she saw Krysty. It was one of Krysty's charges from the kindergarten.

"Auntie Kryssie," the girl said, hurrying over to meet her, a wooden plate still clutched forgotten in her hand.

"Hello, Jessie," Krysty said, leaning down to the girl's level. "Are you helping Mommy and Daddy with the cooking?"

"Yes," Jessie replied, and the adults chuckled behind Krysty. "This is my brother, Daniel. He's at school class. He's six."

So Krysty was introduced to six-year-old Daniel who was at "school class," and she and Ryan were made welcome with mugs of warm mead while Bernie served the food.

"You're new to Heaven Falls," Terrence said amiably. "You come far?"

"I'm from…er, nearby," Ryan said evasively. "Just the far side of the mountains really, but we took the long way getting here."

"That'll make you appreciate it more," Terrence told them both, and Ryan agreed that it had.

Before long, Krysty was called upon to help Jessie go to bed, which left the men alone together. The topic of conversation turned to children and what Ryan and Krysty might be doing in the longer term.

"I don't like to make plans," Ryan explained, "in case they don't work out."

"Don't need to make a big plan," Terrence told him. "You've got a roof over your head, food on the table. That's all you need."

"I guess it is," Ryan mused. "I never saw myself as a farmer, though."

"You should," Terrence told him. "You're good at it.

Natural. Strong. And you don't slack off. I've watched you.
You keep up like that and the Regina will give you *my* job."

"And where would that leave you, Terrence?" Ryan
asked before taking a swig of mead.

"Bitter at you," Terrence said with a laugh in his voice.
"Seriously, we need good men to keep this place running.
We've made a lot of progress, but there's always space for
another good man."

When Bernie and Krysty returned from settling the kids
to bed, they found the two men sitting in silence.

"Terry, what did you go and say to our guest?" Bernie
asked.

Ryan shook his head before Terrence could answer.
"He didn't say anything he shouldn't have. Just got me
thinking."

Krysty shot Ryan a look, recognizing the wistful tone
of voice he had used. "Something on your mind?"

"Something to think about, mebbe," Ryan replied easily.

ON THE WALK home, one too many mugs of mead rushing in their veins, Krysty asked Ryan about what he and
Terrence had discussed.

"Terrence figures I have a life here, if I want it," Ryan
told her.

"That's good," Krysty said. "Do you want it?"

"Do you?"

Krysty stopped on the path through the fields and
looked at Ryan in the moonlight. "Lover, I want us to be
happy. I think that mebbe this place is that happiness."

"Do you think this is the place?" Ryan asked.

"I think this is the place. Chased by muties. Potentially
raped by barons. Mebbe eaten by cannies. Hounded by
wolves." Krysty reeled them off on her fingers. "Do you
think I'd miss all that? Really? Ryan, we're happy here."

Ryan scratched at his nose thoughtfully. "There was something I was supposed to… I forget."

"You're drunk," Krysty told him, smiling her wonderful smile.

Yeah, he was. But it wasn't that. Ryan knew there had been something, something about an explosion. And he had meant to learn more but somehow he had got sidetracked, put it to one side. And now he couldn't remember if the darn thing was important, which probably meant it wasn't.

Ryan laughed, shaking his head and willing the thought away. "I love you," he told Krysty. "If you're happy, then I'm happy."

"I'm happy, lover," Krysty told him, wrapping her arm in his. "I'm so happy."

DOC CONTENTED HIMSELF to taking long walks—or constitutionals, as he called them—across the open fields when he wasn't beekeeping. The mountain air was fresh and the scenery was bewitching. It was hard to find fault with Heaven Falls.

WHEN RICKY WAS let out of the medical faculty on the morning of the sixth day, he came back with Mildred to the shack she shared with J.B. The Armorer was out helping erect another house, which left Ricky home alone with nothing much to do.

"Just rest up, and I'll be back soon as I can," Mildred told him.

"I've done plenty of resting up already," Ricky told her. "I need to get out there, see everyone again. Where are they anyway?"

Mildred didn't know what to say. It would have been nice if Ryan and the others had been here to meet Ricky, but the reality was that they had all become a little distant over the six days since they'd arrived here, and she hadn't even thought to tell everyone that Ricky was coming "home," whatever it was that home meant.

"There's food in the pantry and J.B. usually clocks off an hour before sundown," Mildred explained. "I need to get back to the hospi—the faculty. If you need anything else, pop your head outside and ask around. Everyone's friendly here, they'll help you."

With that, Mildred left, and Ricky found himself alone in a strange building in a strange ville with no idea where anything or anybody was.

Chapter Nineteen

The sixth night was a lot like the companions' first in Heaven Falls. Word went out that a rally was to be held in the center of town and that everyone was expected to attend.

"The Regina calls these things every few days," Terrence told Ryan as they packed up their tools for the day. "Plenty of good grub and drink. It's nothing to worry about."

"Who says I'm worried?" Ryan countered with an easy smile.

The field workers and house builders were let home early, and the nursery where Krysty worked saw its charges collected by their parents an hour or so earlier than usual, which allowed her and her colleagues to leave early, too. The only people still working were the army of cooks, ten in all, who catered to all major events held in Heaven Falls and had been instructed to have fresh food ready the moment the speech ended.

The rally was held in the courtyard outside the Regina's tower. It was a wide-open space lit by flaming bowls that had been arranged at its edges. The burning material had been treated by a chemical additive that colored the flames like a rainbow, turning them a dark red and a rich, leafy green. The flames colored the white towers in flickering new shades and made the whole plaza both eerie and beautiful all at once.

Ryan and Krysty arrived just as things were setting up. They had not called for Mildred, Doc or the others; people were living their own lives here and it didn't make sense to intrude.

Krysty loved the way that the flames illuminated the towers as they walked toward them. "They look like flowers, like red poppy petals amid the leaves."

Ryan placed his arm around Krysty's shoulders and stroked the top of her arm. "This place is all right," he said.

Other people were arriving in twos and threes, parents with kids, friends from neighboring cabins. People began to mingle and gossip while the servers set up the long tables of food.

Doc arrived with Ricky and Mildred. Ricky had never seen anything like this and it came as a wonderful surprise. "Is this place always like this?" he asked.

"Not so far," Mildred told him. She was searching the crowd for J.B. He hadn't been home, and she was wondering where he could have gone to so late in the day.

Jak arrived shortly after that, arm in arm with Charm. Charm had put up her hair in an elaborate design that added five inches to her height. She wore an unadorned, cream-colored dress that hugged her curves tightly and shimmered like silk in the multicolored firelight.

Doc tipped his hand to his brow when he saw Charm and Jak. The albino nodded in reply, his mouth a solemn, fixed line. If there was something between them, it was hard to define.

J.B., the last of the companions to arrive, was still trekking up the dirt path that led into town when the Regina took the stage. She had dressed in a gold-and-black ankle-length dress that rested against the tops of her breasts, revealing her bare shoulders. The top of the dress went down in a point at her navel, leaving her tanned skin ex-

posed. The dress's design featured a black swirl on front
and back that seemed almost to rotate amid the gold. Long
black gloves finished the ensemble, cinched tightly to her
slender arms, up almost to the shoulders.

Most people stood, while a few had taken up sitting positions on the scythe-shaped benches that lined the plaza.
The crowd hushed as the Regina stepped onto a raised platform erected outside her tower. Then she raised her arms
and began to speak in a loud, clear voice.

"People of the Trai," the Regina began with a smile,
"it brings us all great pleasure to come together like this.

"Tomorrow beckons closer every day and we must embrace and conquer it. To see the future, and to shape it into
something glorious—this is the destiny that lies within all
of us, like the seeds within a beautiful flower.

"We must take those seeds—ourselves, our daughters—
and scatter them wide. Together, the Trai can make this
world our world. A better place, a place where strife and
fear are words from history, their meanings all but forgotten.

"Look at the flames burning around you," she said, indicating the burning bowls with a fluid gesture of both
arms. "Light spreads and it conquers the darkness. We,
too, shall spread, and so conquer the darkness that has
gripped this land for generations.

"Already our environment has been tamed. Onward,
like seeds on the wind, and we shall make right the things
that have become wrong. Together. In harmony. In love.

"All love!"

"All love!" the crowd repeated, bringing the formal part
of the evening to a conclusion.

J.B. had heard most of the Regina's speech while wending his way through the towers to the central plaza. He
shook his head at the last few sentences and muttered the

"All love!" sign-off without much enthusiasm. It was all hogwash, wasn't it? Sure sounded like it to him.

Accompanied by four white-robed Melissas, including Phyllida, the Regina moved gracefully from the raised step to one of the long tables of food.

The Regina looked at the table thoughtfully before selecting a fresh-baked loaf that was round like a bun. One of the servers, a man dressed in a simple cream-colored toga, set to cutting the loaf immediately before offering the first slice to the Regina. She tilted her head, and he bowed respectfully as she took the bread. Then the Regina tore a corner of the bread away with her teeth and began to chew. The server watched her with hope and trepidation in his eyes.

"The food is perfect," the Regina announced after a moment. "Let us all eat and so be strong for tomorrow."

A roar of excitement rose from the crowd and before long everyone was lining up at the tables to be served the delicious food and drink. Mead flowed, and sweetened breads and cakes were offered along with cold cuts of meat. The party atmosphere was in evidence, and a band arrived to perform simple folk tunes while the people ate.

J.B. spotted Ryan and wended his way over to him.

"Hey, Ryan, how are things?"

Ryan nodded an acknowledgment as he chewed on a slice of the sweetened bread topped with honey-roasted ham. "S'okay," he said, swallowing.

J.B. eyed the crowd around them with a cautious glance. "You think we could mebbe get away from the hubbub?"

"Something on your mind, J.B.?"

J.B. nodded. "Not here," he said quietly.

Carrying his empty plate, Ryan followed J.B. through the crowd. People were beginning to finish up their feast and some had started to dance. Charm was already in the center of the plaza with Jak, showing him that erotically charged gyrating dance that the local girls seemed to have settled on. Jak, for his part, was transfixed. Ricky, too, had found his way into the dancing, and he was clearly enjoying the attention he was getting as a young and good-looking newcomer.

"Busy place," J.B. said as he and Ryan stepped through the archway and onto the path beyond. It was quieter out here, the sounds of the crowd still loud and the music carrying, but they could talk without being overheard.

"These things are popular," Ryan said easily.

"They're mandatory," J.B. told him. "I was minding my own business today and six people urged me to come along to this thing. Six people."

"They're building something here," Ryan replied. "A sense of community. That doesn't come without working at it. My father knew that."

"What?" J.B. spit. "This place reminds you of Front Royal?"

"They have rules," Ryan said. "It makes everything work."

J.B. sighed. "They got me building houses. They got you picking flowers...."

"Cabbages," Ryan corrected.

"This isn't us, Ryan," J.B. said.

Ryan looked at him, that lone blue eye penetrating the Armorer's gaze like a laser beam. "This is us *now*."

"You told me before not to overthink it," J.B. said. "But I'm looking at you and I'm seeing you *under*-think it, Ryan. Do you remember the bomb? Do you remember why we ended up here?"

"Good fortune brought us here," Ryan said.

"Good fortune never did shit for us, Ryan," J.B. told him bitterly. "Good fortune took a piss on our wounds every time we got shot and laughed at the way it made us hurt. That's what good fortune did. So don't start believing we've got some lucky star looking down on us all of a sudden."

"Pull the trigger, J.B.," Ryan growled. "What are you trying to say?"

"This rally," J.B. said, indicating the plaza with a sweep of his hand, "this whole 'all love, let's spread the message' thing—that doesn't sit well. They say it nicely, but it sounds a lot like an army gearing up to invade somewhere."

"They're not an army," Ryan said.

"We're living in a remote fortress and someone tried to bomb the quickest way out," J.B. said. "I've been all around here—the place is locked up tighter than a drum. They could train an army here and send it out whenever they wanted."

"They're not an army," Ryan repeated.

J.B. shook his head in irritation. "And the bomber doesn't worry you?"

"A madman," Ryan related. "You get them. Even in Front Royal we had malcontents."

"Like Harvey," J.B. said.

Ryan shot J.B. a fierce look at that. His brother Harvey had been power-mad and had slashed Ryan's face and tried to chill him during his deranged quest to take the seat of the barony. Harvey's machinations had sealed Ryan's fate and shaped his life.

"Why don't you come and have a drink?" Ryan said finally. "The mead's good."

"No," J.B. said, shaking his head, "I'd sooner keep a clear head, if it's all the same to you."

"Oil your own blaster, then," Ryan said, and he turned

back to the archway and strode through, returning to the celebration in the plaza.

J.B. watched his friend go, feeling more unsettled than ever. Mentioning Harvey had been a low blow, but it should have provoked more of a reaction in Ryan than it had. Ryan held his anger in check, but to say nothing, to not even comment when J.B. had cruelly mentioned the brother who had cut out his eye…? It didn't ring true somehow. He had known Ryan a long time. Something was up. J.B. just couldn't figure out what it was.

CHARM AND JAK returned to her cottage after the rally and made love. Both of them had been hot for each other at the dance, and it was all Jak could do to keep from tearing Charm's clothes off as she'd danced for him in the center of the plaza. Back home, they coupled in the bed they shared, the covers tossed back and the moonlight playing off the sweat on their bodies. It was a fierce kind of lovemaking, their bodies writhing together like snakes in combat, muscles straining and pushing against one another as they drove each other to greater realms of pleasure.

Afterward, as Jak held Charm close to him to conserve their body heat, she asked him what he wanted.

"What mean?" Jak asked, his eyes focused on a flickering candle by the side of the bed.

"The future," Charm said. "Where do you see yourself in a year's time? Five years?"

"Each day as comes," Jak replied pragmatically. That had been his philosophy for as long as anyone could remember, and certainly since his father had died at the hands of Baron Tourment when he was barely a teenager.

"We could leave," Charm told him, her eyes fixed on his. "Create our own Heaven, like this one, only better. With me as queen."

"And me as king," Jak said, laughing.

"You're strong," Charm said, brushing Jak's sweat-damp hair from his eyes. "We could build something beautiful together, another Home."

"Ville?" Jak asked.

"If that's what you call it. I'd make a good Regina. I'm strong, Jak. I'm ready to lead."

Jak's red eyes flicked to Charm and he seemed to regard her in a new light. "Serious?"

"Yes," she said, nodding. "The Regina tells us we should spread out, bring light to the darkness. Soon it'll be time. Heaven Falls will become too full and people will need to move on. I could lead them, Jak, with you at my side. We could make something wonderful that banishes the darkness forever, just like Heaven Falls. We could do this."

Jak stroked Charm's slender body, a smile on his pale lips. His world had been one of pain and suffering. To hear her talk like this, to hear the promise that their lives together held, made him desire her more, and desire the future they could have.

Charm kissed Jak and they made love until the candle flickered and died, leaving only a thin line of gray smoke fluttering from its charred wick.

Chapter Twenty

Ryan awoke with a head full of mead and thoughts on his mind. The sun was streaming through a gap in the drapes, a bright golden spear of light that drew a shimmering line across the bed and the wall behind it where he and Krysty slept. She was still asleep, naked, the cover pulled up over her shoulder, her face snuggled against his chest.

Ryan looked at Krysty, the light dusting of freckles on her shoulders where she had caught the sun. He was happy with this woman, had always been happy with her. She fed his soul with brilliance, the way the sun fed the seeds to make them grow.

As if sensing his eyes on her, Krysty began to stir, her hand brushing at her nose and her eyes flickering open. "Lover?" she asked, her voice a husky whisper.

"We pulled a mad one last night," Ryan told her, stroking her red hair back from her face.

Krysty smiled. "So that's what's buzzing in my head. Did we dance?"

"We always dance when we're together," Ryan replied. "Even without any music."

Krysty looked at Ryan, her emerald eyes fixed on his lone blue orb. His chin was dark with the start of a beard and his hair was in disarray from where he had slept hard with the alcohol inside him, but he was undeniably handsome. "You look like you were thinking deep thoughts," she said.

"Mebbe I was," Ryan replied easily. "I've learned things here, new skills. Was thinking mebbe I could build us a house for ourselves, out there at the edge of the trees where they're still clearing the earth."

"Build a house?" Krysty repeated, surprise in her tone. "For us?"

"For us," Ryan confirmed. "I don't know... It would take help, I couldn't do it on my own. But the people around here, Terrence and the others—they'd all weigh in if I asked, I'm sure of that."

"And we'd have a house," Krysty said, smiling.

"Yeah, one of our own. Not one that someone else built, but one for us, up here in the mountains, safe."

"Ryan, do you think that's possible?"

"I think we've found a little spot of Heaven here that we shouldn't let go of," Ryan replied.

"I think so, too," Krysty agreed. And there were tears in her eyes.

ARRIVING AT THE nursery, Krysty felt light-headed. She couldn't stop thinking about what Ryan had said, about building a house, settling down. They had been on the road for so long that their goal of living quietly together had become a distant dream, one that a person paid lip service to without ever truly believing. Yet here they were in Heaven Falls, where food was abundant and community was paramount, where safety was not a daily ritual of oiling and reloading blasters but simply existed, untouchable, in the very air around them. They had found perfection.

Andrea was outside the nursery building beating blankets. "Hey, Krys, you look good," she said as she saw Krysty strolling toward the low-roofed building.

"You, too," Krysty said, bemused. "What do you mean?"

"You and that man of yours were knocking back the

wa-wa juice last night," Andrea teased. "I'm surprised you can even see straight."

Krysty smiled. "Who says I can?" Yeah, nothing was going to put a damper on her day this day. Nothing could touch her. She was bulletproof and she knew it.

THE KIDS ARRIVED in their usual groupings, Hailey and her friends clustering around Krysty when they saw her emerge from the little pantry. Krysty sipped on a mug of cool water, conscious she needed to rehydrate herself following the alcohol of the night before. It was a luxury: a hangover that could just be nursed away rather than fought through while a mutie horde chased you toward a cliff face shooting flaming arrows. In a week her life had changed that much—why would anyone go back?

Krysty helped Andrea with the babies for a half hour in the morning. There were only five of them this day, and while it wasn't unusual that one or other kid might swap depending on their parents' rota, Krysty was struck that it was Geoffrey, the little lad who had seemed lethargic before, who was missing.

When Krysty asked about this, Andrea just shrugged. "Little mites get sick sometimes," she said. "All part of growing up."

Not long after that, while the older kids were settling down for their lunch, Krysty took a few minutes to check on the baby room again while Andrea helped serve. The familiar sounds of gurgling and snuffling came from the cribs as Krysty walked down the center aisle. She felt a little like she was walking in a minefield—one false step and all these babies would be set off and start wailing. Stopping by the farthest cot, the one close to the windows, Krysty leaned in and looked at the little girl who lay there.

To her surprise, the girl's eyes were wide-open and she was looking up at Krysty with a dull expression.

"It's okay, sweet flower," Krysty whispered soothingly. "Go back to sleep."

The girl—blue-eyed with blond hair like cobwebs—didn't seem to notice Krysty, and so after a moment Krysty reached in and lifted her gently from her crib.

"There, there," she soothed, rocking the child in her arms. "It's all okay. Nothing to worry about in your tiny little world."

The girl felt limp to Krysty, floppy, like holding a fish. Her eyes were wide but they didn't focus on Krysty, not even when she spoke to her or touched her gently on her little button of a nose. What's more, as Krysty looked, she noticed that the child's belly seemed round, like she'd swallowed a ball.

"I don't think you're very well," Krysty said, still using the same singsong whisper she had used to soothe the little girl.

Just then, Davina appeared in the doorway, backlit into silhouette. "Hey, Kryssie, we need you in here."

Krysty put the baby back in her crib and trotted out of the darkened room and into the main play area. There was a mess of spilled food on one of the tables and an upturned jug was sprawled across the floor, leaking sweetened water all over the boards in a shiny residue. All around, kids were crying and shouting and pulling each other's hair.

"What happened?" Krysty asked, her eyebrows raised high on her forehead.

"From what I gather, Jessie there tried to show some of the kids a trick," Christine explained, the sigh audible in her tone.

Jessie, the daughter of Ryan's friends Terrence and Bernie, was standing in a corner of the room crying while some of the other kids shouted at her. Krysty hurried over and pulled a few of the kids gently aside before leaning down to Jessie.

"Hey, hey, it's all right," Krysty said.

"I spilled it," Jessie said, tears running down her face.

"Not on purpose, though," Krysty told her.

Jessie looked up at Krysty for the first time and the flame-haired beauty saw the relief there in her eyes. "No, not at purpose," she said.

"Not *on* purpose," Krysty corrected her.

THE TRAUMA WAS forgotten by the afternoon, and by the time the parents came to collect their kids everything at the kindergarten was back to its normal level of chaos. As the last of the parents took their two girls home, Krysty excused herself and headed over to the medical tower, leaving Andrea, Christine and Davina to tidy up the last of the toys.

The medical tower's white exterior was turned orange by the setting sun, looking like a shaft of sunlight that had been drilled into the ground like some grand cosmic marker left by a forgotten god. Beside it, the other towers were also glowing red and orange in the sunlight, basking in the last of its warm rays.

Krysty strode past the archways and into the reception area. It was enviously clean in here after the chaos of the kindergarten, and Krysty took a few moments just to enjoy the stillness and the quiet.

Women were hurrying around or discussing this or that patient or case in brisk, clinical terms. Krysty walked over to a group of three women dressed alike in pale apron-like dresses and waved her hand to get their attention.

"Hey, sorry to interrupt…" she began.

"No bother," said one of the women, an olive-skinned

lady with her long hair clipped back in a tight bun. "What can we do for you?"

"I'm looking for a friend of mine—Mildred Wyeth," Krysty said. "She works here."

"Mildred? Sure, I know her," the olive-skinned woman replied. "I'll show you. Can I ask your name?"

"It's Krysty."

Krysty was taken to a second-floor room that seemed to double as waiting area and dining room, where she was told to wait. Shortly after that, Mildred arrived wearing a similar apron-like dress, and she gave a broad smile as she saw Krysty waiting for her.

"Krysty! What brings you to the medical faculty? Nothing bad, I hope."

Krysty made as if to check her elbows and her knees. "Nope, no broken bones," she confirmed with a broad grin. "Actually, I wanted your expertise on something. A little problem I came across at the nursery where I work."

"Fire away," Mildred said, taking a seat beside Krysty.

"The kids are normal enough," Krysty explained. "Nice kids really, full of life. But I noticed a few of the younger ones seem kind of, I don't know, sleepy a lot of the time."

"Sleepy how?" Mildred asked, her interest already piqued.

"It's really the little ones," Krysty said. "Babies. We take them pretty much from birth, so there are a half dozen babies there under two. I noticed one of them was really out of it a few days ago, just lying there like a solid weight."

"Was the child breathing?" Mildred asked with concern.

"Oh, yes, I'd have come to you straight away if he wasn't," Krysty said. "It was more like he didn't have any energy, like a rag doll. Then today, there was a girl—cute thing, pretty as a buttercup—and she looked like she'd eaten too much—her belly was all rounded and she was absolutely out of it. I tried rousing her but she was… Well, she was awake but she wasn't really there, if you know what I mean. Do you think they're drinking mead?"

"No, it sounds like an infection, maybe," Mildred mused, "or a virus. Is it spreading, do you know?"

"I haven't noticed," Krysty said. "Christine—she's one of the other assistants there—she said it's pretty normal, and the kids there go through this from time to time."

"So she's seen it before?"

Krysty nodded. "Her and Andrea, another lady who helps out. They seem to think it's nothing. I just… Children, you know?"

"Yeah," Mildred said, nodding slowly. "They tug on the heartstrings. Have you spoken to Ricky at all?" Mildred added, reminded tangentially of their youngest companion.

"Not recently," Krysty admitted. "Is he still here?"

"No, he was at the dance last night," Mildred said. "Dance! I mean the rally. What do you call that thing?"

"I danced," Krysty said, blushing fiercely.

"Anyway, your kids…" Mildred said, getting back to the topic at hand. "You want me to come over, take a look-see?"

"How hard do they work you here?" Krysty replied. "If you could come over in the daytime then…"

"Tomorrow morning," Mildred stated firmly. "I'll come over during my break and give your kids the once-over. Tell them it's for their own good."

"It is!" Krysty reminded her.

"Good, then I won't be lying!" Mildred said.

"You know how to get there?" Krysty asked. "It's close to the clustered pines out by the west hedge."

"Nursery by the hedge. I'll find it," Mildred confirmed.

JAK COULDN'T EXPRESS in words what it was that he was feeling, but then words had never really been his strong suit. He only knew that he wanted to be with Charm, and that she treated him really nice. The previous night she had spoken about a future together, about them setting up their own ville where she would be the baron.

No, not baron—Regina.

He wanted to be with her. The way she swung her hips when she danced, the way they made love with fury and strength until his muscles burned. He wanted it to last forever.

His need to be close to her had driven him that day, and he had cleared a great square of field—enough work for two men over two days and he had done it in one. But he was wasted there, he knew, clearing fields and chopping firewood from what was left. He wanted Charm to be proud of him, the way she admired his body, his strength. He wanted to use his old skills, hunting skills, chilling skills—the things that Jak Lauren had brought to Ryan's group.

After his shift was over in the field, with his muscles aching from all that he had put them through, Jak stomped into town like a hurricane, making a dead-eye path to the Regina's towering residence in the very center of Heaven Falls.

Words had never come easy to Jak, but he somehow managed to make it clear that he was there to see the Regina and he wouldn't take no for an answer. The Melissa on the door, a sweet-faced brunette called Dorothy, told him to wait on one of the benches outside, where he caught the last of the sun's dwindling rays and listened to the insects buzz and the birds sing. There was green in the skies today, where toxins floated around in wispy clouds that barely had any substance to them, like a sheet of gauze cast over the air. It was fallout from the nukecaust, that terrible day that had changed the world and never seemed to come to an end.

Dorothy came back and accompanied Jak into the Regina's residence. He kept pace with her as she led him up through the tower and into a high room whose windows looked out in all directions, taking in the fields and the houses and the mountains. If he looked really hard, Jak thought he could even see the redoubt where they had arrived a week earlier, just a little mound in the grass, hidden among the trees.

The Regina reclined on a low-backed chair that was more like a bench, picking at dried berries glazed in honey. Her hair was up in an elaborate design that dropped in front of her like the horn of a unicorn, and she wore a yellow dress made up of gossamer-thin layers that seemed to cling to her svelte body like liquid. Her eyes and mouth were striped black with makeup, cast there in thick lines like a painting that was smudged before it could dry.

"You asked to see me?" the Regina stated, phrasing it like a question, though it wasn't.

Jak nodded. "Want help you," he explained. "Am hunter. Am chiller. Could do that. Could protect ville. Feed ville."

"You want to protect the Home?" the Regina asked, raising one perfectly manicured eyebrow.

"Good at it," Jak said. "Could do sec for ville. Chilled bear," he added in afterthought, as though that fact might help him gain her trust.

"The Melissas guard the Home," the Regina explained emotionlessly. "They guard me."

"Could do that," Jak insisted. "Could guard you."

"You want to be a Melissa?" the Regina asked. She was clearly taken aback.

Jak nodded. "Yes. Melissa. Sec man. Same."

The Regina shook her head sadly, chewing on the nub

of a berry. "Only women may perform the sacred duties of the Melissas. Only they may eat the royal jelly. No men allowed."

Jak watched her, unsure what else he could say. "I can guard," he said finally.

"Women only," the Regina repeated. "Order has built this place, and order keeps it safe and assures its growth. Heaven Falls stands in tribute to what can be achieved by following a structure without deviation. To have a man perform the role of a Melissa would be deviation, and that can simply never be."

Jak nodded his understanding, his eyes downcast. "Sorry. Didn't know."

"You were brave," the Regina said, "to come to me the way you have. Someone must have seen this in you."

Jak nodded. Charm had seen it. He just wished he had a way to prove to her how fearless he could be.

And then the Regina said something that surprised Jak, for it was almost as if she had read his thoughts. "She already knows, your woman. She sees the greatness in you and she fosters it, which is what brought you to me. Trust her. Obey her. Let her be your guide. And one day, you shall fly free and prosper in the world beyond, illuminating the darkness, spreading the spirit of the Trai."

Jak left, having failed in his petition to become a sec man. But he left feeling satisfied, as if something had been showed to him that had been obscured. The future was stretched wide-open in front of him, and he would grab it with Charm. Together they would bring greatness and new brilliance to the lands outside these walls.

Chapter Twenty-One

Ricky had come to live with J.B. and Mildred and he had taken the spare room. J.B. didn't mind. The kid was no bother and he figured he might have an ally in all this strangeness while everyone else around him was slowly withdrawing into themselves.

He was wrong.

He had pressed Ricky about a few things over their first couple meals together—breakfast and a subsequent dinner—and Ricky seemed happy, *really* happy. That was how it was with them now, J.B. realized. As if they'd all caught some happiness bug that left Ryan and the others grinning from ear to ear as they went about their workaday lives, digging latrines and building storage shacks for beans or whatever the hell it was they had all been assigned to do.

Ricky got an assignment, too, after a couple days cooling his heels at the shack. The medical woman called Petra had discussed Ricky's health with Mildred. Then Phyllida, the leader of the Melissas who seemed to perform some kind of more general leadership role within the Heaven Falls hierarchy, had come over and told Ricky he'd be picking apples in the fields to the west for the next couple weeks. It was light duty, but necessary, and there was plenty of work to go around. Sometimes it seemed to J.B. that these Trai folks were feeding up an army with all the stuff they grew and preserved and glazed and pickled.

Ricky took to the work well, fitting in nicely with the

mountain community. He didn't bother J.B.; if anything he bothered him a lot less than he had on their days on the road together, which made the Armorer all the more suspicious.

A disease called happiness, infecting everyone it touches. That was how J.B. viewed it, and he was determined not to get sucked in.

While the others drank the sweet alcohol to stave off the chill mountain air, J.B. kept a clear head and drank only water—a lot of it sourced straight from a little mountain stream he had located out to the east, nothing more than a foot-wide trickle passing over the rocks before slipping back under the ground. He boiled the water and stored it, sipping from a metal hip flask he'd carried around with him before they'd settled here in the mountains with the Trai.

Food was plentiful, but J.B. ate sparingly. He worked outside, and they worked him hard, but he didn't want his body to go to fat, and the food here was universally sweeter than he preferred. While the others enjoyed another all-you-could-eat feast in the center of town, with dancing and games, J.B. endured it solemnly from the fringes of the crowd, picking at his food without relish, watching his friends as if they had become strangers, aware that they probably had.

If Mildred noticed a change in J.B., she said nothing. But J.B. wouldn't have been surprised to learn she had noticed nothing, so wrapped up was she in her own work, the herculean task of cataloging and memorizing the thousand-and-one different medicines and potions that the Trai had created and refined from their little selection of ingredients, the herbs they grew mixed with the nutraceutical benefits of the honey.

Mildred seemed dazzled by the whole setup to J.B.'s

eyes, and he couldn't talk with her without her slipping into "shop talk" about this or that remedy, this or that discovery or revelation or healing miracle. The farmhand called Paul, the one whose face had almost gotten torn off by a mutie bear, recovered quickly, and Mildred assured J.B. that the man showed no signs of scarring or pain.

"I'll bet he's real broke up inside," J.B. muttered, thinking about how it had to feel to have your face torn off by a wild animal.

Mildred shook her head. "It's like it never happened," she told him. "The man's a walking, talking miracle."

She didn't mean the man, of course; she meant the medicine that the Trai had applied to heal his wounds. That was the miracle, and it was one that Mildred spoke of taking out into the world, bringing healing to the masses.

J.B. didn't understand how Mildred felt. He couldn't. She had grown up in the twentieth century, that great age of medicine where every problem had a solution, every disease a cure. It had led to a place where men set off nuclear bombs to make their points heard, because not enough of them were dying by the old, natural ways. J.B. wondered whether that was really what Mildred wanted to return to.

ON THE NINTH day, J.B. returned home to a visitor. The Armorer had spent the past three days sawing and whittling wood to build a grain store. It was a big project, but he had been left largely undisturbed, which suited his temperament well. When he returned home, his shoulders ached and his hands felt raw from lugging rough wood around all day.

J.B. sensed the presence before he even opened the door. The door was unlatched—there were no locks in Heaven Falls, but J.B.'s honed instincts kicked in automatically when someone had visited, spotting the telltale signs that the door handle had moved, a boot had scuffed the stoop.

J.B.'s body went to its default mode, and he moved in a crouch, hunching in on himself and reaching into his jacket for the chisel he'd brought home from the construction site. It was a feeble weapon, but it was all the Armorer had now—that and his fists.

Warily, J.B. pushed open the door at fingertip length and stepped back onto the porch. "Who's there?" he demanded.

"Just an old, old friend," Doc replied from inside, his voice as rich and sonorous as ever.

J.B. smiled, slipping the chisel away and stepping into the main room of the shack. He saw Doc sitting by the smoldering fire, his legs up on a low table that J.B. had constructed in his free time.

"What's the news?" J.B. asked, closing the door gently behind him.

"You have a date," Doc began, "in two days' time. A walk-around of the beehives with me and my team. That is, if you are still interested."

J.B. looked at Doc eagerly. "Outside the gates?" he asked.

Doc nodded. "Yes, we will be looking at the external beehives in the morning, just as you had requested."

J.B. leaned down and grasped Doc's hand. "That's perfect, Doc, perfect. I'll be there, wherever you need me. Two days' time, you said?"

Doc nodded. "My place, first thing. We leave about an hour after sunrise."

"I'll be there at dawn," J.B. assured him.

Now all he needed to do was to okay it with his foreman, but he figured that wouldn't be such a difficult ask. His foreman—actually a woman called Helena—was kind of a taskmaster, but she encouraged J.B. to try his hand at new stuff and he figured she wouldn't resent him looking into what other occupations were available here to the Trai. He was a newcomer; he could be expected to have itchy feet.

MILDRED VISITED THE kindergarten on the eighth day and again on the afternoon of the ninth. She wanted to get a clear idea of what was affecting the babies—and something certainly was. While she hoped it wasn't anything too serious, monitoring it over a couple days helped her gain a better idea of the deterioration concern.

The kids were lethargic, just as Krysty had outlined, and they seemed kind of vacant, and couldn't pay attention when she spoke to them. Mildred tried shining the light of a candle with a mirror at the babies in their cribs, but they didn't flinch or show any interest. Mildred suspected that maybe their eye muscles weren't responding the way that they should, part of the lethargy that seemed to have gripped them.

On the afternoon of the second day, Mildred pulled Krysty aside and set out her conclusions over a glass of sweetened water while the older kids played in the enclosed yard.

"I think it's infant botulism," Mildred began, concern on her features.

"Is it serious?" Krysty asked.

"It can be," Mildred confirmed. "Untreated it can lead to paralysis and if that goes to the chest muscles, then a patient can stop breathing."

"That *is* serious," Krysty agreed. "Where did it come from? Is it catching?"

"No. Botulism is an infection of the digestive tract—the

gut," Mildred explained. "It's not contagious. It's caused by impurities getting in during food preparation."

"But it causes paralysis?" Krysty asked.

"Yeah," Mildred said, looking out at the children playing in the yard. "Kids can be more susceptible to it. Infant botulism has its own category in the medical journals."

Krysty looked at Mildred as if the woman were speaking gibberish.

"Old books of diseases," Mildred clarified. "We used to use them before the nukecaust."

"You remember this stuff?"

"A lot of it comes back when you're faced with symptoms," Mildred admitted. "Triggers that old knowledge I didn't remember having from when I was training. You read about a lot of diseases when you're training to be a doctor."

"Where would such a thing start?" Krysty asked, pitching her voice at a low whisper. "And if it's not contagious, why are several children affected? From what the others here have indicated, it seems that they've come into contact with this before. Children have died. It's not unusual."

"The infection's bacterial," Mildred said, "and it generally comes from food getting into the gut and festering the way it does. There are a lot of bacteria out there, swimming around in the air these days. This…outbreak, if you want to call it that, could have come down in a rain shower for all we know."

Krysty looked pensive. "You always told me that most of being a doctor was looking for the obvious. Rain showers aren't obvious."

"Did I say that?" Mildred asked.

Krysty nodded. "Once or twice. So if not a rain shower, how else?"

"The world got messed up six ways to Sunday when

they dropped the bombs, Krysty," Mildred noted. "We shouldn't discount that."

"But the adults are fine," Krysty reminded her.

"Adults are stronger," Mildred said. "They build up immunities. Resistances. Unless…"

"Yes?" Krysty urged.

"Unless the kids are eating something different from everyone else," Mildred said.

"No," Krysty assured her. "Everyone gets the same, pretty much. We get a fresh delivery of bread, honey, cured meats, dried and fresh fruit each day, some other stuff. The tiny ones eat less but we all pretty much—"

"Honey could…" Mildred began and stopped.

"Could what?" Krysty asked.

"Kids don't have the resistance to the bacteria that can exist in honey," Mildred said. "In fact, they used to say that children under twelve months old shouldn't eat anything with honey in it."

"Who said?"

"Medics, doctors," Mildred explained. "Damn it, why didn't I see that? If these babies are eating honey and there's any kind of contagion… Well, they're the ones who'll react. And react just the way you've seen. Lethargic, unable to focus…"

"And the round tummy on the girl?"

"Constipation," Mildred said.

Krysty looked behind her at the shaded windows of the nursery where the babies were held. "So what do we do?"

"Stop feeding them honey," Mildred said. "Change the diet for the little ones."

"And if they already have this botulism infection?"

"Hold all the babies here until I can get them checked properly," Mildred instructed. "Their parents, too. I'll bring Petra and the others in, set up a room at the medical faculty and flush the toxins out of these kids' systems."

Krysty nodded. "I'll do that. And you're sure it's not contagious?"

"Positive. You'll be all right," Mildred assured her as she got up to leave.

That evening Mildred returned with a group of medical assistants and they began to test the children. Mildred was working from memory, but she had found something she recognized and she did all she could to pass that knowledge to her colleagues.

Chapter Twenty-Two

Dawn arrived with birdsong and fingers of sunlight, but there was a tint of yellow to the sky where the pollutants hung.

J.B. was awake before the birds, working through his plan in his mind as he lay next to a sleeping Mildred in the bed they shared. There had been no passion between them in the ten days since they had arrived in Heaven Falls; in fact, they had hardly touched. Mildred had been consumed by her role at the medical tower, and it seemed to J.B. that she was spending all her tenderness there, because when she came home she was exhausted and it was all she could do to stop talking about salves and potions for two minutes straight. J.B. didn't mind. His relationship with Mildred had always been patchy, passions flaring when the opportunities arose. Right now, he had other things on his mind, too, concerns about the walled ville they seemed to have settled in.

Ten days. That was about the longest he and Ryan had ever stuck in one place. Certainly the longest they had been in a place without having a plan to get out again. J.B. had an idea about that, but Ryan wasn't buying it; Ryan just wasn't interested. That nagged at J.B., too, as he got out of bed and dressed.

Once clothed, J.B. shoved his sheathed Tekna combat knife into his waistband and pushed it out of sight. He dearly wanted to carry a blaster but, just now, that was

an invitation to get himself into an uncomfortable line of
questioning he couldn't get out of, or worse, get himself
chilled without any questioning, uncomfortable or otherwise. He crept out of the house, careful not to wake Mildred or Ricky.

DOC WAS EATING breakfast when J.B. arrived at his cabin.

"What is it like out there, J.B.?" Doc asked by way of
greeting as the Armorer slipped through the door.

"Cold," J.B. replied.

Doc showed J.B. the plate from which he was eating.
"Have you had breakfast? Might I interest you in some delicious bread, warmed through over the fire?"

J.B. nodded and took an unadorned slice, cut as thick as
his thumb joint. He needed to eat. The rule of the Deathlands was always to eat when there was food available, because you never knew when it would be available again.
This ville had changed that, but J.B. was planning to go
out beyond the gates this day, and he didn't know for sure
how long he would be gone. He hoped it would just be for
the day, but hope didn't keep a man alive.

Doc added honey to a corner of crust and invited J.B. to
help himself. "You had no trouble, then, joining my crew
for the day?" he asked.

J.B. shook his head. He had told his superior at the
worksite that he wanted to explore his horizons—which
was truer than she realized—and she had been understanding. "A body's got to find the hole where it fits," she'd told
him. "You come back tomorrow and tell me how it went.
Maybe I'll lose a diligent worker or maybe I won't."

Breakfast over, Doc and J.B. left the cabin and trudged
into the center of the ville. All around, people were starting
work. There were burly farmers turning fertilizer on the

fields, construction crews laying the foundations of new buildings and artisans working wood in the workshops.

Doc's fellow beekeepers met them in the shadow of the white towers. J.B. was introduced to the team leader, Jon, and his deputy, Thomas, whose wild brown hair looked like an out-of-control mop.

"J.B.?" Jon queried. "That stand for something?"

"John Barrymore," J.B. told him. "I'm a John, too."

Jon laughed at that and slapped J.B. on the back. "Good man. I have a feelin' we're going to get along all right."

THE BEEKEEPERS STARTED their work by checking on hives inside the walls of Heaven Falls. J.B. had grilled Doc about the procedure on the way over, so he knew what to expect. He was issued a pair of thick gloves that were streaked with varnish but still durable, and he stepped in to help harvest honey from the hives under Jon's watchful eye. Doc was used to the work by now, and he and Thomas worked through two hives each in the time it took Jon to show J.B. the parts of one.

"Think you can handle one on your own?" Jon asked.

J.B. nodded. "Nothing to it," he said. "Like field stripping a blaster. Just gotta remember where all the pieces go."

Jon looked at him askance but said nothing.

IT WAS ALMOST midday by the time the beekeeping crew was ready to check on the outside hives. The morning's work had been continuous, but it was nothing on the physically demanding work that J.B. had been engaged in at the construction sites. The group had stopped for a midmorning snack of sweetened tea made from the leaves of one of the local shrubs, and some dried fruit, though J.B. had found the tea too sweet for his tastes.

As the sun strived toward its zenith, Jon led the group to the main gates and confirmed their duties with the Melissas who stood guard there. J.B. knew both of the women who were on duty, Adele and Linda, recognizing them from his first day in the mountains.

J.B. watched as the gates were drawn back, feeling a strong sense of anticipation as the greenery beyond came into view for the first time in a little more than a week. He eyed the mechanism of the gate, noting how the cantilevers functioned, storing the knowledge away.

Outside, man-made beehives lined the walk up to the settlement wall. Painted white, they were poised like wooden sheep grazing in the long grass.

J.B. followed Jon and the others as they went to the nearest of the hives and began their work.

J.B. worked for a while, taking things slowly and keeping an eye on the sentry post atop the ville gates. The sec women seemed relaxed, which was understandable—there was no enemy out here; tranquillity reigned.

Once he was certain that the Melissas weren't watching him, J.B. left the hive he was tending and spoke with Doc. "I'm going to duck out," he said in a low voice. "Don't know how long I'll be. You figure you can cover for me if Jon starts getting antsy?"

Doc looked sternly at J.B. "I hope you know what you are doing," he said.

"Yeah, me, too," J.B. quipped. Then he went to talk to Jon, explaining that he was prone to headaches sometimes and that maybe the sun had got to him.

"You need to go back inside?" Jon asked, genuinely concerned. "Get some medication?"

J.B. held up his hand to stall the man. "I'll be fine," he said. "I usually find I can walk it off. I'll take an early lunch and clear my head."

Jon agreed that sounded like the thing to do, and J.B. turned and began to stride back toward the gates. It wouldn't do to play his hand too early, he knew. Walking a straight line to the redoubt would attract attention; he had to make this look convincing.

While Jon, Thomas and Doc continued to work, J.B. took a slow, meandering stroll and along the ville wall, kicking at the long grass and occasionally pushing his hat back to rub at his head. Jon asked how he was feeling just once, and before long he had been all but forgotten about. It was then that J.B. changed direction and headed toward the trees that littered the east edge of the valley. It was green there and had plenty of shade—it looked just the kind of place a man with a migraine might choose to sit quietly and rest.

J.B. checked back over his shoulder just once, trusting his instincts that he wasn't being followed and not wanting to give Jon or Tom any opening to catch his eye and call him back. Then he was gone, disappearing among the trees, picking up his pace the moment he was out of sight.

Back at the hives, lunch arrived and Jon and his team took their break.

"What happened to your bud?" Thomas asked as he bit into a sandwich of freshly baked bread and honey-roasted boar.

"He gets these headaches from time to time," Doc said, backing up J.B.'s lie on cue. "I imagine he has found himself a shady spot to lie down somewhere. Probably fallen asleep."

"He's missing out," Jon said through a mouthful of sandwich. "Let's save him some boar."

"He'll appreciate that," Doc said, biting into his own sandwich. There was no question that it tasted delicious.

TAKING A CIRCUITOUS route, J.B. made his way down the slope toward the redoubt. As he got closer, he began to recognize the contours of the land and the positions of the trees from the first time he was there.

Up close, the redoubt looked like a squared-off concrete arch set in a mound of grass, the metal doors wedged half-open and stained with moss and mold, elaborate scaffolding around them. Plants grew at the top of the mound, creepers hanging down over the doors in ineffectual camouflage.

J.B. slowed his pace, slipped behind a tree and eyed the open doorway from forty feet away. There was a figure there, dressed in white and curved like a woman. A Melissa.

That didn't come as much surprise. He had observed the engineering crews leave at dawn on several mornings, usually three or four people accompanied by two Melissas. It tended to be women who went out, but he'd seen one man go with the crew on the ninth day, carrying a huge crate of supplies—packhorse and general hack presumably.

J.B. hunkered down, preparing to wait.

IT TOOK ALMOST four hours before J.B. saw any movement from the redoubt. By then, he had been sitting behind the tree so long that his backside had gone numb; but he didn't shift, aware that every unnecessary movement risked attracting the attention of that guard on the door.

The Melissa emerged without preamble, stepping from the redoubt entrance in a swish of white robes. She was the black-haired one he first met—what was her name? Nancy?

Nancy was followed by two other women who were dressed in plain clothes and carried toolkits that were speckled with paint and oil.

J.B. waited, watching as the group gathered just outside the redoubt entrance. They stood around awhile, chatting just loud enough that their voices carried to J.B. but their words did not. He listened, hiding in the shadows, resisting the urge to keep watching.

Shortly, the tone of the conversation became louder, and J.B. figured someone else had joined the women. Warily, the Armorer peered out from behind his tree. Two more women had joined the group, one of them the blond-haired Melissa called Phyllida. J.B. watched, hand over his brow, masking the glint of the sunlight from his glasses.

The group talked for a minute more while two of the women worked on the redoubt doors, sealing them manually from the outside with a crisscross of tied webbing across the scaffold. Then all five women began to march into the woods, heading back in the direction of Heaven Falls. J.B. shifted position and watched them go. He felt certain they had to have finished their shift, that they were headed home for the day. It was about three-thirty in the afternoon, which meant this work crew would be back home by four, leaving no time for another crew to take over the job, unless they ran a night shift. They'd likely pulled a long shift in the bleak, bomb-scarred interior— little wonder they packed up early. It was a good bet that the redoubt was shut up for the day. J.B. hoped so.

Once he was certain they were gone, J.B. moved from cover and hurried down the slope to the redoubt doors. The doors had been hitched together using some baling wire and strong thread made of canvas. J.B. examined the way the wire had been tied, slipped one end out of a hook that had been forced into the concrete arch and unwound it. In a minute, he had the cord loose and could get to the doors.

J.B. pushed the heel of his hand into the ridge between

the doors and shoved, gritting his teeth as he put his shoulder muscles to work. Had he thought about it, he might have brought some tools, but despite his preparations he hadn't, so it was all down to brute force.

The door groaned on ancient tracks before finally parting a few inches, enough that J.B. could get both hands inside and get a better grip. Then the Armorer steadied himself with spread legs and shoved again, harder this time, until the door inched backward. A moment later the redoubt was open enough that J.B. could step inside.

Within, the redoubt was just the same as he remembered it. Dirty concrete walls with metal plates removed and leaned upright against the leftmost wall, a thin layer of black mold reaching along the floor and up the walls to about the height of his hips.

J.B. hurried through the open room, heading for the corridor that led deeper into the redoubt proper. Overhead lights fired up automatically, sensing the movement.

It took J.B. close to four minutes to navigate the redoubt and find his way to the mat-trans chamber. The redoubt was unmanned; no surprise Melissas waiting to challenge an intruder. J.B. had been confident there wouldn't be— he'd been watching these people the past few days, knew their routines. "Routine will be the death of them," he told himself as he entered the empty control room.

The aisle of desks had been cleared of bomb debris, and shone under the artificial lights. Cracks still scored across the walls, but the dust and dirt had been swept away and a broken section of the flooring had been fenced in using some boxes to prevent anyone tripping on it. The comps were either dead or switched off, but J.B. could see evidence where someone had jury-rigged a new power source.

That meant the control room should be operational at the flick of that switch.

J.B. walked to the mat-trans chamber and peered inside. The armaglass had been patched and resealed; ugly smears of a substance resembling putty ran across the space where the glass had been damaged in the bomb blast. Inside, the floor had been patched, too, damaged tiles replaced with new ones that had been located somewhere in the redoubt, maybe plucked off the walls of another room. Smoke damage blackened the back wall, and J.B. could see where the bomb had gone off. But someone had made a good effort at repairing everything, and checking it over he was pretty sure the door could be sealed shut, which meant that if the mat-trans was operational, it would be able to transfer people and gear to another redoubt.

J.B. stood, studying the repair work. Someone had gone to a lot of trouble to make things right again, someone who wanted an operational mat-trans that could be used when it was needed.

The Trai had rebuilt this thing, which meant they planned to use it. But what did they need it for? Where were they planning to go? In J.B.'s experience, the mat-trans technology was too unpredictable to target a site. He and his companions had used them to travel across the nuke-scarred remains of the United States and to a few places outside, but they had never known where they would end up. Either the Trai had figured out a way to set the destination, or they didn't care where they went—like explorers.

That didn't make sense, either. The Trai had everything they needed here. Fertile land that yielded abundant food and a safe location that had strong natural protection. The Regina had said something at the rally about taking light out into the darkness or some such hogwash, J.B. recalled, but using the mat-trans still seemed awfully random. Who knew where they'd end up?

Unless maybe that was the point of it all, he thought. To end up anywhere. To end up everywhere.

"Shit," J.B. cursed as the realization dawned on him. He had told Ryan that they could be training an army up here in the mountains. If that was the case, then here was the transport for that army, a way to shunt troops out across the Deathlands and to chill all opposition before they even knew what hit them.

Just then J.B. heard a noise behind him and realized that he wasn't alone.

Chapter Twenty-Three

There were two Melissas standing in the doorway to the anteroom. One was Phyllida, their leader, and the other was Nancy, her black hair piled high atop her head. Behind them, the three other women were just filing in.

J.B. watched from where he stood inside the mat-trans chamber, the light through the glass painting the Melissas' white robes red-violet.

"What are you doing here?" Phyllida asked, locking J.B. with a fierce glare.

"Got lost," J.B. responded automatically.

"You're not allowed in here," Nancy stated.

"You broke in," Phyllida added. "We saw where you forced the door."

"I came to see what you girls were up to in here," J.B. replied innocently. "Did some good work."

"You're not allowed in here," Nancy repeated. "No one can be here without the Regina's permission."

"Yeah, about that," he said. "I thought I had permission."

"You don't have permission," Phyllida snapped, striding toward J.B.

J.B.'s hand slipped behind his jacket as he spoke, reaching for the sheathed Tekna blade. "Mebbe I got muddled up somewhere," he admitted.

"You didn't get muddled, Mr. Dix," Phyllida said. "You broke in here."

"Well," J.B. said, his right hand gripping the hilt of his hidden knife, "chalk that down to curiosity. I haven't touched anything. I'll leave now."

"No, you will stay exactly where you are," Phyllida commanded, "with your hands up where I can see them."

J.B. inwardly cursed, but he removed his fingers from the hilt and raised his hands. "Look, this is just a mistake." He tried to bluff. "I thought the redoubt wasn't in use. I was mistaken."

"On your knees," Phyllida said. She was standing now in the open doorway to the mat-trans chamber, blocking J.B.'s only escape route.

"You're real wound tight, aren't you?" J.B. said, making no attempt to obey her order. "Let's just call this a mix-up and leave it at that, okay?"

Phyllida moved then, a blur of motion, her white robes trailing behind her like the afterimage of a torch in the night. J.B. had no time to respond; he tried to step out of her path but she was on him before he had even taken the step, the knife-flat edge of her right hand sweeping through the air and slamming against the side of his neck with a crack.

J.B. staggered back, groaning as pain shot through his neck and shoulder. "What th—?"

Phyllida followed by kicking up and out, striking J.B. high in the chest and knocking him back against the far wall.

J.B. grunted again, sagging there, neither standing nor falling. "Look…" he began.

But the white-robed woman was on him again, swooping at him like a bird of prey, her outstretched arms crossing through the air in rapid blurs before meeting against either side of J.B.'s skull with a blow that sounded like a thunderclap.

J.B. staggered again, but with nowhere left to fall he was trapped against the armaglass wall as the Melissa attacked him. She was moving fast—too fast to be real. J.B. could barely process it, could not follow the speed with which each strike came. He perceived the next one as it began, the blonde woman's tanned left leg kicking up in a billow of white skirts, but before he could block it the blow had struck him in the gut, driving the wind out of him in a painful blurt.

J.B.'s vision swam, but Phyllida kept coming, smacking at him with little blows, each one perfectly placed to hurt him, the attacks striking different parts of his head and body, moving and exaggerating the pain so that it felt as if his whole body was on fire.

The Armorer slumped back against the wall, tasting the blood in his mouth, feeling wetness on his face. The Melissa was standing over him, getting ready to strike again, her robes billowing around her like breakers on the beach.

"No one is to interfere here," Phyllida said, her words hard to hear over the sound of rushing blood coming to J.B.'s ears as though through a broken speaker.

J.B. watched Phyllida move toward him again, tanned skin and white robes blending together in a swirl of gold and white. He felt the blow against his kidneys, figured it for a kick, yelping in pain. Phyllida was saying something else, but J.B. couldn't seem to hear it or to process it; he just knew it was about chilling him, he felt it had to be.

The blond-haired woman swam in and out of J.B.'s whirling vision as he lay on the floor of the mat-trans. He could hear her bare feet slapping against the tiles, could feel the way those movements shuddered through the floor.

The Armorer's hand moved, snatching for the knife hilt once more at the small of his back. As the Melissa closed on him, J.B. whipped out the Tekna combat knife and thrust it upward, driving it not at the woman but at the space he thought she would occupy in the next nanosecond, the space she wasn't when he had begun the thrust.

There was a scream accompanied by the heavy feel of the weight against J.B.'s knife. But he was thinking slowly, struggling to process everything and to just remain conscious. His next move was automatic. He slashed with the knife, pulling it from left to right as though wiping grime from a window, pushing hard against the hilt at the same time with all the force he could muster.

There was another shriek and then a gurgle, and J.B. felt the rush of hot liquid wash over his hand where it held the knife. It was only then that he pulled the knife free.

The woman in the white robes slumped forward, crashing to her knees on the tiled floor, a kind of ticking-bubbling sound coming from her throat. J.B. felt more than saw her as she sagged against him, and he shoved her away with his eyes closed, forcing himself up to stand.

Someone was screaming. Several someones, their voices mingling like some awful choir held in agony. J.B. took a deep breath through his nose and let it out through clenched teeth as he opened his eyes. Phyllida was lying in a pool of blood on the mat-trans floor, her mouth wide and eyes open, the whites turned pink.

J.B. moved forward, forcing one foot in front of the other, agony coursing through him with every step. Phyllida had beaten him hard, sending spikes of pain through his whole body. He focused past it, gazing at the doorway to the control room with the blood-slick knife still in his hand.

"Get back, everyone," Nancy said, placing herself protectively in front of the three engineers. J.B. guessed they had been taking a break when he had seen them exit and lock up, or maybe they had come back after forgetting something. It didn't matter now; he had been injured, and he had to get out of there quick before they regrouped and turned on him.

Nancy glared at J.B. as he staggered forward.

"Get out of my way, girl," J.B. warned.

"Phyllida," Nancy said. "You've…"

"She attacked me, and I'll do you, too," J.B. vowed. "All of you. Now step aside." The initial rush of adrenaline was passing already, and he could feel himself getting weak.

"You've…" Nancy said again.

J.B. glanced back, eyeing Phyllida's slender form where she lay on the blood-streaked floor of the mat-trans. "She isn't dead yet," he told Nancy. "You want to fight me, or you want to save her?"

Nancy glared at him, fury burning in her blue-gray eyes. Then, reluctantly, she stepped aside and ushered the other women away from the door. J.B. trudged through the doorway, shouldering past one of the engineers, the bloody knife dripping in his hand.

"You're a dead man," Nancy told the Armorer as he made his way through the control room and into the corridor beyond. "Run all you like, violator, it won't save you. Not after this."

J.B. ignored her. He had been threatened by meaner people than this, and he was still breathing where they weren't.

As Nancy and the engineers gathered to help Phyllida, J.B. exited the redoubt, forcing himself to keep moving.

J.B. WAS ON the run now. He had made it out of the redoubt without being followed, though each step was fought for past the pain, like swimming through molasses. He had made it topside, got out through the wedged-open door and into the fresh air, and that had kicked in something in his brain, making him wake up and get moving where inside he had wanted to just fall down.

It had been bad luck that both the sec women had come down to check on the mat-trans, he realized as he made his way through the trees and off into an overgrown mountain pass. They had found the open door and had come in numbers to see who had broken into their pet project, which made a degree of sense. At the same time, it had been good for him because it meant he had gotten out alive without meeting another one of the fast-moving Melissas.

And, yeah, what was that about anyway? he thought. That Phyllida woman had moved as though she was high on jolt, faster than the eye could properly follow. J.B. had never seen anything like it.

The Armorer thought about that as he followed a path west, creating distance between himself and the redoubt and the ville. He could make it a few nights up here in the mountains, but without a blaster he wouldn't rate his chances in the land beyond.

And he couldn't leave Ryan. There, he'd said it, at least in his mind.

The tree cover was thick, with tangling bushes budded across the sloping ground like barbed wire. J.B. created a way through it, following the path of least resistance, hacking the odd branch aside with his knife. He checked behind him as he went, placing the redoubt entrance where he thought it had to be, figuring himself to be not that far from the limits of the vast underground facility. They had built them big when they had built them, no question about that. Hadn't done them any good. Most of the people who'd built those redoubts had died in the first few seconds of the nuclear conflict, and what few survived had been too irradiated to make the trek there without keeling over. Shitty way to die, radiation; it sunk into the bones and ate at everything until the body just gave in.

The sun was starting to sink, casting long shadows across the ground, bringing that chill back that J.B. had felt when he had gone to meet Doc that morning. It seemed a long time ago now, and J.B. wondered how Doc was faring without him. Doc was a slick talker when he needed to be; he'd probably come up with something to explain away J.B.'s continued absence.

The tangling undergrowth gave way to an orchard—twenty apple trees clustered in a neat little circle. J.B. stopped by a tree and turned back, watching behind him, searching the long shadows for movement. They'd start following him soon, he knew. Nancy would probably delegate the care of her colleague to the engineers so that she could come for him. She was a sec woman, what they called in these parts a Melissa. Hunting down "violators" was her job.

Moving away from the tree, J.B. kicked his way through the undergrowth, searching for a place to hole up and watch, somewhere he might be able to defend.

Beyond the trees, the side of a rocky incline waited like a hurricane-toppled wall. It was too steep to climb without gear, yet offered good protection from the wind.

J.B. ran toward the rocks, peering over his shoulder frequently to ensure he wasn't seen. There were caves here—no, not caves but dark little depressions that had been carved by rainwater and were just big enough to hold a person. J.B. used his knife to cut away a tangle of briars that he carried with him to the outcropping. He located a good-size hole, one big enough to fit inside, hunkered down and slipped inside, pulling the tangle of green in front of him like a door. The green would act as camouflage, a screen he could peer through without being seen.

Then he waited.

"YOUR FRIEND'S BEEN gone a long time," Jon said to Doc. They were gathering their equipment, circling back toward the towering gates of Heaven Falls.

"What? John Barrymore?" Doc replied. "I believe I saw him return to the Home a couple hours ago now. Did he not come speak to you?"

"'Fraid he didn't," Jon said. "Tom? He speak to you?"

Thomas shook his head as he hefted another pail of honey into the cool box that sat in the fields.

"Well, mayhap he had not wanted to bother you," Doc suggested. "He could obviously see we were busy."

Jon nodded, smiling. "Shame about his headache. You think he'll come back on crew again?"

Doc shrugged. "Who knows? What makes a good bee-keeper?"

Jon laughed. "Patience and a steady hand."

Together, the three-man crew made its way through the open gates and back into the hub of Heaven Falls, thinking nothing more of J.B. and the fact he had gone missing. Doc only hoped that J.B. had found what he was looking for out at the redoubt, and that the man was all right.

NANCY RETURNED TO Heaven Falls with the engineering team and their wounded companion, Phyllida. Nancy carried Phyllida on her own, resting her unconscious body over her arms, managing the weight with apparent ease. Phyllida's virgin-white robes were stained red with blood and, while Nancy had done what she could to patch up the woman, she was still losing a lot of blood.

One of the engineers called Deirdre hurried ahead to

ensure that the gates were open by the time they arrived. Alerted, a medical team hurried to meet Nancy as she entered the gates, and they rushed Phyllida to the medical tower. Word was sent to the Regina, and shortly thereafter she came to find Nancy at the medical faculty to discuss what had happened.

"We found one of the newcomers in the mat-trans," Nancy explained. She was standing at the doorway to the room where the medics were working on Phyllida, her brow furrowed with concern.

"A newcomer? Which one?" the Regina asked.

"The one with the hat," Nancy told her. "Dix."

The Regina nodded, her blond ringlets brushing like a pendulum across her shoulders. "The others have found their places, but Dix has been restless since he first arrived," she said. "He petitioned to join one of the honey-harvesting teams. That's how he got out."

"An oversight," Nancy said, "but one that can be corrected, my Regina. I will see to it personally."

"Take a squad," the Regina said. "You're Chief Melissa now, until Phyllida is ready for service again."

Nancy nodded in understanding. "As you will. All love."

"All love," the Regina responded.

THE SUN WAS low when the women came looking for J.B. There were five of them, each dressed in the gossamer-thin white robes of the Melissas. The robes billowed around them like mist, and the last rays of the sun highlighted the curves of their supple bodies beneath as it peered through the material. They had tracked J.B. via the path in the undergrowth, following the signs he had left in his haste to get away from the redoubt. He hadn't had time to cover his tracks; his body ached and it was all he could do to hide.

J.B. had rested in the bolthole all afternoon, the agony

of the beating he had received turning to a persistent ache. Nothing was bleeding, nothing was broken, and for that he was grateful. His ribs ached, though, and he figured there would be bruises there if he looked in the light, but he dared not step out from cover, for fear that someone would see him. So he had remained in the shallow hole all that time, watching through the curtain of brush as the afternoon shadows had grown longer, the once-vibrant grass turning a deep olive as the sun set.

Despite the pain, J.B. was alert. He spied the women as they made their way through the trees, their robes catching the breeze and whipping up behind them. Fanned out to cover as much ground as they could, there was about fifteen feet between one woman and the next. He couldn't make it out between them; they hadn't left enough room for that. They would swarm him the instant he showed himself.

J.B. watched from his bolthole as the women came closer, and he recognized three of them. One was the second Melissa from the redoubt—Nancy—her black hair piled high on her head. Accompanying her were Adele and Linda, plus two others he didn't know by name but recognized from his travels around Heaven Falls. He was outnumbered with nothing to use against them except one lone knife.

He had to get away from them, and do it quickly. What he had seen in the redoubt, the inhuman way that Phyllida had attacked him—the *speed* with which she had assaulted him—was something uncanny. J.B. had to assume that the others could do the same.

He watched through the foliage as the women came closer, closing in on him.

Chapter Twenty-Four

The Regina had called a rally at sunset. Everyone was expected to attend.

The rally was held in the plaza outside the Regina's tower, torches burning around the edge to illuminate the space as the sun slid below the horizon. It took thirty minutes from when the Regina had decided to hold the rally to everyone in Heaven Falls arriving.

Ryan and Krysty stood together in the crowd as the Regina took the stage, actually a raised platform outside her tower. Illuminated by the burning flames, their cheeks seemed to glow, and their eyes were alight with adoration for the benevolent leader of this paradise on Earth.

The Regina wore a wrap dress of bloodred with a matching headdress that ended in a sharp spine at its apex. The dress and headpiece was wound with black material, around and around in a series of thick stripes. Two white-robed Melissas stood in front of the stage, one to either side, surveying the crowd with stern expressions.

"My people," the Regina began, her arms held aloft, "my children. I have gathered you this eve with terrible news. A violator walks among us. A violator has lived with us—passed himself off as one of us—for many days. The man showed his true face today when he tried to kill one of my precious daughters."

A rumble of dismay buzzed through the crowd. A dark-haired young man dressed in a toga handed a flat wooden box roughly the size of a shoebox to the Regina with a bow. The crowd waited on tenterhooks as the Regina opened the box and removed the single item that rested within. Then she held it aloft, and a rumble of shock and revulsion went through the crowd. It was a lone item of clothing—the familiar white robes worn by the Melissas—only this one was stained with blood, fully two-thirds of it turned red.

"Phyllida, leader of our Protection Sisters and my most precious daughter, was almost killed," the Regina announced to the horrified crowd. "She lives only because she is strong—made strong by the royal gift."

Watching, Krysty turned to Ryan, pulling him a little closer. "It's terrible," she said. "I thought this place was safe."

"So did I," Ryan said, a mixture of emotions rushing through him.

Still holding aloft the bloodstained robe, the Regina continued. "Fear not. The attack was perpetrated outside the Home, in the mat-trans unit where daughters work. The violator who did this remains beyond our walls.

"We are hunting him down even now. A squadron of Melissas has been dispatched to end his reign of wickedness."

"It's like William all over again," muttered a woman close to Ryan.

"Who is this violator?" cried a woman at the front of the crowd. All around, other people in the audience repeated the question.

"The violator's name…" The Regina paused, waiting for the crowd to quiet. "The violator's name is J. B. Dix!"

A roar went through the crowd. From somewhere close by, Ryan heard a man's voice say, "I worked with him! That guy was always kinda off."

"Me, too," said another, this one a woman. "J.B. never

wanted to contribute to the Home. He kept going off by himself."

Ryan looked to where the voices were coming from and realized that more people were saying similar things about J.B. A wave of dissent was sweeping through the crowd—everyone seemed to know J.B. and everyone seemed to have had their suspicions.

"Ryan?" Krysty prompted, touching his arm.

Ryan saw the look of confusion on her face, illuminated by the flickering flames.

"Can it be true?" Krysty whispered. "You've known him longer than any of us. Could J.B.…?"

Ryan fixed her grimly with his cold eye. "Yeah," he said. "It's true. I can feel it. That bastard's going to ruin our Home."

FIVE MELISSAS CLOSED in on the rock wall past the orchard. It was obvious that this was as far as a person could run in that direction; after that he or she would have to climb and it was a near-impossible task to scale that wall once it became vertical just above head height.

They moved almost silently, foot over foot, their white robes fluttering around them like mist. J.B. winced as they settled on the little indentation in the sheer rock wall where he had been hidden less than five minutes before. He had moved when he'd seen them approaching, using the cover of dusk to scramble out of the hole and under the dense cover of the tangled bushes. It seemed scant cover now, with five Melissas prowling the scene.

In the lead, raven-haired Nancy turned briefly, hissing something to her colleagues. They had him. Or so she thought.

J.B. hunkered down behind the tangled briars, the knife clutched tightly in his hand, his breathing shallow and silent. They were just feet away. All that they needed to do was to turn and they would have him. He watched as Nancy took the lead, sidling up to the wall by the bolthole, then moving like lightning to peer within. J.B. should have been there, but he wasn't.

She moved on, meticulous and logical, checking each crevice in turn, backed by her sisters in sec. J.B. hunkered lower, holding his breath, recirculating the air in his throat, letting out only the faintest whisper of breath when he really had to.

Five minutes felt like a lifetime. The women checked every inch of that slate-gray outcropping, checked each hole twice over to be sure they hadn't missed something in the last of the twilight. By the time they were done, it was dark—the kind of dark it only got in the mountains, when there weren't even shadows, just blackness.

One of the women lit a torch made of plaited brambles. It burned slow with a sweet, musky scent that sat heavy on the air. J.B. watched the flickering flames from his hiding place in the bushes, cupping his hand over his glasses so that they wouldn't reflect the brightness and give his position away.

It seemed to take forever, but finally the women moved on. J.B. watched as they passed his hiding place under the thick tangle of foliage. The closest stepped just eight feet from J.B.'s face; he watched her bare feet pass, their contours ever-changing shadows from the flickering torch.

"The violator must have gone up the mountain," one of the women proposed. "It's the only place left to run."

"There's nowhere to go from there," another replied. J.B. recognized it as Adele's husky voice. "Chances are a bear will get him, or a wolf."

The women continued to discuss this as they moved out of earshot. J.B. just lay there in the dirt for a long, long time, watching the flaming torch retreat, turning from a burning ball to a tiny speck that winked in and out of existence as the search party moved through the trees.

So they figured him dead, or as good as. Maybe they were right, J.B. thought. He didn't know this territory, and he'd heard about the mutie bear that had almost chilled Jak and his group. The only thing he could do was get back to what little protection the bolthole in the mountainside had given him and try to get some sleep, trusting that the Melissas wouldn't come back until morning.

Slowly, J.B. crawled out from under the bushes and trudged back to the outcropping. He sank down into the crevice and pulled a tangle of bushes over the entrance, enough—he hoped—to hide him.

"Dark night," J.B. muttered, sinking into the dirt, his body aching from Phyllida's assault. "Dark fucking night."

MORNING CAME WITH a shock of brightness, waking J.B. like an inquisitor's lamp. He grunted as he placed the glasses on his nose. His side ached where Phyllida had attacked him, and what was more his gut was grumbling that he hadn't eaten in twenty-something hours.

Ignore it, J.B. told himself.

He peered through the screen of brambles, searching the underbrush and the inclined plain that lay beyond. There was no one there, just a few early birds hopping around as they searched for grub. After batting the camouflaging bramble aside, J.B. used his arms to wrench himself up from the gap in the rocks and out into the dawn. The air smelled fresh.

J.B. pissed in the bushes, careful to cover the evidence with dirt. Then he made his way from the outcropping that had been his bed, using the sun to navigate, making his way west, away from Heaven Falls.

Two hours later J.B. hit a snag. The mountains had herded him in a southwesterly direction thanks to various impassable tracts of rock that ran vertical or at an acute angle that no man could climb. Now J.B. found himself in an alleyway between two towering rocks, at the end of which was a ravine that spanned seventy yards before the path restarted. Up close, the ravine looked bottomless.

"Hello?" J.B. called, cupping his hands and leaning toward the ground.

There was silence for a ten count before his voice finally echoed back to him, deeper and fuller.

Yeah, there was no passing this, not without climbing gear. Mebbe someone built a bridge somewhere, J.B. speculated. He turned and retraced his steps until the narrow corridor of rock opened up again, giving him new options to explore.

J.B. SPENT THE rest of the daylight exploring the mountains around Heaven Falls. He stayed alert to patrols, though he only saw one, and that was at such a distance that he could avoid it with ease. He was also careful not to stray too close to the walled settlement itself, checking his location by marking trees with his knife to create a kind of artificial border around the ville that he would not cross. He ate fruit and berries that he found in abundance on the trees and bushes, and washed and drank from a couple springs he came upon.

The day was cool but not unbearable, and it actually felt quite warm when he walked in the sunshine. J.B. followed a number of routes that fed into dead ends, either abruptly meeting a cliff wall or a drop that no human could survive. By 4:00 p.m. he had reached the conclusion that Heaven Falls was akin to an island, it was so remote. There was no easy way to leave the territory, or indeed to enter it, and short of climbing gear he was pretty much stuck here.

"Well, that explains the need to get the mat-trans working," J.B. muttered, peering out across a wide chasm at the next nearest section of the mountain range. The wind whistled through that chasm, and J.B. noticed the rad counter he wore on his lapel was flickering close to red, which meant that whatever lay beyond was a hot zone. Probably a nuke had landed here and blasted new holes in the mountains, which went some way to explaining why the region had become so cut off.

J.B. clambered back across a shallow incline of slate-gray rock and slipped down to the grass beneath, leaving the chasm behind him. He was trapped here, the same way he had felt trapped in the ville of Heaven Falls itself.

Safe for now, J.B. halted close to the bottom of the outcropping and sat, pulling on his boots until he could slip them off. Having removed his boots, J.B. wiggled his toes and then, still on the rock, lay back and felt the sun beating on his face. He lay there awhile, feeling the tiredness in his weary feet, letting the sun's warmth soothe them.

As he lay there he went over all that had happened in his mind. A man called William had placed an explosive in the mat-trans with the intention of blowing it up. The mat-trans had only been working a few hours or days, having been brought back into operation by the Trai. The logical conclusion was that William didn't want the Trai using it for whatever they had planned, which meant he'd known what they were planning.

"He was an engineer," J.B. said aloud, letting the thought sink in. It was the only thing that made sense— only the people of the engineering squads were allowed to visit the redoubt, and very few people would even know that the redoubt was there.

"Mebbe the Melissas, too, but the Regina said they were only women, so William wasn't sec."

So William had been part of the engineering crew, perhaps providing some muscle where the women couldn't move something. That made sense—for one, it explained how William had known what the mat-trans was going to be used for, and how he had come to form his objection.

Question was… What was the mat-trans being prepped for?

"Escape," J.B. said automatically.

The Trai had really lucked out with this location. The soil was fertile and the land around the settlement was abundant with plant life, fruit and other consumables. Furthermore, they had livestock—they had either brought it with them or had bred it from what was living here when they'd arrived. J.B. could only speculate about that, but he guessed the Trai had begun as maybe three or four families that had taken to the mountains for safety. They had probably gotten here using climbing gear, or had possibly moved in before the fissures had opened up.

But their society was trapped now, as much as if they had been on a remote island in the middle of the ocean. They wanted out. Their leader spoke about bringing light to darkness, sending her people out to enlighten the Deathlands. That sounded an awful lot like invasion to J.B., and that worried him. Mebbe, he thought, that was what had worried Bomber William, too. Mebbe the guy hadn't bought into the Regina's rhetoric about shining beacons into the darkness. But why?

There was another question, a crucial one given the way this society was run. The Trai were obedient and loyal to the Regina, and at first glance that was because they were happy. Why not? They lived in paradise. But J.B. couldn't help wondering if there was something more to it than that. The way Ryan had become disinterested in why William had blown up the mat-trans—that wasn't like Ryan Cawdor, and J.B. had known Ryan for a lot of miles of road, all the way back to their days working with Trader. Ryan was a hard man, a stone-cold chiller when he had to be. Something wasn't right.

J.B. pushed himself back up to a sitting position and reached for his boots. His first priority was survival, and the only way to do that was to go back to the place he knew—the hellscape beyond the tight mountain constraints of Heaven Falls. He would need gear to do that, either by crossing one of those ravines or risking the mat-trans for one jump, which meant he needed his weapons. And he needed his friends.

Boots on, J.B. stood and eyed the line of trees that dotted the slope leading back to Heaven Falls. He would have to break in and get his gear. Mebbe he could make Ryan and the others listen to him.

JAK WAS LYING naked in bed with Charm. Her shift had finished after lunch, and Jak had come home early. They had made love as the sun turned orange and sank low outside the open window, turning their conjoined shadow into a long, undulating black beast that stretched across the far wall of the bedroom. Now they sat in bed, the covers pulled across their legs, eating bread dripping with honey. The bread was freshly baked, part of Charm's ration as a Melissa. It tasted good, the honey so sweet it made you wince to eat it.

"We looked for your friend," Charm said as she licked honey the color of her hair from her lips. "Nancy thinks he probably fell into one of the great chasms, but there's no sign of a body."

"No body?" Jak repeated with concern.

"He's violated the Regina's love," Charm assured Jak. "He won't come back. If he does, we'll execute him."

Jak nodded. "Chillin' good," he said. It was what violators deserved, and Jak would be all too happy to pull the trigger. He ate the last bite of bread and honey, then turned to Charm and kissed her, the honey on their tongues mingling as they did. Chilling violators was good.

Chapter Twenty-Five

It was past midnight when J.B. returned to Heaven Falls. Unseen, he had traveled by the scantest sliver of moonlight peeking between the clouds, picking his way in a long ellipse around the ville walls until he reached a steep, cliff-like incline of mountain that overlooked the ville itself. He had scaled that unforgiving slope, grazing the palms of both hands as he struggled for purchase on the sharp rocks. Then J.B. had followed a narrow trail that, at times, was no wider than the heel of his boot, walking as fast as he dared in places where only hardy gorse and mold could cling. The ville came into view below him, lifeless, asleep, the only signs of movement in the sentry post that dominated the tall gates and three or four torches burning among the fields. J.B. held his body low to help his balance, his arms outstretched like a wire walker, until he saw a space where he could drop down.

J.B. came down in a run, the kind caused by a slope that was too steep, the kind where you either ran or you rolled, dropping back into the settlement from just beyond the trees to the east. There was a chasm twenty feet beyond that, and J.B. could hear the disquieting rustles of creatures close by as he made his way from the open rocks to the cover of the trees.

No one stood guard. The Trai believed their home to be impregnable and, besides, there should be no one around to break in like this. He was the only one, and he was taking a heck of a risk coming back here after what he had done.

The only things out here besides trees were three bee-hives, man-made structures painted white and standing on four table legs, their occupants asleep. J.B. made his way past them toward the edge of the trees and the arable fields that lay beyond.

The narrow slice of moon granted just enough light to turn the world a muzzy gray. J.B. spent a long time waiting silently in the trees that backed onto the fields, watching those fields and the tiny wooden cabins that dotted the distance, assuring himself that no one was walking around or running an organized patrol. The place was quiet, the only noises coming from the skittering insects' legs as they rummaged through the disturbed soil left by the farming.

He was still a long way from home. J.B. had been housed, along with Ryan, Doc and the others, in a row of widely spaced shacks over to the west. J.B. kept close to the tree cover, walking the line that divided Heaven Falls from the straight drop that ran all along the south.

Seven uneventful minutes later J.B. was within sight of the shacks. He made his way not to his cabin but to Ryan's. It was the east-most and the easiest to access, and he needed Ryan's backup now if he was going to survive here in a hostile ville.

Ryan's shack was silent, the wooden exterior licked with silver moonlight. J.B. followed the dirt path past the trees and up to the stoop, always alert to danger. He took a moment to check the area close to the shack and saw Ryan's tools where he had left them on the back stoop: a spade and a digging fork, tines caked with dirt. Then J.B. worked the catch on the back door in silence before slipping inside.

J.B. stood alone in the darkened interior of the shack, controlling his breathing. He was in the kitchen space, but like the shack he shared with Mildred and Ricky, that space opened up to the main living area, beyond which were the bedrooms.

KRYSTY WOKE WITH a gasp, going on full alert.

"Ryan," she whispered.

"What is it?" Ryan asked, the drawl of sleep still in his whispered words.

"Someone's here."

"What?" Ryan asked. He was awake now. His time spent in the Deathlands had trained his body to wake up at the first hint of danger. He was reaching for something on the bedside cabinet, a pocketknife he had used to whittle wood when he had been working with the construction crew. The knife was three inches long, its handle barely long enough to fit in Ryan's big paw. It would do.

Krysty looked at the door to the bedroom. The door was ajar, not fully pulled closed. A whisker of moonlight painted the frame and the door's edge, casting a line where it stood open.

"Out there," Krysty whispered, pushing the covers aside and placing one foot on the floor. She was naked, and the moonlight cutting through the drapes painted a silver sheen on her skin, tracing her outline in ghost white.

Ryan slipped from the bed, too, naked, padding across the room on silent feet. Krysty met him at the end of the bed and the two of them motioned to the door together.

"It's safe here, lover," Ryan reminded Krysty as they stood at the door, ready to cross.

"Then be safe," Krysty whispered back.

Ryan went first, pulling the door back just enough to pass through it, the pocketknife held low to his side. Ryan spotted the figure in the darkness, lounging in the chair that backed onto the kitchen at the same moment that the man spoke.

"I didn't want to wake you," J.B. said from the chair, tipping the brim of his hat in greeting, "but I'm glad you're here now. Would have been a long night's wait otherwise."

Still holding the pocketknife, Ryan stopped, placing his body in front of Krysty's as she stepped from the bedroom behind him. "Krysty heard you, J.B.," he said.

"Krysty," J.B. said in acknowledgment. "You both want to get some clothes on? There's some things I need to discuss."

Ryan glared at him. "You shouldn't be here. You're a violator."

"That sounds like I been playing patty-cake with someone's daughter," J.B. responded with a shake of his head. "Get your clothes on, friend. Let's talk this out."

Ryan stood there, waiting while Krysty went back into the bedroom and eased into her jeans and red blouse. He wouldn't take his eye off J.B., and the Armorer saw something in his friend's expression that he did not like.

"You have a problem?" J.B. finally asked.

"You're the problem, J.B.," Ryan said. "The Regina has pronounced you a violator of her love. We saw what you did to that Melissa. You shouldn't have come back."

J.B. couldn't believe what he was hearing. "Ryan, we've been buddies for a long time," he said, keeping his voice low. "What the fuck are you saying?"

"The Regina said—" Ryan began.

"No!" J.B. interrupted. "Screw the Regina! We've had each other's back for as long as I can remember, and now you're coming at me with this attitude?"

Ryan sneered. "They don't need an Armorer here," he said as Krysty rejoined them. "Weapons are outlawed. You're an anachronism who's lived out his time."

"There are things going on here, Ryan," J.B. replied. "Bad things just below the surface."

"Says the man who doesn't belong," Ryan growled.

J.B. glared at him from the chair, wondering what had got into his best friend. Finally, he spoke, and though his eyes remained on Ryan he addressed Krysty.

"Krysty? Do you agree with this, what Ryan is saying? Is this how it is now?"

Krysty's body language was taut as if she was about to launch into a fight. "You should leave," she said.

"Exactly what I was planning," J.B. said, "but I was hoping you two would come with me. Seems that's not in the cards."

"That's right," Ryan snapped.

"So—what?" J.B. asked. "You got a cozy, perfect life here in this vision of heaven and I don't fit in. You don't want anyone messing it up. Is that it?" When Ryan didn't answer, J.B. continued. "There's no such thing as a perfect place, Ryan. We've seen too much of the Deathlands to fall for that."

"You need to leave," Krysty said.

"If you go now," Ryan added, "I won't chill you. For old times' sake. That's what I owe you. But you can't stay here. You can't stay in Heaven Falls."

J.B. shook his head in disbelief. "You've changed, Ryan," he said. "They've got to you. You've changed and you don't even see it."

"We found our Home," Ryan replied. "Why would we let that go?"

J.B. moved from the chair then and left, striding to the back door without looking back. "Because it's a sham," he said as he stepped onto the back porch.

Ryan and Krysty stood watching the back door for a

long time until Krysty reached for Ryan and pulled herself close. "Is he gone?" she asked.

"For now," Ryan assured her. "But if that violator's still in Heaven Falls at sunrise, the Melissas will find him and chill him."

Krysty nodded sadly. There was nothing worse than seeing a respected friend fall from grace.

Chapter Twenty-Six

Outside, the cold had become colder, or so it seemed to J.B. Perhaps that was just the feeling of isolation, manifesting in an abrupt sense of mourning. How long had he known Ryan? Fifteen years? Longer? They had fought back everything that hell on earth had to offer, chilled muties and barons and sickos and psychos, saved each other's life more times than either of them could count. But now Ryan had turned on him. Ryan and Krysty both. As though something was controlling them, forcing their actions.

J.B. crept through the trees, always keeping from the main tracks so that he wouldn't be seen. It paid for a wanted man to be cautious.

He spotted the first patrol he had seen since he'd arrived back in the ville. One of the Melissas was walking down the path toward him, a flaming torch of entwined briars held aloft in one hand, her white robes of office glowing like water in moonlight. J.B. slipped behind a tree and stopped, pulling himself flush to the trunk.

The woman in white continued to stride toward him along the path, the burning briars lighting her way. J.B. suspected she was patrolling—he watched as she peered left and right, running the torch along the dark space beyond the path to check what or who was there.

J.B. watched the burning torch flicker between the trees as the Melissa made her way slowly along the track. She stopped every few seconds as she checked another area, illuminating the shadows between the trees. J.B. slinked back farther, huddling close to the tree that hid him.

It took five minutes until the torch disappeared, the Melissa with it. J.B. leaned his head back against the tree trunk and dragged in a deep breath, calming his nerves. He was alone in enemy territory, with just a single combat knife for protection, and every hand was turned against him, even those of his friends. He needed to get out of here, and soon. But without his private armory, that sounded like foolishness. Even if he made it out alive, he still had the Deathlands to contend with, and crossing them without a blaster made no sense.

Another patrol was coming. J.B. spotted the torch flickering in the trees. Without another thought, he turned and strode down the path away from the light and toward the other shacks.

J.B. needed somewhere to hide, at least until he could figure out a way to get his blasters back and get out of this nut ville for good. He could return to his shack, gather his belongings, maybe make a break for it. That meant leaving Ryan and Krysty and the others behind. And then there was Millie and Ricky. Mildred was so enamored of the medical accomplishments the Trai had achieved that she likely wouldn't leave, certainly not without Ryan's say-so. And Ricky could be a little hair-trigger when it came to intruders. So no—his hut was out for now.

Doc, however— Well, Doc was alone and had been ever since Jak had left to live with the sec woman. Doc would be home right now, likely asleep and most probably alone.

Hurriedly, J.B. made his way to the old man's cabin and let himself inside. There were no locks in Heaven Falls, which was either commendable or foolhardy. Just now, J.B. was merely glad that he could come and go as he pleased, at least until someone spotted him and forced him into the endgame.

It was dark inside, strips of moonlight filtering in through the drapeless windows. J.B. stood stock-still in the doorway for a half minute, watching another torch pass along the path where a Melissa patrolled, before pulling the door closed behind him as silently as he was able. He could hear Doc inside, snoring from the bedroom. Once the door was closed, J.B. crept swiftly through the living area of the shack and stopped at the door to the bedroom, which stood wide-open. Doc didn't awaken; he was lying on his back, snoring loudly, his mouth wide-open.

J.B. smiled when he saw the old man deep in sleep, and he felt a twinge of guilt as he called quietly to wake him. It took a few tries before Doc roused, and he seemed confused for a moment as J.B. stood in his doorway.

"Jolyon, are y—?" Doc said then stopped. "John Barrymore? Is that you there?"

"It's me, Doc," J.B. confirmed.

The old man was awake right away, sitting bolt upright as if someone had sent a jolt of electricity through him. "You are a wanted man," he pronounced. "You must not be here."

J.B. quieted him with a gesture. "Doc, I need a place to stay. Just for tonight. There are patrols out there, and I'm unarmed. If they catch me now, it'll end badly." He didn't need to add for whom.

"John Barrymore," Doc said, the concern thick in his voice, "you cannot be here. The Regina has branded you a violator, and I have seen the evidence of what you did to that poor woman—"

"That 'poor woman' attacked me," the Armorer explained, taking a step into the darkened bedroom. "She tried to chill me with her bare hands."

"That sounds terribly alarmist." Doc pondered. "I am certain that—"

"Doc, listen to me," J.B. pleaded. "I just went through all this with Ryan and Krysty. I don't know what's come over you, but you have to remember what we are to each other. How we stood firm and protected one another."

Doc looked at J.B. where the moonlight cast him like a bust in the doorway. "This is an awfully dangerous path you have chosen to tread, John Barrymore," he said finally. "I am not sure that I can countenance having a violator in the Home."

"The Home or *your* home?" J.B. challenged.

"The…" Doc stopped himself, shaking his head. "It doesn't matter. I want you away from here before trouble descends on both of us. I am already having to answer questions about what happened with you yesterday when we went out to tend to the hives. What do you think will happen to me if they find you here?"

"What do you think will happen to *me?*" J.B. returned sharply. "Doc, I'm calling on you to help me—for everything we've been through. I need a place to hide out for the night, that's all. Once the sun's up, I figure I can pass through the farms with the workers and get out of here, and I won't come back."

"Where will you go?" Doc asked.

"Far away," J.B. said. "You don't see it. Ryan doesn't see it. Millie doesn't see it. But this place, these people—there's a wrongness here I can't explain. They're gearing up to move into the Deathlands, mebbe take control of it."

"By the Three Kennedys, you are delusional!" Doc insisted. "The Trai are good people. They have welcomed us into the Home and you have abused that friendship with this…this paranoia!"

"No, I haven't," J.B. told him. "You want me to explain

it? Well, I can't. But I can see it—in you, in Ryan, in the others. Everything here feels like a blaster out of balance, and none of you can see it. None of you can see how much you've been suckered in."

"These are the ravings of a madman, of course," Doc said calmly.

J.B. shook his head in exasperation. "Doc, I'm asking you as a friend to hide me. I'll be out of your hair right after breakfast, and you won't see me again. And if someone comes here between now and then, I'll testify that I broke in and I'm holding you against your will. Please."

Doc thought for a moment and then a smile appeared on his face, a flash of perfect teeth in the moonlight. "You *did* break in," he pointed out.

"I walked in the door," J.B. said.

"Without being invited," Doc elaborated.

"Well, if it bothers you, get a bastard lock."

Doc agreed that J.B. could stay as per the terms he had laid out, and so the Armorer took the bedroom that Jak had vacated a week earlier and stole what sleep he could. It was a restless kind of sleep, and his mind kept racing with nightmare thoughts of the mat-trans and what would happen if the Regina captured him. In his dream, the Melissas swarmed on him and hoisted him high above the towers until the Regina feasted on his flesh before welcoming her people to join in. He awoke with the sunrise, his body covered in sweat.

BY THE TIME morning came J.B. had a concrete plan. Under Doc's sufferance he would remain in hiding in his cabin until midmorning. By that time, the Armorer could be reasonably certain that Mildred and Ricky would have departed the cabin he'd shared with them to attend their respective jobs at the medical tower and orchard. With them gone and their shack deserted, J.B. could sneak back in and retrieve his weapons from the lockbox undisturbed, hopefully without running into a Melissa patrol. Once re-armed, J.B. intended to get out of Heaven Falls as fast as he could, utilizing the same mountainous track he had used to get back here. He could remain up there until the cover of night, at which stage movement would become less risky and he could return to the redoubt and hopefully reactivate the mat-trans. The Trai were almost finished with the repairs when he had looked a day and a half before; it was entirely possible they had the unit operational again by now.

One aspect of J.B.'s plan that didn't sit comfortably with him was leaving Ryan and his other companions behind. They had been a team for a long time—more than that, they had become a family. But he had tried to reason with Ryan, had remonstrated with Doc, and nothing had seemed to change their minds about this mountain society. He had seen how Mildred enthused about the medical faculty and her role there, seen how Ricky seemed happy and care-free for the first time since J.B. had met him. Whatever had affected his one-time allies, it had gotten them well and truly hooked. As such, J.B. would have to leave alone, and console himself with the fact that Heaven Falls was safe and that his former companions would not come to any harm there. That wasn't much, but it was what it was.

J.B. outlined his intentions to Doc as the white-haired old man splashed water on his face and prepped to shave.

"I am not comfortable with this, John Barrymore," Doc insisted, lathering his face with soap.

"I'll be out of your hair in two or three hours," J.B. assured him, leaning against the frame of the little wash-room. "You won't see me for dust after that."

"And good riddance," Doc muttered, loudly enough for J.B. to hear.

The Armorer looked at the scarecrow-like old man, thinking of all that they had been through together. "I always figured we'd go down in a hail of bullets," he told Doc. "Never like this."

Doc turned and glared at the Armorer with a piercing stare. "Well, you've made your decision. Stick with it and leave us be."

J.B. nodded. "I'll do that." He stepped away from the doorway then and paced back into the main room of the shack, taking a seat in one of the wooden chairs. The whole situation was a mess, and he had an inkling that if he riled up Doc too much the old coot would turn him over to the Melissas.

Doc joined J.B. a few minutes later, the skin of his chin a little redder where he had shaved. J.B. sat with his outdoor jacket on and his fedora in his lap, playing idly with the headband. He looked up at Doc sullenly as the old man entered the room in undershirt and pants.

"You should eat something before you depart," Doc said. It was conciliation to the friendship they had shared, and J.B. could not help but be surprised by it.

"That's mighty generous of you," J.B. said. He stood, tossed his hat onto the chair and strode across to the kitchen area to help the old man prepare breakfast.

"You have a long day ahead," Doc said as he reached into a cupboard for one of several clay pots of honey he had stored there. "I do not rate your chances out in the wild, but I will not be a party to your death through starvation."

"Nice that you care," J.B. said bitterly, taking a knife from the counter and working it into the crust of a half-eaten loaf.

Doc seethed at the comment, placing the pot of honey

on the countertop with a thump. "You ungrateful wretch!" he snarled. "We came to the Trai with nothing and they welcomed us to the Home with open arms. They have shared everything with us—food, shelter, things that are hard to come by in this world—and they ask nothing of us in return but that we help farm and build, help them grow. We have been welcomed into paradise without question. But you, sir, are the serpent in the Garden of Eden." Doc thrust his outstretched finger into J.B.'s chest.

"You're wrong, Doc," J.B. insisted, "but it won't register with you. None of you. You've got yourself so suckered into this Heaven Falls scam that you've forgotten that the only place heaven can fall is into hell!" He shoved Doc back and stepped away from the counter.

The old man stumbled backward, his arms flailing as he was batted into the wooden counter. His flailing limb caught the contents of the counter and in a second the bread, knife and flask of honey fell to the wooden floor. The flask shattered with a loud crash.

Doc stood there reeling while J.B. glared at him, shocked at what they had come to. "I'll go," J.B. said, reaching for the handle of the back door.

"You should," Doc said angrily.

As J.B. turned the doorknob something on his lapel caught his eye. The tiny radiation meter that he wore there had suddenly flickered into the hot zone. "What!" J.B. muttered.

For a moment the Armorer stood unmoving, staring incredulously at the rad counter. Then he turned back to the kitchen, his gaze racing across Doc's face and the room around him. Something had just changed and that something had set the rad counter off. J.B. scanned the room until his gaze settled on the ruined breakfast that lay strewed across the floor. Without a word, he leaned down, bringing the lapel of his jacket close to the shattered honeypot and half-finished loaf. The rad counter went into overdrive, warning its user that the radiation here was very high.

"The honey," J.B. whispered after a moment. "The stupid bastards have been feeding on radioactive honey."

Chapter Twenty-Seven

Doc stood over J.B. as the Armorer stared at the spilled honey, the rad counter on his lapel showing the needle hard in the red zone.

"John Barrymore?" Doc said. "What…are you doing?"

Kneeling on the kitchen floor, J.B. stared at the glutinous honey as it began to inch slowly across the floorboards where it had spilled. "There's something in the honey," he stated.

"You fool! I *eat* that honey every day," Doc snapped at him.

J.B. looked up, the concern clear on his face. "I'd stop. Right now."

Doc struggled to process what J.B. had just said, the bewilderment and frustration clear on his lined face. "What is it you are saying?" he demanded.

J.B. stood and brushed the old man aside, reaching for the cupboard where the kitchen supplies were stored. There were three unopened pots of honey standing on the shelf. J.B. took the leftmost and uncapped the lid.

"John Barrymore Dix!" Doc snapped. "This is madness! What do you think you are—?"

J.B. ignored the man, opening the pot and bringing his radiation counter close to the revealed contents. "This honey is irradiated," he stated calmly.

J.B. grabbed the next flask and uncapped it while Doc watched.

"This, too," J.B. said. "Probably they all are."

"How can this be?" Doc demanded. "I help harvest this honey. It's made by bees all around Heaven Falls."

J.B. shrugged. "Fallout from the nukes, mebbe. Whatever caused it has entered the food cycle at some stage. Could even be in the pollen that your bees are collecting."

"They are not my bees," Doc said defensively.

J.B. brushed the objection aside. "We need to get this out of your house right away," he said, snatching up the open pots of honey and marching to the open back door. "Do you have more?"

"What?"

"More honey!" J.B. snarled. "Do you have more?"

"I…I have a jar in the bedchamber," Doc admitted. "I work with the honey, it is entirely proper that I…"

"I'm not accusing you of stealing it, Doc," J.B. told him as he threw the clay pots out onto the grass. "Listen to me. Don't you understand? This shit you eat is red-hot with radiation."

Doc stood there openmouthed, trying to comprehend J.B.'s words.

J.B. was back at the cupboard. He grabbed the last pot of honey and launched it overarm through the open back door, smiling grimly when he heard it shatter on the ground outside. "You said you had more in the bedroom," he growled. "Show me."

Bewildered, Doc led the way to his bedroom and pointed to the night table. It featured an extinguished candle on its top and a shelf set midway below. There was a four-inch-tall clay jar resting on the shelf, a sheet of muslin cinched around its open top with a string. J.B. grabbed the pot and marched to the front door of the property— the nearest exit. He pulled the door open and prepared to toss the clay vessel away when he stopped. Walking along the dirt path not twenty feet from him were two Melissas: Linda and another he did not recognize. They spotted him at the same moment as he saw them.

"Violator!" they cried as one.

J.B. reacted as swift as thought, dropping the pot on the stoop and slamming the door closed. Then he spun and grabbed Doc as the old man came ambling out of his bedroom.

"Where's your blaster? Quickly!" J.B. demanded.

"I-it was put away."

"Where?" J.B. growled, but he had already spied the lockbox located outside the washroom and he marched toward it.

Doc followed, glancing back at the front door. "What is going on? What did you see?"

J.B. slid down on his knees and worked the catch of the lockbox, pulling the lid up. Inside there was Doc's commemorative LeMat and a handful of bullets, and beside it was Jak's Colt Python, which the albino had left behind when he'd moved out of the property. J.B. grabbed both, checking the barrel of the Python with a professional eye. It was still loaded the way Jak had left it. Naturally suspicious, Jak had doubtless put the blaster away with the thought he may need it in a hurry.

"That untrusting son of a bitch!" J.B. said, smiling as he raised the loaded Colt in a steady, one-handed grip and targeted the front door. It felt good to have a blaster in his hand again; the weight was just right, like a missing limb replaced.

"Doc, you need to get down," he said, his eyes fixed on the door.

An instant later the front door swung open and Linda came striding into the cabin, her brunette locks fluttering behind her in the breeze. J.B. squeezed the Colt's trigger and sent a .357 slug straight through the woman's forehead. The boom of blasterfire sounded surreal after so long without it; almost two weeks away from the carnage of the Deathlands had changed everything.

J.B. watched grimly as Linda fell backward, a red smear materializing dead center between her eyes.

The other Melissa was just outside, and hearing the report of the blaster she stopped, horrified. J.B. was on his feet immediately, bringing the blaster around and trying to get a bead on the white-robed woman where the frame of the door obscured her.

"Violator!" the Melissa shouted. "Place your blaster on the floor right now."

"Not going to happen," J.B. snarled as he sent a bullet through the room toward her.

The bullet clipped the edge of the door frame by the Melissa's face, sending a shower of splinters into the air. The woman screamed, leaped back and brushed the tiny flecks aside, her eyes screwed tightly shut.

J.B. kept moving, striding across the room with the Colt Python extended in front of him. Doc had stepped aside when the shooting began, and he looked bewildered as J.B. passed him.

"This is yours," J.B. said, thrusting the LeMat blaster into Doc's gut as he strode past.

Doc's hands bent around the weapon in surprise.

"Don't shoot me in the back," J.B. told him without turning.

Then the Armorer was at the door, his eyes scanning the exterior for the second Melissa. It was still early, an hour or so after sunrise, and Heaven Falls was still waking up. People could be seen in the distance, heading off to the farms, the medical faculty or the construction sites.

There was a little mist between the trees, hanging low like bleached cotton candy.

J.B. peered left and right, trying to find the woman who had ducked away from his shot. She was dressed in the flowing white robes of a Melissa, and she had hair styled the way they all wore it while on shift, red locks piled atop her head with twisting curls wafting down past her ears. That red hair and white dress should make her easy to spot, J.B. thought, and yet he could not see her. She had been here not five seconds before—there was nowhere she could have disappeared to.

Then J.B. heard the noise coming from above and behind him, and he spun and ducked in the same movement as the unnamed Melissa leaped down at him from her hiding place on the roof of Doc's cabin. J.B.'s swift reaction saved him from a broken neck. Instead, the woman in white collided with the top of his left arm with the force of a hammer, and the two of them sank to the dirt in a tangle of limbs.

Shifting his weight, J.B. tried to scramble away, to put enough distance between himself and his attacker to take a shot at her. But her body was on him, the weight of it dragging at his waist and legs where she had dropped. She reached up for him with slender arms, her hands hooked into claws. J.B. batted her hands away with his left hand, whipped the blaster around and tried to aim. The Melissa swiped at the weapon's muzzle, jarring it with such force that J.B.'s hand shot upward and he almost lost his grip on the weapon entirely.

The woman followed up with a brutal knee to J.B.'s kidney as she clambered up his body and reached for his face.

"Violator!" she raged. "You are an offense to the Regina's love!"

J.B. saw the woman's hand reaching for his face with

sharp nails. He turned his head as the nails struck, felt them bite against the flesh of his cheek half an inch beneath his eye socket. Then his hand was up and he snagged the Melissa's wrist, twisting it and forcing her to curtail her attack. The Melissa shrieked with surprise, her weight shifting so that it no longer pressed against J.B.'s legs.

The Armorer scrambled out from under the flailing Melissa, powering across the dirt away from the shack, trying to generate some distance from his attacker in a crouching run. The Melissa followed, her teeth bared, setting her arms back for balance as she sprang after J.B.

He whipped the Colt Python around, targeting his pursuer. She was six feet behind him, her bare feet slamming against the ground as she gave chase. The Melissa started her leap as J.B. squeezed the trigger, and he watched incredulous as she sprang into the air and brought her feet above head height as his blaster spit its deadly issue. The bullet soared past where the Melissa had been, cutting through the air before embedding itself in the wall of Doc's cabin, two feet from the open door. Then the Melissa's foot snapped out and caught J.B. under the chin, striking with such force that his head jounced up and backward and suddenly his legs gave way beneath him.

Still running, J.B. caromed to the ground with a burst of dislodged dirt. The Melissa landed three feet away, right foot then left touching the ground milliseconds apart, sliding and spinning as she met the soil.

The woman in white turned to face J.B. even as she landed, but he recovered enough to send another bullet at her. The bullet was angled upward, targeting the Melissa's chest where the robes met beneath her tanned cleavage. It should have been over then, the bullet drilling through the woman like boiling water on snow, but somehow she managed to twist aside, faster than the eye could follow.

J.B. saw it but couldn't understand it—the way the woman seemed to whirl in place to let the bullet slip behind her. He had seen that quickness once before, when the Melissa called Phyllida had attacked him in the redoubt before he had stabbed her.

Could they all do that? Could they all move at super-speed when they needed to? The thought filled the man with horror.

The Melissa charged at J.B., pivoting on one foot while whipping her other leg back to kick him in the skull. Lying in the dirt, tasting soil in his mouth, J.B. saw that foot cut the air toward him in a pale blur. And then he heard what sounded like a crack of thunder, and suddenly the foot was no longer coming at his face but rather sailing over his head, spewing blood.

J.B. watched, stunned, as the Melissa toppled to the ground beside him, screaming in agony. There was blood on her right leg and the section below the knee was missing entirely, just a ragged hunk of bone and strips of dangling flesh remaining. The rest of the leg and foot landed a moment after she did, fifteen feet to J.B.'s right, on the other side of him to the Melissa.

Doc stood a few feet away, the secondary barrel of his LeMat pistol swirling smoke where it had discharged a burst of buckshot like a shotgun. He had his shirt on now and his frock coat, and his lion's-head swordstick leaned against the front door to his shack.

J.B. processed all of that in a fraction of a second, even as he began to move. He scrambled forward with the Colt Python in his hand, slapping its snout point-blank against the screaming Melissa's head. He looked away as he pulled the trigger, feeling the blaster buck in his hand as it delivered a mercy bullet to the woman's brainpan.

Then J.B. strode back toward Doc's shack where the old man was returning to collect his swordstick.

"It seems we have much to discuss," Doc said as J.B. caught up to him.

"Yeah," J.B. agreed, "but not here. People will have heard that thunderclap of yours, and they'll come running."

"I do not doubt it," Doc acknowledged, his eyes already roving the path and the trees beyond for signs of new enemies.

J.B. slipped past him and into the shack. "Just let me get my hat and the rest of Jak's bullets," he explained. "Then we can get out of here and mebbe figure out what the hell is going on."

Doc agreed. Where previously it had been just J.B. against the whole of Heaven Falls, now things had changed. Now there were two.

Chapter Twenty-Eight

J.B. and Doc hurried through Doc's cabin, grabbed the fedora and Jak's spare ammo and slipped out the back door. It didn't pay to be out front anymore. The sounds of those gunshots would attract attention, and if they didn't then the bodies surely would. The paths around here were well used and it was the busiest time of the day, when the locals went to their designated assignments—the corpses wouldn't stay unnoticed for long.

J.B. said nothing to Doc as they passed through the back and into the woods beyond. They moved swiftly, slipping into the shadowy cover of the trees that ran in a narrow band between the cabins and the crop fields. The trees were dense enough to provide cover for now, but J.B. didn't rate their chances in staying hidden there for an extended period. He had something else in mind.

Once they were out of sight of Doc's shack, J.B. halted and Doc stopped a pace away. Already they could hear the sounds of alarm as the first corpse was found. It wouldn't take long for a patrol to be organized to hunt down the fugitive Armorer.

J.B. reloaded the Colt Python as he spoke to Doc. "What brought on the change of heart?" he asked, keeping his voice low.

"You know, I think it was automatic," Doc admitted. "Seeing you tussling with that woman brought to mind the number of times we have been in combat together, and I think my brain slipped into its default setting of assisting you."

J.B. gave Doc a cockeyed smile as he heard this. "And what about now?" he asked. "Are you with me?"

Doc shook his head slowly. "My every neuron is telling me that you are a violator to the Regina's love and that you should be turned in and chilled. I cannot lie to you."

"But…?" J.B. prompted.

"Love can be a tricky emotion at the best of times," Doc said wistfully. "I want to do the right thing out of love for the Regina, but seeing the way that slip of a girl fought you—the speed and ferocity with which she attacked— weighs uncomfortably in my mind. I believe that you have stumbled upon something here that the rest of us did not see. Perhaps we cannot see it. So I am trusting you, even though my every fiber tells me to chill you."

J.B. reached out and grasped Doc's hand, shaking it firmly. "You're a good man, Doc," he said. "When all this has played out, I can assure you you'll have made the right choice."

Doc nodded. "I hope so. Now then, where do we go from here? The ville is on high alert for your presence, and presumably it will be for mine now, also."

"Not yet it won't," J.B. corrected him. "There were two witnesses to that altercation, and we chilled both of them. Right now, all anyone knows is that you aren't in your cabin, which could just as easily mean you went off to do some hiving early."

"Hiving?" Doc asked.

"Honey collecting, whatever you call it."

"Irradiated honey," Doc stated. "That is what you found, is it not?"

"I'm piecing it together," J.B. admitted, "and I don't have all of the facts. But there's something in that honey that's been messing with your head, and it has not just affected you. I saw Millie and Ricky get sucked into this thing, too, and Ryan nearly chilled me when I went to speak to him last night. If I'd stayed longer, he or Krysty would have."

"Jak has been rather preoccupied," Doc mused. "He left the shack we were sharing without a word a few days ago. It struck me as strange, but I did not press it."

"And you've all been eating honey," J.B. said.

"Not just honey," Doc pointed out. "They ply us with mead at the rallies—that is beer made from honey. Then there are the cakes, the dried fruit glazed with honey, the honeyed water. I did not even think about it."

"Why would you?" J.B. asked. "Food in abundance—no wonder this place felt like paradise."

"It still feels like paradise in my heart," Doc admitted. "But why has this…mental recalibration not affected you?"

"I've been getting my water elsewhere," J.B. said, "and helping myself to fruit off the trees whenever I got the chance, mostly because I took to checking out the ville limits and skipped out on the lunch ration. I probably just ate less of the standard diet."

"So where do we go now?" Doc asked.

"The honey's got some sort of psychoactive property," J.B. stated, "probably because this whole area got showered with nuke fallout all them years ago. It's probably in the plant life and so the pollen that the bees are gathering is riddled with it. That's my best guess."

"They have a huge store of honey," Doc said. "Years' worth. I think it has become an addiction with the Trai."

"Yeah, that makes sense," the Armorer said. "The setup here is very obedient, and it's efficient, too. People—groups—have designated roles."

"Like a beehive," Doc said in realization.

J.B. adjusted his glasses as he thought. "A while back, you told us that *Regina* is another word for queen."

"Latin," Doc confirmed. "Are you proposing that the Regina is some kind of…human queen bee?"

"I think so," J.B. said. "You feel intense allegiance to her, trust her every word, believe in her love for you and for the people around you."

Doc nodded uncertainly. "Please go on."

"Bees are a female-led society, right?" J.B. said. "You have the queen and then what? Come on, Doc, you have book smarts."

"The worker bees are female," Doc recalled, "while the males are drones used for menial tasks, including reproduction."

"The most menial task of all," J.B. opined sourly. "The Trai have set up Heaven Falls the same way. They call this place the Home, the same way bees probably think about their hive. Women do all the important stuff—the child protection, the medicine, the sec duties—while guys like you and me get to chop wood and harvest food."

"The level of agreement in this ville is so absolute that it is fanatical," Doc said. "It is like a hive mind."

"And what happens next?" J.B. asked. "How do bees set up new homes?"

"They swarm," Doc said. "A new queen is born one day, and she departs with a few members of the hive, swarming to a new location beyond the limits of the original hive's domain."

"This place is cut off by quakes and mountains," J.B. said. "They're all but impassable. That's why the Trai need the mat-trans. The new queen must be reaching maturity. They're gearing up to swarm."

"Or new queens," Doc said. "Plural."

J.B. looked at Doc with concern. "Does that happen?"

Doc shrugged. "We might assume that it could. You have seen the way the young women flaunt themselves at the rallies. Tantalizing their would-be mates through… My goodness!"

"What?" J.B. demanded, seeing sudden realization cross the old man's face. "And keep the noise down, Doc, okay?"

"Do you not see?" Doc said. "The dance. The… This…" He showed J.B. the dance that the Trai women performed at the gatherings, mimicking the way they thrust their butts out and shook them. "That's a waggle dance."

"A what?"

"It's the way that bees communicate," Doc explained. "The waggle dance conveys information to other bees. These people have adapted it into some form of mating ritual, most probably without even realizing it."

"Human bees," J.B. said sourly. "People thinking like insects."

"And do you know, I have only now realized why the Melissas are so called," Doc told him. "It is Latin— Melissopalynology is the study of pollen and spores in raw honey."

"You know this how?" J.B. asked.

"I know Latin," Doc explained. "It is an ancient language that operates by strict principles. Once one knows those principles, it is a simple process to break down compound words into their component parts and—"

"Yeah, fine," J.B. interrupted with a raised hand. "Look, Doc, I'm a fugitive here and you will be soon, too. That means we need to move quickly if we're going to get everyone out of here alive."

"What are you proposing?" Doc questioned.

"You saw the way that Melissa fought me," J.B. said. "These people are superstrong, superfast. They're superhuman, and I guess that's something to do with the honey they eat. Mildred told me about the medical properties they've tapped, used some miraculous salve on my hand where I cut it..."

"Honey can have very strong health benefits," Doc confirmed.

"If these people swarm, then the whole of Deathlands and beyond could fall to an army of superstrong, human bees," J.B. said. "Now, I'm not much of a one to worry about who's chilling who out there, as long as it isn't me who's getting chilled, but hive people wiping out the rest of humanity—that's going to end in a bad place for all of us."

"I could return to the honey storage tower and break the vessels there," Doc proposed, but already he could see it was a colossal task, one that he would be restrained from long before he could make any serious dent in the supplies. "No, forget that. I could not do enough."

"No, not while you're a fugitive," J.B. said, "I need you to get Ryan and Krysty. You can still move freely. You should be able to get to them and convince them what's going on."

"Convince them how?" Doc asked. "You told me that you had already approached Ryan with your suspicions not eight hours previously."

"Doc, I've known you for a long time," J.B. said, "and even now you still come up with words I have never heard anyone else say. If anyone can find a way to convince Ryan, it's you."

"I am a modestly accomplished orator," Doc said uncertainly. "But I would dearly regret ruining the life that Ryan and Krysty have begun to build here for themselves, a life of peace so richly deserved."

"It's time to piss on their parade, Doc," J.B. said calmly. "The people here have become insects. In their reasoning.

In their actions. Ryan and Krysty have been here only two weeks, same as you. You came back from that and they will, too, if you can convince them. Mebbe the Trai were beekeepers once who got this junk in their systems and stopped thinking rationally. You want that to happen to our friends?"

Doc nodded in understanding. "I shall find Ryan and I shall do my utmost to convince him. And what will you do?"

J.B. gestured toward the edge of the wooded area. "I'm going to get my weapons back," he said. "I figure I'm going to need them."

HIDING THE LEMAT blaster beneath the folds of his coat, Doc made his way at a brisk trot to the nearby shack that Ryan and Krysty occupied. There were people all around, hurrying to their designated roles. Doc saw them differently now, knowing that they were worker bees fulfilling the tasks given them by their queen. It was disconcerting, made more so by the fact that Doc dearly wanted to join them and fulfill his own designated role, and so enjoy the adoration of the Regina.

"No," he muttered to himself, shaking his head. "You are not this. It is not you." He hurried on, willing away the all-consuming desire to serve the Regina.

Doc didn't stop hurrying until he had reached Ryan's front door. Doc thought of his wife, Emily, and his children, Rachel and Jolyon, reminding himself that he was a man and not a drone, never that.

He knocked at door with the silver lion's-head handle of his swordstick. Krysty opened the door a few seconds after, and she smiled when she saw Doc standing there.

"Doc Tanner, as I live and breathe," Krysty said. "What are you doing here?"

Krysty was dressed in her usual ensemble, but she looked different to Doc, the way she had tied her hair back in a neat ponytail, hair that he knew was alive and that hurt her to cut or to fuss with overmuch. To see her looking prim and proper like this, her rough edges smoothed down, made Doc wonder at how much they had all changed without even realizing it during their stay in Heaven Falls.

"Krysty," Doc said, barging his way none too gently into the house, "I need to speak with you and with Ryan on a matter of grave urgency. Is Ryan still here?"

Krysty seemed oblivious to Doc's fretful manner and merely stood aside and let him in. "He's just through in the kitchen, finishing up the dishes."

Doc strode through the main room to where Ryan was standing at the countertop wiping two plates with a damp cloth.

"Ryan Cawdor doing dishes!" Doc observed. "Will wonders never cease!"

Ryan looked up. "Doc, you're here early," he said. "I was just leaving for the farm."

"Forget that," Doc told him. "We all need to talk, right away."

Krysty had followed Doc through the shack and she stood on the far side of the counter, looking at him with concern. "What's happening, Doc?" she asked.

"We have all been duped," Doc stated.

MEANWHILE, J.B. QUIETLY made his way back to the cabin where he had lived for almost two weeks, sticking to the cover of the trees that ran parallel to the path. He slowed his pace when he got within sight of the cabin, scanning the door and windows, checking for signs of movement within. J.B. didn't emerge from cover until he was almost to the shack, having waited a minute or so for the path to become clear of travelers. When he finally emerged, J.B. pulled the brim of his hat low over his eyes to try to disguise his features.

He trotted up to the front door and pushed it open without a knock of warning, striding across the main room even as Ricky and Mildred looked up from the two chairs that furnished the room. They were just starting to eat breakfast. Each held a plate, two slices of toast dripping with honey.

"J.B.!" Mildred cried. "What are you doing h—?"

J.B. lashed out, knocking the plate from her hand. It sailed into the wall above the hearth, crockery shattering, uneaten bread strewed across the floor. "Stop eating," J.B. said. "Both of you. Now!"

Ricky looked dumbstruck by the command and by the appearance of the Armorer after he had been branded a violator. "Y-you shouldn't be here, J.B.," he stuttered.

J.B. reached down and snatched the plate from Ricky's lap, even as the lad went to take a bite from his toast.

"Drop it," he said. "For both your sakes, listen to me."

Mildred got to her feet, her hands clenching into fists. "The Regina told us that you tried to chill Phyllida," she said. "I saw with my own eyes the state you left that woman in. It's down to advanced medicine that she's alive now."

J.B. turned to her. "She's still alive?" he asked. "Black dust!"

"So you did do it!" Mildred said with a shock.

Before J.B. could explain, Mildred's right fist snapped at him, knocking him right in the nose. He staggered back, his left hand going to his face.

"Violator!" Mildred cried, and Ricky took up the chant.

With his free hand, J.B. reached into his waistband at the small of his back and pulled Jak's blaster loose, aiming it at Mildred and Ricky. "You both had better settle down," he instructed. "We've got a lot to get through and not much time to do it in. Now, why don't you sit by the fireplace and I'll tell you all about how mixed up and wrong you've got it."

Reluctantly, Mildred and Ricky sagged into their chairs, their eyes locked on the blaster in J.B.'s hand.

"That's more like it," J.B. said once they were seated. "Now, let's see if I can get this right…"

And with that, J.B. began to explain his tale of the irradiated honey with its psychoactive properties, of how the society of the Trai had become entangled in the thought processes of the honeybees, and how the companions had become brainwashed into accepting the hive mind as normal.

Once he was done, J.B. backed away from his one-time friends and sat on the lockbox where they had stored their weapons. He waited, uncertain of how his one-time allies would respond.

"WE ARE IN considerable danger here," Doc explained as he stood with Ryan and Krysty in the kitchen of their simple shack. "The people of Heaven Falls are under the mental command of an insidious power, one which has begun to enslave us, too, and which, I suspect, plans to take over the whole of the Deathlands."

Astonished, Ryan placed the plate and dishcloth he held on the countertop. "What are you saying? This sounds like the kind of crap you spouted back when we first found you."

"I can assure you that this is not crap," Doc stated firmly. "All of us have been feeding on a psychoactive agent that has blunted our capacity for reason. I have seen evidence of this, and while I know how hard it must be to accept what I am saying, I must ask that you try."

"Doc," Krysty said gently, "did J.B. come speak to you?"

Doc nodded. "I did not believe him, either, but then I saw something that profoundly changed my mind."

"What changed?" Ryan demanded.

Doc looked around the kitchen, his eyes searching for a cupboard or storage larder. "Do you have honey here in the house?" he asked.

"We just finished up some on toast for breakfast," Krysty confirmed, bemused by the old man's question.

"Where?" Doc demanded. "Where do you store the honey?"

Ryan reached under the counter and brought out a familiar clay pot, the exact same style of pot that Doc's honey had been stored in. "If you're staying to eat, I really have to get to work," Ryan insisted. "You're welcome to help yourself to whatever—"

"Ryan, no! Concentrate!" Doc demanded. He understood Ryan's yearning to be at work, could feel that same call in his mind where the Regina had assigned him a crucial task that would demonstrate his love for her. "Do you still have your rad counter?"

Ryan nodded, his brow furrowed in confusion.

"Get it!" Doc commanded.

Ryan looked at the old man blankly, and Krysty shook her head sorrowfully. "Are you sure you're all right, Doc?" she asked gently, clearly concerned for his sanity.

"Just get the rad counter," Doc insisted. "Now!"

Taken aback by the vehemence in the old man's voice, Ryan strode past him and reached for his coat where it hung on a hook beside the front door. He plucked at the rad counter as he strode back, a skeptical expression on his face.

"Okay, Doc," Ryan said. "Here it is."

The old man removed the muslin lid of the honeypot and used a spoon to scoop out a small portion of the russet-gold contents. The honey glistened there on the spoon, shimmering like liquid sunlight. "Test it," Doc told them.

"What do you mean?" Krysty asked.

"The radiation content," Doc said. "Test it."

Ryan looked uncertain, but he leaned in with the simple rad counter and held it close to the spoon. In a moment, the circular, button-like display had flicked from green to the rich red danger zone.

"What is it?" Ryan asked as he watched the display change.

"The honey is irradiated," Doc said. "Maybe all the food here is. That is certainly not beyond the realm of possibility. The radiation has been affecting our minds—and not just us. All of the Trai are in its thrall."

Krysty gasped incredulously. "This sounds—"

"I know how it sounds," Doc interrupted. "I, too, am struggling to accept the evidence that has been clearly presented to me. And the only reason I can come up with regarding the conflict I feel is that this is the truth, and that my conflict is with the way that this satanic substance has toyed with my emotions and my capacity for rational thought."

Ryan and Krysty stared at Doc, their mouths agape.

"I am so sorry," Doc told them.

"Why?" Krysty asked.

"Because you thought that you had found the perfect retreat," Doc said, "the one thing that you have strived for—and that you have dearly deserved—for so long. I am sorry that I had to come here today and take that away, and I hope, when all of this is over, that you see that I was right to do so and that you will find it in yourselves to forgive me."

Ryan stared at the open pot of honey, and he ran the rad counter over its lid, watching as the indicator light changed color. "This is hard to take in," he admitted. "When J.B. came here last night, I thought he was insane." He looked up at Doc then, as the rad counter went from orange to red over the mouth of the pot.

"Is it the truth, Doc, or are you insane, just like him?"

"John Barrymore is your oldest friend," Doc replied. "If he was insane and you were in your right mind, you would stand by him and do all you could to help him regain his senses. The fact that you have not should tell you more than anything I can say."

MILDRED AND RICKY were struck dumb by J.B.'s speech. They sat there staring at him for more than a minute, not saying a word. J.B.'s gaze flickered to the windows, making sure no more Melissas were coming to restrain or chill him.

Finally, Mildred spoke up, her voice cracking over the first few words. "Is this true, J.B.? Is the honey really a drug that's got into our system and made us think in a different way?"

"I believe so," J.B. told her. "I don't have any more evidence than what I've seen with my eyes, and the fact that it's hot with radiation. But, Millie, if I'm right and I left you behind, then it wouldn't have been worth me being right."

Mildred could not help but smile when she heard that. "That is the most romantic thing you have ever said to me," she said. "Kind of makes me wonder if you might not be in your right mind even now."

"I oiled your blaster while it was in storage," J.B. told her. "That's proper romance in my book. Something that keeps you alive."

"There are no blasters in Heaven Falls, J.B."

"We're about to overturn that law," J.B. replied. "And we're going to do it together, I hope."

Mildred looked ponderous as she weighed J.B.'s revelations, while Ricky seemed torn. He idolized J.B. and had followed him into that mutie nightmare out in California two weeks ago. Whatever life he had discovered here, whatever the Trai had offered or promised, would it ever compare to the life of adventure that the Armorer led? Ricky didn't think so.

"I'm with you, J.B.," Ricky said, a look of anguish on his striking features.

"Good lad," J.B. said. "Millie?"

"My head's telling me not to trust you," Mildred admitted, "but my heart knows you'd never lead me astray. I'm with you, J.B., but for goodness' sake watch me, because if what you've told us is true, then this shit is rewiring my brain and I might just shoot you in the back when you turn around."

"Point accepted," J.B. said. Then he moved from his seat atop the lockbox and, crouching beside it, opened it up and withdrew their weapons. In a moment, Mildred and Ricky were armed for the first time in two weeks, while J.B. had his miniarsenal back. To the Armorer, it felt a lot like another old friend had returned to the fold.

"My instinct is to fight," Ryan admitted, his lone eye fixed in challenge on Doc. "To fight you, to fight for what me and Krysty have built here. To fight for the Regina and for the love she spreads."

"Ryan, please…" Doc began, reaching surreptitiously for the LeMat blaster beneath the tails of his frock coat.

"I have spent my whole life fighting," Ryan continued,

"and now, finally, I've found somewhere where that's not a way of life. And you know what—you've come to us with this story about brain poison in the food, and you've asked me to believe you and all I want to do is fight. But the thing is, I haven't wanted to do that for weeks, not since we got here. And that's not me. I know that and I should have seen it. You're right—I would stand by J.B. and do all I could for him if I thought he had gone crazy, just as I would stand by Krysty and Jak and all of you. Just as I *have* stood by you."

"An old man should be excused his eccentricities," Doc muttered with embarrassment.

"J.B. kept telling me about the bomber and I dismissed him," Ryan said angrily.

"Ryan?" Krysty piped up when he fell to silence.

"They got us," Ryan told her. "They got us good. Whatever is going on in this ville, it's tried to change us and—fireblast!—it damn near succeeded. Krysty, we've gotta leave. We've got to get away from this madness because it's a madness none of us can see happening, and that's the kind that chills you."

There were tears in Krysty's eyes now, and her lip trembled. "The children," she whispered. "They have been dosing their own children with this…this *poison*. I saw how it affected them, made them sick. But I didn't realize what it meant."

Reaching across the counter, Ryan stroked the side of Krysty's face and neck gently. As he did so, he unclipped the band that held her hair in place, setting it free. "Now we'll fix it," he said. "All of it."

Then Ryan popped the rad counter onto the lapel of his shirt and he began to give out instructions. "We're going to need our blasters," he said.

"I'm already ahead of you," Doc admitted, flashing the LeMat at Ryan from its hiding place beneath his coat.

Ryan smiled.

And now the two were six.

Chapter Twenty-Nine

Ryan and Doc found Jak out in the eastern edge of Heaven Falls clearing the scrub to reclaim the land for farming.

"Best you stay here, Doc," Ryan suggested.

Doc nodded. "Quite. I would not want to crowd the lad."

So while Doc remained at the edge of the field, Ryan trudged across the dirt toward Jak where he worked with two other laborers. Jak looked up as Ryan's shadow crossed him.

"We need to talk," Ryan said, pitching his voice low.

"What 'bout?" Jak asked.

Ryan almost smiled at that. Jak had lost none of his rough edges from living with the Trai, and his speech style was as reticent as ever. "Away from here," Ryan said, gesturing to an overgrown bank of grass at the edge of the cleared space.

The young man nodded once and followed Ryan.

"Jak, we got trouble," Ryan said. "It takes a little figuring, but it's nasty and it's affecting us all."

"Trouble?" Jak asked, canny eyes flicking to his companions still toiling in the field.

Ryan explained the whole story about the irradiated honey and how the caste system of Heaven Falls reflected that found in a beehive, how the Trai were following the behavioral patterns of honeybees and how J.B. suspected they intended to swarm and conquer the Deathlands.

When Ryan had finished, Jak stared at him in disbelief. "Charm chose me," he said. "Trust me. We in love, Ryan."

"She's duped you," Ryan said, shaking his head, "the same way they've duped us all. Mebbe she saw something in there that frightened her, or mebbe the Regina did. Mebbe they needed to keep you under control."

Jak lunged at Ryan then, driving the knuckles of his left fist into the taller man's jaw.

Watching from across the field, Doc winced and considered stepping in. But no, Ryan would have to deal with Jak his way. If Doc waded in now, it would seem that the two men were ganging up on him, and the argument would be lost.

Ryan grunted, and his hands came up to deflect the second blow that Jak attempted. The one-eyed man sidestepped, blocking Jak's left fist with his right hand, meeting the wrist and pushing the blow up and forward, forcing Jak to compensate or lose his balance. Jak never lost his balance in a fight.

The anger was clear in Jak's face, his usually sullen expression replaced by a fiery hatred. He took two quick steps back then charged at Ryan, growling like a beast as he came at him. The other men in the field had been alerted by the noise, and they hurried over to see what was going on.

Ryan stepped aside as Jak came at him, holding up both forearms to take the force of the albino's charge. It was a powerful blow, and the power behind it knocked Ryan so that his boot heels slid on the freshly turned soil.

"Jak, listen to me," he commanded. "This isn't helping."

But Jak was fired up now. "No help," he snarled as he swiped at Ryan with his right fist.

Ryan moved swiftly, grabbing Jak's arm as the fist connected with the top of his chest. "Ugh!"

Then Ryan pulled, stepping backward and dragging Jak off his feet. The albino youth seemed to skip along, his toes scraping the top of the soil before slipping down to his knees. Ryan let go then, breathing heavily, watching.

The two laborers could not believe it. They asked what was going on, who started it, why they were fighting—but Ryan ignored them, while Jak was as typically reticent as he had always been.

"Calm down and think," Ryan told Jak. "We've been friends too long for this."

Jak pulled himself up from the soil, crouching like a coiled cougar. He sprang without warning, driving toward Ryan like a dart from a blowgun, issuing a savage growl from his throat.

Ryan was forced on the defensive again, blocking Jak's attack as best as he could but still taking a powerful blow to the chest. He grabbed Jak's shirt as the albino slammed into him, using it like a handle to hoist Jak into the air and toss him aside.

"I helped you out in Louisiana when Baron Tourment tried to execute you and me both," Ryan stated as Jak rolled over and over in the dirt.

Jak was up in an instant, running at Ryan once again. The one-eyed man braced himself, adopting a defensive stance.

Six feet from Ryan, Jak sprang into the air, kicking his right leg toward his former friend's face. Ryan responded without thinking, bringing his right arm up to block the blow, taking the full impact there with bone-jarring force.

"And when Christina died," Ryan said as he rolled with the blow, staggering backward.

Jak went hurtling in the opposite direction to Ryan, slammed into the ground and rolled over twice to bring himself back up to a fighting crouch. Ryan saw the knife blade glint in his hand where he had slipped it from its hiding place in his sleeve.

"And Jenny," Ryan said. He saw something in Jak's expression change as he said the name of the daughter Jak and Christina had had: a softening of the anger, a rush of sorrow. And then he knew what to say. "I lost Dean—*my* son. I know how it chills you inside, Jak. I know how that void must hurt even now. But if you turn your back on your family, the void only gets bigger. In the end, all we have is family."

Jak's scarlet eyes were fixed on Ryan, and for a long moment he did not move or speak. Then, as Ryan watched, Jak slipped his knife back into its hidden sheath and nodded fractionally. "Tell," he said.

Ryan stepped forward and offered Jak his hand, helping the albino up from his crouch. They were both covered with dirt as they trekked across the field to where Doc was waiting. The two farmhands who had worked with Jak had a hundred questions to ask, but neither man offered any answers.

J.B. TOOK THE other companions to the redoubt without incident, following the same rocky pathway that he had taken to regain entry into Heaven Falls and keeping to the cover of the trees as much as they could. J.B. was accompanied by Ricky, Mildred and Krysty, and all of them stayed on high alert as they came within sight of the mound that housed the hidden redoubt.

J.B. had his minibinoculars up to his eyes as they came within sight of it and he scanned the doors, the bulky satchel he carried resting against his hip. "The doors are open," he told the others. "Last time I came here they'd posted a Melissa on the door and there was a team inside working on the mat-trans. I can't see any sign of… Wait, there she is. Cute little blonde."

J.B. passed the binoculars to Ricky.

"I see her," Ricky confirmed. "It won't be hard sneaking past her, either."

When Ricky pulled the field glasses from his eyes he saw that J.B. had his M-4000 shotgun cradled in his hands. "No time for negotiation," he said. "Krysty, Mildred— you're covering the exit. Anyone comes in or out who isn't one of us, you pop them. This is life or death, as usual. Ricky, you're with me."

Ricky hurried after the Armorer as he marched downslope, pulling his reproduction De Lisle carbine from beneath his jacket.

Ten seconds later they rounded a tree and appeared in the open, twenty feet from the redoubt entrance. The blonde in the white robes looked up with surprise to see two armed men standing there. J.B. didn't let her thought process get any further than that. It was kill or be killed. He squeezed the trigger of his shotgun, sending a lethal cloud of buckshot into the woman's gut and peppering the wall behind her.

The Melissa fell back, collapsing on the floor.

"Now they know we're here," J.B. stated grimly. "You got to hit them quick because they move like lightning if you give them a chance. And, Ricky, it's us or them."

"Gotcha," Ricky acknowledged.

The two men stepped over the dead body and marched deeper into the redoubt, automatic lighting flickering to life with each step.

"TRICKED," JAK GROWLED, shaking his head in frustration. He was walking with Doc and Ryan along the main path of Heaven Falls that led into the ville center. Doc thrust his swordstick ahead of him with each step, warily watching the few other people using the path, wondering if they suspected anything.

"We were all taken in," Ryan said quietly. "J.B. figures the Trai are going to swarm soon, use the mat-trans to settle a new colony and expand their territory. Once they get one mat-trans jump behind them, it'll be child's play for them to keep moving, keep setting up colonies, eating up every bit of space."

Jak looked thoughtful. He was recalling the conversation he had had just a few days before when he and Charm had been making love.

"We could leave," Charm had told him, her eyes fixed on his. "Build our own Home, like this one, only better. With me as queen."

"And me as king," Jak had replied, laughing.

"You're strong," Charm had said. "We could build something beautiful together, another Home."

Not a home, Jak realized. A hive. He had said he would be her king but she had never agreed, only told him how she would make a fine Regina. Doc had told him that the word meant queen, as they'd walked toward the ville center. It made a warped kind of sense now, the way the conversation with Charm had gone.

Jak recalled something else, too, how the wound on Charm's leg had repaired very quickly and without any medication. "Bee people strong," he said warningly.

"I have seen them move very fast," Doc added.

"Me, too," Jak said. He was recalling the incident outside the redoubt, when he had first seen the Melissas as they'd chilled the bomber. They had attacked as a group, and they had moved with uncanny speed and grace. It had struck him as odd then, but the further he had gotten away from that incident the more he had forgotten about it. There was so much he should have questioned but hadn't. If what Doc had said was right, then the honey in the diet was making them all docile and obedient to the Regina, open to her suggestions. That made sense, albeit the sick kind.

"Charm trick me, Ryan," Jak said. "Got fix it."

Ryan nodded. He understood how Jak felt. Where the rest of them had been taken in by the miracles around them, Jak had been specifically targeted by one of the Melissas, the so-called daughters of the Regina, and kept almost as an obedient puppy. It had to burn him up inside.

Doc reached into his frock coat and pulled out the blaster that J.B. had handed to him before they'd parted to attend to their separate tasks. It was Jak's Colt Python, reloaded and oiled by J.B., the safety carefully set. "I foresee that you shall likely be requiring this," Doc said.

Jak nodded, taking the blaster with an expression of glee.

"Keep that hidden, Jak," Ryan reminded him. "You know the ville rules."

Jak slipped the blaster into an inside pocket of his jacket, pressing at it so that the jacket's folds hid the bulge. Once he was satisfied, he trotted a little faster to catch up with Ryan and Doc.

The gleaming white towers of Heaven Falls peeked over the tree line where they waited up ahead.

THE REDOUBT WAS eerily quiet after the sound of the shotgun blast. J.B. and Ricky moved swiftly, their weapons in hand, ready for an attack.

"Perhaps if we look around the upper levels we'll find something that will blow up," Ricky suggested. "That way we won't need to mix it up with whoever's down below."

J.B. shook his head. "I admire your style, kid," he said, "but it won't work. We need to clear this place of bee people since it's our escape route. We leave the Trai in here and they could seal the place up and then we're screwed."

"Couldn't we walk out of the mountains?" Ricky asked.

"Far as I can see, this whole area got hit by missiles and quakes pretty hard," J.B. told him. "Quakes probably came about because of the missiles shaking seven shades of piss out of the terrain. Net result is this here is a land island—there's no way out unless you plan to grow wings."

Ricky shook his head. "Not me," he said. "These people have tried to make me mutie enough for one week."

They started to descend a stairwell. As they got closer to the lowest level Ricky became a little more nervous, and J.B. worried that Ricky was going to do something rash and give their position away. He remembered his dream, and the way Ricky had almost got himself chilled out in California.

"Settle down, kid," J.B. whispered as they neared the bottom of the stairwell. "Whatever happens now, trying to second-guess it will only get you chilled. We need to react and watch each other's backs."

Then they were at the door. Without any discussion, J.B. positioned himself on one side while Ricky held himself back, centering the door in the sights of his De Lisle. J.B. nodded to Ricky just once, then pulled the door open and shrank back. A figure moved through the doorway as it opened, dressed in white robes that danced around her lithe body like mist.

Ricky pulled the trigger on the De Lisle, sending a .45-caliber bullet at the Melissa. She moved faster than he could imagine, leaping up toward the next level of the staircase even as his blaster boomed. The shot whizzed through the air where she had been a nanosecond before.

Standing to the side of the door, J.B. moved, too, aiming

his blaster at the fleeing target and sending a cacophonous explosion of buckshot at the fluttering white robes. His shot missed, too, and the Melissa seemed to slip behind the cover of the next level like a cloud passing the sun.

J.B.'s breath came out in an audible "Whumph!" as the Melissa swung around on the aged metal banister and kicked him high in the forehead.

The Armorer crashed backward, his hat flying from his head.

"J.B.!" Ricky shouted, whipping his blaster around for another shot.

"No, Ricky, the—" J.B. began.

Moving like lightning, the Melissa delivered a second kick, this time to J.B.'s jaw. It struck so hard that the Armorer's teeth clacked together with an audible snap.

Ricky tried to take aim, but then he heard something behind him and realized what it was J.B. had been trying to warn him about. Behind him, framed in the open doorway of the stairwell, stood another Melissa. Adele. Before Ricky could switch targets, the dark-skinned Melissa was on him, her hand flattened into a wedge as it cut toward his throat.

Chapter Thirty

Ricky reeled backward at the strike, choking on his own breath as he tumbled against a wall.

Three of them! J.B. realized. One on the door and two down here. No, check that—at least two down here.

He was still recovering from the other's attack. J.B. brought his shotgun around and squeezed the trigger without aiming, sending a brilliant burst of buckshot at Adele as she slipped into the stairwell after Ricky. He watched with grim satisfaction as the white-robed woman did a twisting dance on the spot, the buckshot slapping against her right side.

But Adele recovered with the swiftness of lightning, switching targets and pouncing at J.B. in the blink of an eye. The Melissas were bastard resilient, J.B. knew, but he didn't have any other option; as she sped toward him, J.B. squeezed the trigger again, sending another lethal burst of fire at her.

The other Melissa was scrambling up the stairwell, feet swishing out, bounding from step to wall, clambering upward monkey fashion. Ricky was just recovering, and he brought his De Lisle carbine up to take a shot at the escaping woman. "I got her," he choked, the words coming out rough where his throat had been struck.

J.B. was knocked back against the wall by Adele, and the M-4000 shotgun in his hands angled upward, pointing uselessly toward the ceiling as the woman attacked. The

Armorer took a blow to the face, another, then heard something crack inside his nose. He ignored it. Adele moved in a blur, striking out at him from feet away, each blow precise and vicious, like being lashed with a whip. J.B.'s glasses slipped from his face as the woman struck another painful blow there, and the Armorer cried out in agony.

"Violators die by the Regina's command." Adele spit in his face. "Die, violator!"

"That's not in the plan, girl," J.B. snarled. As he spoke, he shifted his weight, thrusting his left leg out and hooking his foot behind the leg of his attacker as she continued toward him. Then he pulled his leg back quickly, and Adele lost balance as her foot was pulled out from under her.

The Melissa crashed backward, her skull striking the metal banister with a bell-like clang. J.B. stepped forward, raising the M-4000 and pointing it at the woman's face as she struggled to recover. He pulled the trigger and Adele's face was turned into a bloody ruin, her brains exploding out the back of her skull.

Ricky was at J.B.'s side, the tension clear on his face. "The other one got away," he croaked. "We should go after her."

"No," J.B. advised as he plucked his glasses from the floor. "Krysty and Mildred are up there. They'll stop her before she gets back to the ville."

Ricky looked as if he would contradict that, clearly frustrated at letting the Melissa go.

"You have to learn to trust your friends, kid," J.B. told him, wiping Adele's blood from his glasses on his shirt before replacing them on his nose. "Loners don't last long in this world."

Ricky accepted J.B.'s advice with a nod.

Leaning down, J.B. snatched his hat from the floor.

"Might be more Melissas out there," he said, indicating the stairwell door. "We aren't out of this yet."

"I thought you didn't want to chill anyone you didn't have to," Ricky said.

J.B. shrugged. "Sec men or women choose the life," he said grimly. "They know the risks."

Ricky reloaded his De Lisle.

MILDRED AND KRYSTY were waiting in the trees close to the redoubt when the Melissa appeared. They had rearmed themselves, Krysty with her Smith & Wesson .38 revolver, Mildred with her trusty Czech-made ZKR 551 target pistol. Even now it seemed strange going back to weapons after almost two weeks of tranquillity in Heaven Falls.

Mildred spotted the woman first, seeing the glint of her trailing white robes as she hurried through the garage-like area of the redoubt toward the pulled-back door. "Look alive," she whispered to Krysty. "We've got company."

The women watched as the Melissa exited the redoubt, moving at a sprint.

"No sign of J.B. or Ricky," Mildred said, concerned.

Krysty watched the Trai woman hurrying up the slope that led from the redoubt entrance. "No time to worry about them now," she whispered. "Melissa's making a beeline for Heaven Falls."

"Beeline," Mildred muttered with a shake of her head.

Then Krysty and Mildred stepped out from cover, weapons raised as the dark-haired Melissa came sprinting almost straight toward them.

"Freeze!" Mildred shouted.

The Melissa changed direction, moving at a blur.

Mildred pulled the ZKR's trigger, sending a .38 round at the sec woman. "Stop her," she shouted to Krysty as she loosed the bullet.

Impossibly the Melissa weaved out of the bullet's path, her white robes swirling around her like surf in a whirlpool. Mildred cursed as her shot went wide.

Krysty steadied her grip on her blaster and took a deep breath, one hand cupped beneath her wrist as she tracked the running woman in the white robes. Then, letting out her breath slowly, Krysty pulled the trigger and sent a single shot at the retreating woman as she sped past them, just twenty feet away. The bullet left the chamber and powered from the Smith & Wesson's muzzle with a bang of propellant, the smell of cordite immediate in the air.

The Melissa reacted to the sound, bringing one hand up and—incredibly—batting the bullet aside as it drilled through the air toward her. There was a thunderclap of noise as her hand met the bullet, knocking it away before it could strike her.

Krysty and Mildred watched the display with incredulity. This woman had just swatted a bullet from the air, moving with such speed that it could not harm her.

"Holy...! Bees move fast, I guess," Mildred said breathlessly. "We've got to—"

"On it!" Krysty said, running after the Melissa.

Krysty's hair trailed behind her like a flame as she ran, chasing the white-robed woman. The Melissa moved incredibly fast, her arms pumping in a blur, long legs eating up the distance with every step. She was heading for the settlement, no doubt to raise the alarm. Krysty had to prevent that. If she didn't, if the warning made it through, then Ryan, Doc and Jak would be in danger, either captured as they tried to enter the honey store or simply found guilty by association.

Krysty's cowboy boots pounded the ground, the blaster clenched tightly in her fist as she dashed up the grassy incline. The Melissa was moving too fast; she would never catch up.

Still running, Krysty raised the blaster, steadying her breathing as she drew a bead on the fluttering white robes ahead as they weaved between the trees, sending a .158-grain lead slug up the hill toward the retreating figure. The shot missed, clipping a low-hanging tree branch in a shower of sawdust.

The Melissa reacted to the shot, however, spinning on her heel to see who was following.

Krysty shot again, sending another slug at the dark-haired woman as she spied her. The Melissa leaped, her right hand snapping out to slam against the trunk of the tree next to her, using the force of the blow to swing herself around and out of the path of the hurtling bullet.

Krysty continued sprinting, hurrying up the slope as the Melissa dropped back down to the ground and adopted a combat stance.

"Violator!" the Melissa said accusingly, flexing her fingers in readiness.

Krysty tossed her blaster aside as she approached. It was useless against her fast-moving foe, and she wanted both hands free for what she was about to do. As she ran, she chanted a familiar prayer. "Gaia, help me in my time of need. O, Earth Mother, hear my plea!"

It was like being struck by lightning, ten thousand volts racing through Krysty's body in the blink of an eye. That was the Gaia power, drawn up from the earth and bringing the woman alive in a way no one else could ever know. She felt her muscles burning with energy, felt her strength increasing, the force inside her growing. Behind her, Krysty's sentient hair crackled with energy, spreading out from her head in jagged tangles of fiery red, so bright that they seemed to glow in the sunlight.

Then Krysty was on the Melissa, powering at her like a charging bull. The Melissa leaped, vaulting over the woman, one hand slamming down against her back. Krysty felt the blow—it was powerful and it seemed to echo through her rib cage—but she shrugged it off and changed direction, readying for her follow-up attack. The Gaia power made her almost invulnerable, and while it could not be tapped for long, while it flowed she felt invincible.

The Melissa landed in a billowing cloud of robes, turning in a superfast blur to face Krysty.

"Violator!" she repeated. "You betray the love of the Regina!"

Krysty charged once more, twisting her body to bring the crook of her right elbow around and slam it into the Melissa's face. The sec woman responded with lightning quickness, blocking the blow with both hands and throwing Krysty off balance.

The redheaded beauty rolled away, bumping against the ground in a tight ball. The Melissa saw her advantage then and she pressed it, kicking one perfectly tanned leg at Krysty's face as she recovered from the fall.

Krysty moved quicker, reaching out with her left hand and snagging the Melissa by the ankle as that bare foot rocketed toward her face. The movement was sudden, so sudden that the Melissa didn't have time to counter. Her kicking leg stopped in place with such abruptness that she toppled over, falling forward and pushing all of her weight against her hip and knee joints where Krysty held her leg.

The Melissa shrieked, dropping to the ground.

Still holding the woman's ankle, Krysty grabbed higher up the same leg with her other hand. Then she moved both her hands in a brutally swift use of counterforce, snapping the woman's tibia and fibula bones with a hideous crack.

The Melissa shrieked again, not just from the pain but from surprise. She didn't expect Krysty to match her move for move, countering her blinding speed with such incredible strength. Her speed came from imbibing the royal jelly, where all the Melissas got their power.

Krysty eyed the woman, scanning for weapons. She had none—of course she didn't, that was the rule of Heaven Falls, and why would she ever need one given her superhuman speed? Krysty's power was ebbing, though. Krysty moved swiftly from the Melissa, hurrying over to where she had tossed her blaster barely a minute before. The Melissa was cursing her, calling her a "violator" between her gasps of pain.

Krysty spotted the sheen of her .38 blaster glinting in the grass, and picked it up from the ground. Behind her, the Melissa was struggling back to her feet in a display of incredible bravery and agony. Her leg was ruined, the tip of the tibia bone jutting through the skin beneath her kneecap, strands of blood running from the wound like a map of the Nile.

Krysty turned as the Melissa began limping toward her, and raised the blaster in her hands. "I'm sorry it's come to this," Krysty said in a voice that didn't sound like hers. "In another world, one more meal and we could have been sisters."

With that, Krysty pulled the trigger, blasting a single bullet from the weapon—not at the woman's head but low in her gut where she could not move swiftly enough to avoid it. The Melissa hobbled in place as the bullet struck, sinking back to the ground with a screech of pain.

Krysty walked across the grass and delivered a second shot to the Melissa's forehead from just a foot above her, silencing her screams in an instant. Then she sank to the ground, clutching herself, the .38 still in her hand. The power of the Earth Mother was retreating from Krysty's body and with its departure, she would become as weak as a kitten.

J.B. LED THE way through the last corridor of the redoubt with Ricky covering his back. They took it slow, wary of an ambush after what had happened in the stairwell. Noise echoed from the concrete walls, the sounds of metal against metal, the low roar of what J.B. knew from experience was an acetylene torch.

"They're trying to patch up the mat-trans," J.B. told Ricky in a whisper. "I wonder where they got the knowledge to do that?"

Ricky looked confused. "Why didn't they stop when the guards came to investigate the gunshots?"

"Probably they're programmed not to," J.B. reasoned. "What do you feel like you should be doing just now? Be honest."

Ricky closed his eyes in thought for a few seconds. "Picking fruit," he said. "To prove my love for the Regina."

"Exactly."

They reached the control room without incident. The lights were on, and two engineers were working on the mat-trans while a third had removed the front panel of an operating console and lay on her back wielding a screwdriver, her head peering up at the revealed interior.

J.B. leveled the shotgun and spoke in a loud voice. "Nobody move."

The trio looked up at the intrusion and saw J.B. standing there like some grim angel of death.

"Violator! It's the violator!" shouted one of the women inside the mat-trans chamber, pointing at J.B.

"Yeah, it is. I am," J.B. confirmed. "But since you ladies aren't armed and we've already taken out your sec crew,

I would strongly recommend you play it cool and not try anything dumb."

The woman under the console pushed herself up, clenching the handle of the screwdriver so that its blade pointed downward. J.B. didn't hesitate; he stepped forward and thrust the snout of his shotgun into his adversary's breastbone. The woman toppled back on her butt, still clutching the tool.

"Drop that," J.B. said, "because next time I won't hesitate to send you on the next train to the coast."

The women exited the mat-trans chamber, determined looks on their faces. Ricky saw them move and he sent a bullet their way from the De Lisle, aiming the blast high.

"My friend asked you not to move," Ricky said. "Do that again and he'll stop asking so nicely."

The women finally seemed cowed by that, and they all sank to the floor and sat with their hands behind their heads.

"We bumped into three Melissas," J.B. told them, his blaster trained on the women. "You come here with any more'n that?"

"No," said the woman who had been working at the open console.

J.B. believed her. For one thing, he had monitored the engineering teams as they'd exited Heaven Falls each morning, and he knew they tended to travel in a three-to-two Melissas ratio. The third guard this day was a sign that they had become more wary after the last incident here, but in a ville this size they wouldn't have very many sec people to spare.

A brief discussion followed as Ricky and J.B. decided what to do with their prisoners. Ricky was worried they would escape, but J.B. told him that wouldn't matter so long as they didn't destroy the mat-trans. He proposed they secure their hands and then escort them to the surface, where they could be tied up until the companions returned. It would keep them out of trouble and prevent them alerting the Trai to the insurrection that J.B. and his crew were about to launch.

"What about wild animals?" Ricky asked. "Tied up like that, anything could just—"

"They can take their chances," J.B. cut in. "Their sec crew tried to chill us. I think we're showing more mercy than they should expect."

Ricky searched the engineers' equipment until he found some unused electrical cable. While J.B. held a blaster on the women, Ricky bound them tightly by wrist and ankle, giving them just enough movement so that they could walk but not run.

Once Ricky had finished, J.B. surveyed the mat-trans and grilled the prisoners about its status. One of the women confirmed that it was now operational.

Ricky and J.B. escorted the women through the redoubt and searched for explosives. The redoubt hadn't been stripped of supplies, and they found many packs of MREs, as well as magazines of ammo in various calibers. J.B. snagged several that would fit his weapons, and some spares suitable for the other companions. Bullets were hard to come by in the Deathlands—you grabbed what you saw when you saw it.

Soon after, they found a stash of explosives, and J.B. took some time deciding what best to use. He chose several detonators and pocket-size plas-ex charges, which looked like lumps of clay and could be molded for ease of use. He placed the explosives and a few other choice items into his trusty satchel and then he and Ricky escorted their prisoners topside.

Mildred and Krysty were waiting for them outside.

Krysty was sitting on a patch of grass with her head bowed low.

"She okay?" J.B. asked.

"Had a little scuffle with a friend of yours," Mildred explained. "Dark hair, white dress. You know who I mean?"

"Old sparring partner," J.B. confirmed with a nod. "Gave us the slip."

"She was a fast mover," Mildred said. "Krysty tapped into the Earth Mother to restrain her."

"They're all fast movers," J.B. stated grimly.

The companions tied the three engineers to separate trees, far enough apart that they could not help one another and could only converse by shouting. Then they set off back to Heaven Falls, using the high paths that J.B. had discovered less than a day before. They could only hope that Doc and Ryan had managed to persuade Jak to join them, and that all three were still safe as they put their part of the plan in motion.

WITHIN HEAVEN FALLS, Ryan, Jak and Doc waited in the plaza between the towers. They occupied one of the benches while Doc explained how the honey was stored.

"There are six levels to the storage facility," Doc said, pointing out the tower that contained it. "Each one is filled floor to ceiling with clay vessels containing honey."

"Six levels?" Ryan mused.

"Five or six," Doc confirmed. "I did not go up to the topmost level, but from my brief exposure to the interior I would confirm that, at the very least, the bottom two stories are full with the third floor close to capacity."

"Lot honey," Jak said.

"It forms the core of the Trai's diet," Doc reminded him. "The cakes and pastries they eat, the mead they drink, even the sweetened water."

"Brain messin' goo." Jak spit. "No good."

Ryan shielded his eye from the sun as he watched the doorway to the storage tower. "I can see two women in there," he said quietly. "Guards?"

"I believe so," Doc confirmed. "My superior gave them some specific information before we were allowed inside."

"What information?" Ryan asked.

"Regrettably that was something that I was not privy to," Doc told him.

"How many guards?" Ryan asked. "Just the two?"

"Yes, but the door can be locked," Doc told him. "Furthermore, there may be people inside who are in the process of delivering or removing honey for use by the ville."

"This is the heart of the infection," Ryan told his companions. "We need to be certain that it's destroyed. That means someone needs to go in there and eyeball it."

"Me," Jak said. "Owe them."

Ryan shook his head. "No, it'll take two people to cover the hives and you're fastest, Jak. Doc, you know where all the hives are located?"

"Yes. But they are painted white and easy enough to spot," Doc confirmed. "Jak should have no trouble."

"Good," Ryan said, reaching down to grab his Steyr Scout longblaster, which he had brought with him wrapped in a blanket to disguise it. "You and Jak work in opposite directions. I'll take on the store. This honey trap's about to burn."

Chapter Thirty-One

The journey back to Heaven Falls took longer than J.B. had hoped. Krysty had little energy left after drawing on the Gaia power, and she kept needing to stop to rest. Eventually, Krysty urged the others to go on without her.

"I'll catch up," she said. "Better that Ryan has some backup than none."

J.B. couldn't argue with that reasoning, nor could the others.

After making sure Krysty was comfortable sitting on a mossy log in a thicket, the Armorer, Mildred and Ricky continued over the high mountain path, picking their way across the sharp rocks as they hurried back to Heaven Falls.

Once they were in sight of the gates, J.B. pointed out the beehives that ran in twin lines along the exterior wall.

"I'm going to ask you to duck out of the main event," he told Ricky. "I need a man to set fire to the hives. Think you can do that?"

Ricky looked uncertain. "You sure you won't need me in there?"

"Mildred can cover my ass," J.B. assured him.

"Not for the first time," Mildred teased.

Ricky handed Mildred the extra plas ex he'd been hauling, then scrambled down the steep outcropping, taking care not to be seen.

WITHIN THE VILLE, Doc was following a similar task to Ricky's. He had lit one of the smoking cloths that were used by the beekeepers to dull the bees' senses while they gathered the honey, and now made his way around the ville counterclockwise, setting fire to the hives. Jak was performing the same task following a clockwise direction.

The fires were slow burning, and it wasn't until Doc was almost a third of the way around that someone noticed that the hives weren't just smoldering—as if they were being smoked by a harvesting crew—but were actually on fire. Before long, the alarm went up, but Doc's actions were overlooked. He was known as a beekeeper and no one thought to question why he would be carrying the same smoking cloth that he and his colleagues regularly employed in their workaday business.

Working from northwest to southeast, Doc had reached the east wall hives when someone finally came to question him. That someone was Jon, his beekeeping supervisor, who happened to be working at a nearby hive in the otherwise empty field. He clearly didn't register what Doc was up to, and was simply surprised to see Doc at work.

"I heard you were sick," Jon said. "That nice medicine lady—Molly, is it?"

"Mildred," Doc said.

"Yeah, she came and told me early this morning," Jon explained. Already a respected healer in the ville, Mildred had been sent to spread a little disinformation before the companions had split off to enact their plan.

Doc took a deep breath. "As you can see, I am feeling far more sprightly now," Doc explained, "so I hurried to catch up with the day's tasks."

Jon eyed Doc skeptically. "Where are your gloves?" he asked. "And what have you been collecting the honey in?"

As he spoke, his eyes flicked over Doc's shoulder to

a beehive that stood just a little distant, and he saw the dark smoke pouring from it. "Hey, is that hive burning?"

"Where?" Doc said, turning to see where Jon pointed. As he did so, he flipped his swordstick up and around, rapping it with force into Jon's groin.

The beekeeper let out a gurgle and sank to the ground. Standing over him, Doc swung the swordstick again, smashing it hard on the side of the man's skull. Jon said something unintelligible and sagged in the grass, unconscious.

"Sorry, my friend," Doc lamented, "you were a rather good boss and deserved better than that. But time is not my ally today."

"Hey!" The cry came from across the field. Doc looked up and saw Jon's curly-haired partner, Thomas, running toward him. "Hey, what the heck did you just do?"

Doc twisted the silver lion's-head handle of his swordstick and readied to draw the blade that was hidden within. Thomas stopped a few feet away, staring in shock at Jon's body where it lay in the grass, swelling already evident at the side of the man's face.

"You hit him, Doc," Thomas stated. "I saw you do—"

In a swift movement, Doc drew the blade and slashed it across Thomas's chest, tearing shirt and skin.

"Get back," Doc warned.

Thomas stood there incredulous, looking at the line of blood that had appeared across his chest. "Why did you…?" he muttered. And then he swayed in place and sank to his knees, his hand clasping the wound on his chest. It was a common enough reaction, one that Doc had seen many times before—a person didn't know how to react when his or her blood was suddenly spilled.

Taking advantage of Thomas's momentary shock, Doc stepped closer and unholstered the LeMat, using the grip like a club against the back of the beekeeper's skull. Thomas collapsed to the grass, unconscious.

There was no time to lose. Doc had to keep moving, setting light to the hives while his allies continued with their own parts of the plan.

LIKE DOC, JAK worked around the ville as fast as he could, setting fire to the beehives. He moved swiftly, using a flint and tinderbox to light a fire before sprinting to the next hive.

Jak had set light to twelve hives before someone noticed what he was doing and gave chase.

"Hey, what do you think you're doing?" a woman asked. Jak didn't know her name, but he had seen her around. A supervisor in the construction projects, she was tall with long limbs and blond hair so pale it was almost white.

Jak didn't even stop. He merely glanced back at the woman before working the flint and tinder over a rag to light the next hive. Behind him, smoke was beginning to churn in the air above Heaven Falls from the burning hives.

"I asked you a question, man," the woman demanded, now standing over Jak. When he ignored her, she reached down for the crook of his elbow as if to pull away a small child.

Jak turned then, thrusting the burning rag at her face. The woman shrieked and backed off, the burning rag setting her hair on fire.

"Keep away," Jak warned her as she slapped at her burning hair.

Three minutes and four hives later, Jak became aware that people were approaching, a whole group of them, walking determinedly in step. He looked up from his work at the next hive and saw Charm leading four other women across the flowers toward him. She was dressed in her

Melissa robes, but the other women looked like farmers or construction types.

"Jak, my love, what do you think you're doing?" Charm demanded. "Put that down."

Jak closed his eyes, allowing her silky voice to wash over him, dropping the flint and tinder as he felt the urge to trust her. He wanted to trust her, believe her, *obey* her. He wanted all of that, in some deeply buried part of his mind. But he had to ignore it; she was as much a victim as he was.

"Jak?"

"Honey poisoned," Jak said, keeping his eyes closed. "I save you. Save all."

"Jak, you're sounding like a madman." Charm practically cooed the words, and Jak felt her shadow cross over his face as she reached for him.

Jak lashed out, not looking but sensing where his lover was. Charm gasped with surprise as Jak's swipe struck her under the chin.

"Jak, please…" she began.

The albino opened his eyes then, two bloodred orbs reflecting the flaming rag in his hand. "Charm don't see," he said. "None see."

"I was going to be your queen," Charm rasped.

"Not queen," Jak told her. "Queen bee."

And then Jak drove the clenched fist of his left hand into the side of Charm's head with sudden force. Charm saw it coming at the very last instant and she tried to avoid the blow, but there was nowhere for her to go. Jak's fist hit her with a blunt thud, striking her temple where it was most sensitive. He watched as Charm keeled over and sprawled on the ground, her white robes fluttering around her in the wind. She was semiconscious, her eyes flickering, only the whites showing.

"Check her," Jak told the other women.

One of the women stepped forward, a fierce expression on her face. "You lunatic!" she bellowed. "You're defiling the Regina's love!"

Jak thrust the burning rag at the woman, forcing her to step back. As she did so, he reached across his body with his empty left hand and pulled his Colt Python from its hiding place at his right hip. The woman's eyes were still on the flaming rag as the blaster appeared in Jak's hand, and he waved it in a controlled arc at the group.

"Keep away," Jak told them. The alternative was obvious enough.

RYAN WAITED FIFTY yards from the honey store, leaning back in the shade of an adjacent tower, watching the twin guards who stood within the shade of the door. He could smell the smoke now as it wafted over the mountain ville, and the sounds of shocked discovery were echoing from the distance where the Trai people were beginning to realize what was happening. The two white-robed women in the storehouse doorway were aware that something was going on, too. Ryan saw them peer excitedly from the door, discussing what they could see.

"Come on," Ryan urged quietly. "Step outside and take a look."

The two women, one blonde, one redhead, talked and pointed, spotting several sources for the plumes of smoke that were tangling together in the skies above Heaven Falls. The redhead stepped into the courtyard and paced a little way out to get a better look.

Unseen in the shadows, Ryan lifted his longblaster to his shoulder, shucking the blanket that had disguised it. He followed the redhead through the crosshairs, waiting until she was in line with the blonde at the door. When she was, he stroked the trigger on the weapon and a 7.62 mm bullet drilled from the barrel and hurtled through the air, piercing the redhead's throat without pause.

The blonde looked up at the noise, turning as she saw her colleague drop to the ground.

Still hidden in the shadows, Ryan shifted his aim slightly, centered the blonde in the crosshairs and fired. He watched emotionlessly as she dropped to the ground in the doorway. Ryan lowered the Steyr and sprinted the fifty yards of open courtyard to the store-tower doorway. He could hear shouting coming from all around—people discovering the burning hives, maybe questioning the sound of his blaster shots that had echoed like cracks of thunder across the ville. He kept moving, hurrying through the open door, into the darkened, warren-like interior.

A woman was standing at the far end of the corridor. Ryan pulled his SIG Sauer P-226 handblaster from its holster and snapped off a shot, one-handed. The woman sank to the floor, her death barely seen in the unlit corridor.

Open doors ran along both sides of the corridor, Ryan realized. At the sound of his blasterfire, a head bobbed out from one of the doorways. Ryan raised his SIG Sauer, but the figure ducked back inside the storeroom.

"Get out," Ryan shouted as he scrambled past the open doorway where he had seen the face appear. It was a woman, he saw now, dressed in a shift covered by a pale apron, its color difficult to discern in the poorly lit room. Behind her, lining every wall, Ryan saw the great clay containers of honey. "If you want to live, get out."

The woman looked at Ryan, then at the SIG Sauer in his right hand, the scoped longblaster in his left. "Y-you can't have blasters here," she stammered, shocked.

"Out!" Ryan shouted at her, gesturing with the handblaster.

The woman stood defiant for a moment, so Ryan fired a shot over her head. The report was loud in the enclosed space, and the bullet penetrated a clay cylindrical vessel shelved at shoulder height. Ryan watched as honey began to drool from the holed vessel, while the apron-wearing woman finally took her cue to leave, sobbing as she tottered past him on suddenly unsteady legs.

"Right," Ryan growled as he looked around the towering storeroom at all the clay cylinders of honey. "Time to shut down this sweet op."

J.B. AND MILDRED approached the ville from the east, scrambling down the almost vertical rock face where the mountains met the fields. As they descended, they could see the plumes of smoke clouding the air, billowing in tufts from the burning hives.

"Looks like Doc's been busy," Mildred said.

J.B. looked around, searching for any sign of the old man. A scarecrow-thin figure was hurrying across an adjacent field, the tails of his coat flapping in the breeze. "There he is," the Armorer said, pointing. "Go get him and meet me at the towers. Ryan should be there, and we have some last bits of business to conclude."

Mildred agreed, and she sprinted across the field with the ZKR 551 target pistol in her hand. The time for stealth had passed—now there were only life-and-death decisions to be made.

SURROUNDED BY ALL that honey, Ryan was starting to feel giddy. The stuff was irradiated, produced from pollen that had been doused in the fallout of the nukecaust. It had spoken to him when he had believed the Regina and the society that she had created. But now— Now it made him feel light-headed and nauseous simply being this close to it.

Ryan looked around the storeroom, calculating how many rooms like this that the tower had to hold. Doc had said that there were probably six levels in all, and that three of them were almost full. There was enough honey here to feed a settlement the size of Heaven Falls for years—perhaps even a decade, if it didn't spoil. They were stock-piling it—that was obvious. Perhaps they planned to take some with them when the Regina's chosen ones left the hive to swarm. Perhaps they planned to dose up the entire Deathlands, make everyone see things from the point of view of the hive mind. Ryan and his companions had been in Heaven Falls two weeks, and in that time they had become subsumed by the strange culture that the Trai had created. It didn't take much; a little longer and they never would have left, not even after J.B. had come to tell them what was happening. They would have just chilled him.

"Two weeks to lose your humanity," Ryan muttered, shaking his head.

Holstering his handblaster and slinging the Steyr, Ryan paced over to one of the shelves and ran his hand along it. It was made of wood, and so was the wall behind, which meant once he got a blaze started, the whole place would go up in flames.

Ryan moved swiftly, checking the other rooms of the storage unit, searching for anyone else who might get accidentally caught up in the inferno he planned. He hadn't come here to chill people. Whatever was going on in these folks' heads, it wasn't really them—he could vouch for that by his own experience, the way he had become docile and had very nearly turned on his oldest friend. He would chill if he had to, but he would not be a party to genocide.

Ryan reached the wall ladder and moved up into the second story of the storage tower.

MILDRED HAD BEEN joined by Doc, and they took a different route into the ville center. Around them, hives were burning, sputtering smoke into the air. Bees were exiting their hives in great clouds, their angry buzzing sounding like some colossal power saw cutting through the air.

Doc pulled his coat up over his head, moving in a crouch. "We have riled our insect friends," he said, shouting to be heard over the buzzing.

"Just keep moving, Doc," Mildred urged. "J.B. found enough explosives for all of us."

As they hurried up the dirt trail toward the central towers, Jak appeared from a line of trees, having cut across the ville. "What happen?" he asked.

"The whole place is coming down," Mildred told him, handing Jak detonators and several blocks of plas ex.

"What target?" Jak asked her as the three companions jogged up the dirt incline and reached the seven towers.

"Here and here," Mildred said, pointing. "Doc, you take the one at the back. J.B.'s handling the central tower."

"What about you?" Doc asked.

"Medical faculty," Mildred told him. "Good luck."

With that, the three allies split up, running toward their chosen targets. Mildred could not help but feel a pang of regret at having to destroy the medical tower. The Trai had developed such knowledge and insight. They had created a society of superbeings with the ability to heal quicker than a normal person thanks to their steady diet of honey, and had employed royal jelly to create the superfast Melissas. There was so much that Mildred could take from here, so much she still had to learn. She should save the Home....

No, she thought as she reached the medical building. That's the honey talking, twisting my thoughts. It's evil, pure evil. Insect reasoning trying to override my rationality.

She strode into the medical tower and saw Petra crossing the lobby.

"Mildred," Petra gasped, "what's going on out there? I heard screaming."

Mildred raised her ZKR. "You'll be hearing a lot more unless you get everyone out of here right now."

Petra's eyes boggled at the sight of the blaster. "You can't—"

Mildred pulled the trigger, sending a single bullet into the floor between the woman's feet. "Only the first one's a warning shot," she said. "If I shoot again, no amount of medicine will fix what will be left of you. Got it? Now clear the faculty. You have two minutes."

Petra ran, rushing to get everyone out of the medical tower.

J.B. APPROACHED THE central tower where the Regina made her home. Three Melissas stood guard there, including raven-haired Nancy. J.B. stomped toward them, shotgun in hand.

"Get out of here if you want to live," J.B. snarled.

"Violator!" Nancy shrieked. "How dare you set foot in Heaven Falls after what you did to my sister-in-arms."

J.B. wasn't going to argue. He simply pulled the trigger, sending a wad of buckshot at the white-robed woman as she stepped from the doorway.

Nancy leaped, spinning through the air as the shotgun's discharge raced toward her, passing over its deadly issue. She landed eight feet from J.B., and he snapped the trigger again as she danced toward him. Nancy slipped past the blast with a fraction of an inch to spare, the shot peppering the side of the Regina's white tower.

The other Melissas were out of the tower now, too, running at J.B., a fourth one joining them from wherever she had been posted within. People peered down from the overhead walkways, dismayed by all that was happening in their peaceful, ordered community.

J.B. ducked as Nancy leaped at him, her right leg sweeping up to kick his head. Had it met, J.B. had no doubt that the blow would have taken his head from his shoulders; as it was, his reaction time was just enough to slip him beneath its punishing blow.

The Melissa followed up with a second kick, pivoting on her right leg as it met the floor and snapping out with her left. J.B. grunted as Nancy's heel met him high in the chest, sending him lurching backward. He stroked the M-4000's trigger again, sending another burst of shot at his attacker.

Nancy weaved in place, letting the wide burst of fire zip past her by the slimmest margin. Then the other three Melissas were with her, swarming on J.B.—swarming like angry bees.

Chapter Thirty-Two

And then everything started to blow up.

Black smoke poured from the honey storage tower and, simultaneously, two of the nearby towers exploded, their bases erupting into flame.

J.B. was thrown to the ground by the force of the blasts, and around him all four Melissas tottered and fell as if caught in an earthquake.

Seconds later, the Regina emerged from the palace tower in a sweep of yellow-and-black robes. "What is happening?" she shrieked. As she did, her eyes swept across the panorama of devastation—the Melissas, her personal guard augmented by the powers of royal jelly, lying on the ground amid billowing trails of smoke, the flames licking at the lower levels of two of the nearby towers, the dark smoke emanating from the precious honey store.

"My honey!" she cried, her eyes fixing on the last of these. "My…honey!"

Lying on his back in the dirt, J.B. struggled to make sense of things. He saw the Regina moving in a blur of yellow and black toward the honey store, and he took a moment to fire his shotgun. The Regina leaped the discharge without even turning, her awareness augmented to superhuman levels by her constant imbibing of the irradiated honey. Out of ammo, J.B. watched her go, her long golden skirts trailing behind her like a pointed tail, the black stripes running up her slender body.

Then Nancy recovered from where she had fallen, and she stomped toward J.B. as he reloaded the M-4000.

INSIDE THE HONEY store, Ryan ran a flaming torch along the wooden walls of the lower level, setting light to everything he could as he backed toward the exit. The torch was made from the blanket he had used to disguise his Steyr, wrapped around a hunk of wood he had broken from a door frame in one of the rooms. He had already been through the whole storeroom, checking to confirm there were no other people working there, and had tipped as much of the honey from the clay containers as he could without slowing his pace. Now black smoke billowed all around, flames licking the wooden walls, and the whole atmosphere was heavy with the cloying sweetness of warmed honey.

Ryan could still make it out through the main door. He had plotted a route before starting the fires, moving backward through the tower, ensuring that the space behind him was not alight. But the fire was spreading fast, running up the walls and sending red-gold tendrils into the final corridor.

There was a pop as the flames caught a knot of wood close to Ryan's ear, and a burst of sparks spit across the floor. He had done what he could; it was time to go.

Tossing the flaming torch into the open doorway of the closest storage room, Ryan turned. He saw her immediately—the woman in the yellow-and-black dress, marching down the warren-like corridor toward him as black smoke painted the air. The Regina had arrived to save the honey or to chill the man who had destroyed it.

"Violator!" the Regina railed. "After all I have given to you and your friends, you spurn my love. After all I gave, without asking a thing in return."

"You asked everything," Ryan told her. "You asked for

our humanity, our will, our very souls. You're just too caught up in the mind poison to see it."

"You've destroyed what it has taken years to build and to harvest," the Regina thundered, blocking the narrow corridor. Ryan's only exit was past her, *through her.*

"We're saving you," Ryan told her, "from a fate you can no longer comprehend." As he spoke, he reached for the SIG Sauer holstered at his hip.

"Saving?" the Regina snarled, gesturing to the flames. "With destruction? This is the way of the old world, Ryan, not our glorious new age. The days of destruction are over—harmony shall rule humankind."

"Your glorious new age is at an end, your highness," Ryan said, raising the SIG Sauer to target the Regina. "Aborted before it can spread any further." He fired, sending a single 9 mm Parabellum bullet at the Regina's forehead.

The Regina blurred, her head moving so swiftly to avoid the bullet that it seemed as if there were three of her standing in the smoke. Then, in less than a heartbeat, she had traveled the length of the burning corridor and was on top of Ryan. He gasped, seeing the blur of the woman's arms as they cleaved the air to bat his SIG Sauer aside.

MILDRED PLACED THE charges the way J.B. had shown her, depositing them around the medical tower working from the center outward and targeting the major support beams. She set the timer for ninety seconds.

As the timer began its countdown, Mildred took one last look around the lobby. It was sterile in its cleanliness, free of dirt and debris. The Trai had found something special here, used it to the advantage of everyone, securing wonderful health for all. But it had come at a price—the lost of their individuality.

For a moment Mildred wondered if she might take some of the medicine from one of the rooms with a view to studying it, synthesizing it, perhaps recreating it. But no. It had to be destroyed. Everything here had to be destroyed. It was the only way to be sure they had stopped the evil from spreading.

Mildred stepped from the tower as the timer reached sixty seconds and ran out into the burning plaza beyond where the other towers were beginning to crumble in on themselves amid eight-foot-high flames.

It was over. Heaven was falling down.

OUTSIDE THE VILLE walls, Ricky was preparing to set light to the last of the hives, covering it with a liquid accelerant he and J.B. had found in the redoubt. Behind him, eleven hives belched dark smoke into the air in trailing streamers, their occupants burning up within, just a tiny percentage escaping the fury of the infernos.

As Ricky finished smothering the last hive with accelerant, two Melissas sprinted toward him from their sentry post at the ville gates. Ricky remembered the altercation in the redoubt, remembered everything that J.B. had told him about these women and their phenomenal speed, and he whipped off two quick shots from his Webley, shooting straight from the hip.

One Melissa went down, her flowing white robes fluttering around her like fog. But the second seemed to jump over the bullet meant for her, leaping high in the air and coming down just feet from where Ricky stood.

"¡Madre di satanás!" Ricky breathed, and he fired again, sending another .45 slug toward the beautiful, pale-skinned woman.

The Melissa stepped back, flicking her left hand out in a move that resembled a judo chop. Ricky heard a whip crack of air, and suddenly his bullet was zipping uselessly away in a new direction where the woman had knocked it from its trajectory.

"Impossible," Ricky muttered, raising the Webley and reeling off another shot. He moved the weapon left and right as he fired two bullets at the fast-moving woman.

Kicking one heel against the ground, the Melissa leaped up and over Ricky's head. As she did so, one of the bullets clipped her right leg and a trail of blood followed as she soared through the air.

Spinning to follow her, Ricky threw the last of the accelerant at the Melissa as she landed beside the hive. At the same time, he pulled the trigger of his blaster again, sending another bullet screaming from the chamber—but this time he aimed not at the Melissa but at the ground where he had spilled the accelerant. The bullet struck the accelerant and, before the superhuman sec woman could even register what was happening, she lit up like a human torch, shrieking in untold agony.

Ricky stepped back from the blaze, watching as the woman went up in flames. She stumbled on unsteady legs for a moment before crashing into the beehive. The accelerant on the beehive caught fire in an instant, and suddenly the conflagration was doubled, turning from the single figure of the flaming Melissa into a funeral pyre. The burning forms of bees rushed at the woman as their artificial nest blazed, stinging her before crashing to the ground as blackened husks.

Ricky watched all of this without emotion, quickly reloading his Webley revolver. Behind him, the last Melissa stared with sightless eyes, a red-rimmed hole in the center of her forehead where Ricky's first bullet had chilled her. Speed wasn't everything—ruthlessness could win the day in the Deathlands. Survival was everything, and he had learned that from the best.

RYAN WAS DOING all he could to avoid the punishing attacks of the Regina in the burning honey store. The woman moved in a blur, faster than Ryan's eye could follow. It was all he could do to block as she kicked and punched him backward, forcing him deeper into the burning tower.

A savage kick to his chest sent Ryan tumbling back, and he slammed against a burning wall as black smoke billowed around him. He struggled away, patting at his smoldering coat, sinking to the floor.

"You still love me," the Regina stressed. "You still feel the love that will save you."

Ryan did. He could feel the emotion tugging at him— adoration for this woman who was trying to chill him.

No. I have to see past it, Ryan reminded himself. Have to remember what this woman is—what all these people have become.

"You will obey me," the Regina instructed. "You will execute the violators of my law—for love is stronger than the bonds of friendship."

Slumped by the burning wall, Ryan's hand slipped to the sheath on his thigh, and he tried to remember what it was he had been thinking before the Regina's words started buzzing in his mind.

Adoration is not love. Blind devotion is not love.

The Regina stood over him as the walls burned, red- gold flames highlighting her perfectly coiffed blond hair. "Love me," she instructed.

"No," Ryan snarled, powering his fist up with all his strength until it met the Regina's jaw with a loud crack.

"I love Krysty," Ryan told the Regina as she stumbled back, astonished.

"Die!" the Regina yelled, leaping for Ryan, her hands hooked like talons.

Ryan let her drop onto him, using her weight to thrust the blade of his panga into her gut. "You first," Ryan replied, forcing the blade in deep.

J.B. HAD RELOADED and blasted off a single shot from the M-4000 before Nancy reached him. The blast had been almost at ground level where J.B. was lying in the dirt, and Nancy had stepped over it easily. Then she was on him, yanking the Armorer from the ground with one powerful hand, swiping his blaster away with the other.

"Violator!" Nancy screeched. "Look at the damage you have caused." She slapped his face, left then right then left again, forcing J.B. to turn his head. "Do you have anything to say for yourself before I execute you in the name of the Regina's love?"

"Going to…thank…me," J.B. muttered through bloodied lips, "tomorrow."

Nancy pressed her free hand against the Armorer's face, shoving his glasses aside and pushing her fingers against his eyes and under his lips the way a man would grab a predark bowling ball. J.B. fought to get free, but the woman was impossibly strong, and her grip on his clothes held him above the ground so that he could not get any leverage. He growled through gritted teeth as he felt the woman's fingers press against his eyeballs.

And then, without warning, another explosion rocked the ville, and J.B. felt Nancy's grip loosen. It was the medical faculty blowing up and caving in on itself, the last but one tower to be destroyed by the companions.

J.B. took advantage of his foe's momentary surprise, kicking out against her shins with all the force he could muster. He felt her grip slip from his face and he kicked out again, launching himself from her grasp and tumbling back hard against the ground.

There were three other Melissas with Nancy, and when J.B. looked he saw them stalking toward him.

"And me without my shotgun," he muttered as he reached into his jacket for his other weapon of choice, a Mini-Uzi.

As he did so, the Melissas swooped toward him, white robes billowing like wings, dancing across the ground like birds taking flight. In that moment, J.B. could not deny that they looked beautiful—the perfect idealization of the human form, angels descended from Heaven. He raised the Uzi and held down the trigger, sweeping the weapon in a swift arc.

THE REGINA SQUIRMED at the end of Ryan's blade as he wrenched it across her stomach, creating a ghastly, bloody wound.

The Regina was fast, but speed couldn't save her up close like this. No amount of superhealing was going to stem the flow of blood that rushed from the awful rent in her gut.

Ryan stepped away, yanking his blade free. The Regina collapsed, her mouth stretched open in silent agony, blood cascading down her torn dress.

"Your empire's over," Ryan told her as flames licked at the wooden walls and ceiling of the narrow corridor. "Your dream of spreading is finished."

The Regina looked at Ryan with desperate eyes, her hands clenched around the wound in her gut. "Love me," she croaked. "Love the Home."

"No," Ryan told her as he wiped the blood from his blade and sheathed it. "I'm going to burn it down."

Ryan stepped over the fallen queen and hurried down

the burning corridor, running toward the exit where daylight shone through the flaming doorway.

BULLETS WERE FLYING everywhere. J.B. zipped through a whole magazine just keeping the Melissas at bay.

But bullets were coming from another direction, too—and more than one, in fact.

Mildred, Doc and Jak had joined the fight, gathering at the plaza after completing their respective missions. It was like shooting fish in a barrel—the companions were the only ones who were armed, and while the rest of the population of Heaven Falls had finally realized that their best option was to run away unless the Regina told them different, it left the superhuman Melissas fending off an attack from all fronts.

Rearmed, Jak threw two of his leaf-bladed knives, and they drummed into the throat and breast of one of the Melissas.

Doc fired his replica LeMat, sending a devastating .44-caliber lead slug into—and through—another Melissa's back, turning her guts into offal in a blinding flash.

Mildred showed more finesse than her companions. As the towers collapsed around the plaza, she reeled off carefully placed shots at Nancy and the other remaining Melissa, clipping one of them in the flank but missing the fast-moving Nancy by an inch.

Nancy flew at J.B. in a rush of speed and anger. The Armorer dropped back, feeling the ground slam against his back and shoulders as he tossed the empty Uzi aside. Then the Melissa was on him, clawing at his face like a wild animal. J.B. punched her hard in the gut, and she momentarily fell back. As she did so, Jak drilled a throwing knife into her right eye socket, ending the Melissa's attack.

At that moment Ryan came crashing through the flaming doorway of the burning storage tower. His clothes were blackened with smoke and so was his face, the skin red beneath. He was clearly exhausted. But he was alive.

The one-eyed man staggered away from the burning tower as it began to lurch behind him. And then, as J.B. watched, a second figure emerged through the fire, her trailing dress alight with flames.

"Ryan!" J.B. shouted in warning.

Ryan turned but he was slow now, exhausted from all he had been through. The Regina of Heaven Falls, the queen bee, was on him in an instant, her burning flesh reaching for his.

But it only lasted an instant. Another figure was there, one that had not been there just seconds before, and this one, too, had brought flames with her: the flame-red locks of her flowing hair. It was Krysty, running at speed through the debris of the crumbling towers. She met with the Regina just as the woman reached for Ryan, body slamming into her like a speeding freight train hitting a cow that had strayed onto the tracks.

The Regina lurched backward, her feet scrambling for purchase on the ash-strewed ground. Krysty kept moving, knocking into the woman again, driving her fist into the Regina's jaw.

"Stay the hell away from Ryan," Krysty shouted. "Get out of our heads."

The Regina crashed back into the crumbling storage tower, the fire licking at her flesh and clothes. Standing in front of her, Krysty pivoted and kicked, driving her booted foot into the woman's wounded belly. The Regina hurtled back through the doorway of the tower and the flames roared brighter, hiding the doorway forever behind their burning curtain.

A loud crack shook the air, and Krysty turned and ran,

grabbing Ryan by the collar of his coat as she did so. Behind them, the storage tower crumbled in on itself, its integrity ruined by fire, collapsing in a pillar of flame.

Krysty threw Ryan to the ground, holding her hands over his head to protect him as clay pots and cylinders went firing in all directions, shattering on the ground. The other companions did likewise, protecting themselves from the death throes of the burning building.

Chapter Thirty-Three

After that it was just mopping up and dealing with the loose ends. The innocent people of Heaven Falls had scattered to the mountains as the towers crumbled, too scared and disorganized to fight Ryan and his companions. Where once they had worked together, without the Regina they were nothing, their reasoning lost in a miasma of confusion, like waking from a coma dream.

J.B. set the last of the charges at the tower that had served as the Regina's palace, though truly there was little need. The central tower had taken a lot of damage from the buildings that had burned and collapsed around it, and it was already so ruined that it looked as though it would fall over in a strong breeze. While he primed the charges, the last occupants of the tower were ushered out, mystified by what had happened.

Krysty apologized to Ryan for leaving things to the last minute to come help him. "I had to wait to gain the strength to summon the Earth Mother's power," she explained.

"And you did—just in time," Ryan told her, his face still black with soot. "Nothing like an old-fashioned firefight among friends to shake you out of a daze, huh?"

Krysty laughed at that, and helped Ryan brush ashes and dirt from his clothes.

Ryan had been sucked into this plot, and Krysty knew

she had been part of the reason why. "We thought we'd finally found heaven on earth," she said sadly.

Ryan shook his head. "No," he told her. "I've already found that—and I find it again each time I look in your eyes."

WITH KRYSTY'S HELP and Mildred's know-how, J.B. concocted a herbicide that would destroy the plants in the immediate area around Heaven Falls, a kind of scorched-earth insurance. Krysty brought her knowledge of all things botanical while Mildred figured out what to substitute given what remained in the limited stores of the farmers. For his efforts, J.B. brought a working appreciation for the napalm he had sourced from the redoubt, which he assured the women was the best herbicide known to man.

After that, the companions regrouped and made their way back to the redoubt.

"I GUESS THEY were muties," Ricky said as the companions strode across the mountain path.

Behind them, the fires were burning out of control in the place that had once been Heaven Falls, the columns of red flame making it appear more like a vision of hell now.

"They were still changing," Mildred confirmed, "mutating as we watched."

Leading the way, Ryan slipped through the open doors to the redoubt, the Steyr held horizontally over his shoulders. "Humans turning into something else," he said. "Never let it be said that this world isn't full of surprises."

"And every one of them a new horror," Doc declared, though there was a light, mocking tone to his words.

Bringing up the rear, J.B. and Jak stood at the redoubt doors for a moment, checking that they were not being followed. The three women who had been repairing the mat-trans were still tied to trees scattered around the entrance, but J.B. was okay to leave them. He wasn't one to leave an enemy close behind him. They would free themselves in time, or someone would come for them. There were plenty of folks wandering the mountains now, with the destruction of their ville. Someone would stumble on them before very long.

"Lock up," Jak said, intruding on the Armorer's thoughts.

"Yeah," J.B. agreed, reaching for the makeshift pulley system that had been used to operate the door. He used his knife blade to cut the ropes, then he and Jak pulled the door closed for the last time.

"Did you ever wonder why that guy tried to blow this place up?" Krysty asked the others as they reached the control room.

"He broke the conditioning," J.B. declared, "same way I did."

"People can be allergic to honey," Mildred told them all. "That's not so unusual. If that was the case with William, he would have chosen a different diet from the others and would not have become sucked into the whole queen-bee-and-worker-drone setup."

"Mebbe," J.B. said, "or mebbe he just didn't have a sweet tooth for honey. *That's* what saved me, anyhow."

"Saved us all," Ryan said. "And thanks."

J.B. met Ryan's gaze and he saw something there he hadn't seen in a couple weeks: friendship. "You sure you don't want to chill me for wrecking the life you and Krysty had going?" he asked.

Ryan shook his head. "There's a better life out there. For all of us. I'm certain of it," he said.

"Then let's find it," J.B. said, stepping into the mat-trans with the others. "Together."

"Together."

Ryan entered the chamber last and closed the door, wondering, as he made his way to Krysty's side, whether the mat-trans would work. He had no need to worry. As he sat beside his lover, the mat-trans powered up, and in a moment the companions were gone in the blink of an eye.

* * * * *

The Executioner
Don Pendleton's
NIGERIA MELTDOWN

Nigeria hinges on the verge of a revolution after a secret terror group is discovered

When Washington learns a secret military brotherhood is plotting a revolution in Nigeria, they know they need to act quickly. Mack Bolan is teamed up with a few men from the Nigerian military, but not only is he dodging bullets from the terror group, someone on his team has been hired to kill him. Closing in on the brotherhood in the heart of the jungle, he'll have to rely on his instincts to take down the leaders and disarm the traitor when he strikes.

GOLD EAGLE

Available January wherever books and ebooks are sold.

The Executioner®
Don Pendleton's
BREAKOUT

A secret syndicate profits by freeing ruthless criminals...

When notorious killers and drug lords break out of a maximum-security penitentiary, it soon becomes clear that these weren't escapes; they were highly organized rescues. A covert organization is selling prison "insurance," promising to bust criminals out of jail for a hefty price. With the justice system in shambles, Mack Bolan steps in as an undercover rival insurance salesman, hiring his own team of con men. But he'll need more than his war skills to destroy the operation's kingpin.

GOLD EAGLE®

GEX423

Available February, wherever books and ebooks are sold.

AleX Archer
RIVER OF NIGHTMARES

The Amazon never shares its secrets without a price...

Archaeologist Annja Creed has a full crew in tow as her TV show, *Chasing History's Monsters*, prepares for an in-depth exploration of the rain forest's most guarded secrets—including a magical child and a slothlike beast. But an opportunity to tread off the beaten path proves too tempting to ignore, and Annja leads her crew into an uncharted world that's both alien and dangerous—a world that attracts the morally corrupt with promises of wealth and power. A world that will steal the one thing Annja needs to survive: *herself.*

Available March wherever books and ebooks are sold.